I0885162

# *In Five Years*

*A Novel*

Rebecca Serle

ATRIA PAPERBACK
New York Amsterdam/Antwerp London
Toronto Sydney/Melbourne New Delhi

ATRIA PAPERBACK

An Imprint of Simon & Schuster, LLC
1230 Avenue of the Americas
New York, NY 10020

For more than 100 years, Simon & Schuster has championed authors and the stories they create. By respecting the copyright of an author's intellectual property, you enable Simon & Schuster and the author to continue publishing exceptional books for years to come. We thank you for supporting the author's copyright by purchasing an authorized edition of this book.

No amount of this book may be reproduced or stored in any format, nor may it be uploaded to any website, database, language-learning model, or other repository, retrieval, or artificial intelligence system without express permission. All rights reserved. Inquiries may be directed to Simon & Schuster, 1230 Avenue of the Americas, New York, NY 10020 or permissions@simonandschuster.com.

This book is a work of fiction. Any references to historical events, real people, or real places are used fictitiously. Other names, characters, places, and events are products of the author's imagination, and any resemblance to actual events or places or persons, living or dead, is entirely coincidental.

Copyright © 2020 by Rebecca Serle

All rights reserved, including the right to reproduce this book or portions thereof in any form whatsoever. For information, address Atria Books Subsidiary Rights Department, 1230 Avenue of the Americas, New York, NY 10020.

This Atria Paperback edition October 2025

**ATRIA** PAPERBACK and colophon are trademarks of Simon & Schuster, LLC

Simon & Schuster strongly believes in freedom of expression and stands against censorship in all its forms. For more information, visit BooksBelong.com.

For information about special discounts for bulk purchases, please contact Simon & Schuster Special Sales at 1-866-506-1949 or business@simonandschuster.com.

The Simon & Schuster Speakers Bureau can bring authors to your live event. For more information or to book an event, contact the Simon & Schuster Speakers Bureau at 1-866-248-3049 or visit our website at www.simonspeakers.com.

*Interior design by Alexis Minieri*

Manufactured in China

1 3 5 7 9 10 8 6 4 2

Library of Congress Control Number: 2019027133

ISBN 978-1-6682-0375-0

## Also by Rebecca Serle

*Expiration Dates*

*One Italian Summer*

*The Dinner List*

### YOUNG ADULT

*Truly Madly Famously*

*Famous in Love*

*The Edge of Falling*

*When You Were Mine*

"With masterful storytelling and all the ingredients of a romantic comedy, Rebecca Serle weaves a story far deeper than the genre typically dares to go. *In Five Years* isn't simply a book you will read; it is a book that will change you."

—Jenny Mollen, *New York Times* bestselling author of *I Like You Just the Way I Am*

"The story takes us in unexpected directions with twists and turns, but much like Dannie has to adapt, so do we as readers. In Serle's capable hands, it's worth the ride."

—*Bookreporter*

"I love books that are secretly about female friendship, not romance, and this sweet, heartbreaking charmer certainly fits the bill. You'll be texting your best friend chapter by chapter, revelation by revelation. Devouring this charged romance of sorts, I could easily picture it on the big screen starring Anna Kendrick or Alison Brie—you heard it here first."

—*Mashable*

"Emotional hooks alongside humor and self-awareness will remind readers of Jojo Moyes's *Me Before You* or Taylor Jenkins Reid's *Maybe in Another Life*."

—*Library Journal*

"I read it in one late night. Very, very clever. And lovely. The end is EXACTLY what it should be."

—Anstey Harris, author of *Goodbye, Paris*

"*In Five Years* is more than just a love story; it's a half dozen of them, none quite what you expect. Heartwarming, heartbreaking, and hard to put down, it's a novel about romance, friendship, the magic of good bagels, and what happens after you get everything you always wanted."

—Laurie Frankel, author of *New York Times* bestseller and Reese's Book Club pick *This Is How It Always Is*

"Serle's whimsical tale is book club catnip."

—*Publishers Weekly*

"A charming love story . . . *One Day* meets alternate-universe vibes."

—*theSkimm*

"When smart, thoughtful writing pairs with a compelling, ingenious plot, I am hooked and so very happy. It's been a long time since I read a novel in two sittings, but as soon as I started *In Five Years*, I was a goner. Loved it! Brava, Rebecca Serle."

—Elinor Lipman, author of *Good Riddance*

"Rebecca Serle has a way of blending a little bit of magic into the everyday, and *In Five Years* is her best book yet. . . . Prepare to be an absolute wreck upon finishing this unbelievably satisfying book. Your book club will freakin' love it."

—*HelloGiggles*

"A heartwarming portrait of a broken heart finding a little healing magic."

—*Kirkus Reviews*

"I just finished *In Five Years* and—my heart—oh! What a clever, beautiful, special book. The writing is stunning, the concept is so original—it just has everything going for it. I loved every page."

—Beth O'Leary, author of *The Flatshare*

Praise for

# *In Five Years*

"What would you do if you glimpsed your life five years from now—and found that it was different, in every way, from what you hoped for and expected? Rebecca Serle pairs this inspired premise with deft, propulsive prose and characters who feel as real as friends. *In Five Years* is as clever as it is moving, the rare read-in-one-sitting novel you won't forget."

—Chloe Benjamin, *New York Times* bestselling author of *The Immortalists*

"*In Five Years* is a profound tale of unconditional love and anguish with a touch of the mystical and mysterious. Deep, abiding friendship and loyalty are portrayed along with heartbreak."

—*New York Journal of Books*

"Heartbreaking, redemptive, and authentic in all the ways that make a book impossible to put down—I fell in love with this story. In five years, I will still be thinking about this beautiful novel."

—Jamie Ford, *New York Times* bestselling author of *Hotel on the Corner of Bitter and Sweet*

"I adored *In Five Years*; it's so poignant and tender. It broke my heart—such an unusual idea executed brilliantly, I didn't see that twist coming! I'm a sucker for great love stories, and this one is just lovely. A keeper on my shelf!"

—Josie Silver, author of #1 *New York Times* bestseller and Reese's Book Club pick *One Day in December*

"Serle takes a fairly generic rom-com setup and turns it into something much deeper in this captivating exploration of friendship, loss, and love."

—*Booklist*

*For Leila Sales,*
*who has lit up the last five years,*
*and the five before them.*
*We dreamed it because it had already happened.*

The future is the one thing you can count on not abandoning you, kid, he'd said. *The future always finds you. Stand still, and it will find you.* The way the land just has to run to sea.

—MARIANNE WIGGINS, *EVIDENCE OF THINGS UNSEEN*

Coming over the bridge to Manhattan.
Pie.

—NORA EPHRON

# Chapter One

Twenty-five. That's the number I count to every morning before I even open my eyes. It's a meditative calming technique that helps your brain with memory, focus, and attention, but the real reason I do it is because that's how long it takes my boyfriend, David, to get out of bed next to me and flip the coffee maker on, and for me to smell the beans.

Thirty-six. That's how many minutes it takes me to brush my teeth, shower, and put on face toner, serum, cream, makeup, and a suit for work. If I wash my hair, it's forty-three.

Eighteen. That's the walk to work in minutes from our Murray Hill apartment to East Forty-Seventh Street, where the law offices of Sutter, Boyt and Barn are located.

Twenty-four. That's how many months I believe you should be dating someone before you move in with them.

Twenty-eight. The right age to get engaged.

Thirty. The right age to get married.

My name is Dannie Kohan. And I believe in living by numbers.

"Happy Interview Day," David says when I walk into the kitchen. Today. December 15. I'm wearing a bathrobe, hair spun up into a towel. He's still in his pajamas, and his brown hair has a significant amount of salt and pepper for someone who has not yet crossed thirty, but I like it. It makes him look dignified, particularly when he wears glasses, which he often does.

"Thank you," I say. I wrap my arms around him, kiss his neck and then his lips. I've already brushed my teeth, but David never has morning breath. Ever. When we first started dating, I thought he was getting up out of bed before me to swoosh some toothpaste in there, but when we moved in together, I realized it's just his natural state. He wakes up that way. The same cannot be said of me.

"Coffee is ready."

He squints at me, and my heart tugs at the look on his face, the way it scrunches all up when he's trying to pay attention but doesn't have his contacts in yet.

He takes a mug down and then pours. I go to the refrigerator, and when he hands me the cup, I add a dollop of creamer. Coffee mate, hazelnut. David thinks it's sacrilegious but he buys it, to indulge me. This is the kind of man he is. Judgmental, and generous.

I take the coffee cup and go sit in our kitchen nook that overlooks Third Avenue. Murray Hill isn't the most glamorous neighborhood in New York, and it gets a bad rap (every Jewish fraternity and sorority kid in the tristate area moves here after graduation. The average street style is a Penn sweatshirt), but there's nowhere else in the city where we'd be able to afford a two-bedroom with a full kitchen in a doorman building, and between the two of us, we make more money than a pair of twenty-eight-year-olds has any right to.

David works in finance as an investment banker at Tishman Speyer, a real estate conglomerate. I'm a corporate lawyer. And today, I have an interview at the top law firm in the city. Wachtell. The mecca. The pinnacle. The mythological headquarters that sits in a black-and-gray fortress on West Fifty-Second Street. The top lawyers in the country all work there. The client list is unfathomable; they represent everyone: Boeing. ING. AT&T. All of the biggest corporate mergers, the deals that determine the vicissitudes of our global markets, happen within their walls.

I've wanted to work at Wachtell since I was ten years old and my father used to take me into the city for lunch at Serendipity and a matinee. We'd pass all the big buildings in Times Square, and then I'd insist we walk to 51 West Fifty-Second Street so I could gaze up at the CBS building, where Wachtell has historically had its offices since 1965.

"You're going to kill it today, babe," David says. He stretches his arms overhead, revealing a slice of stomach. David is tall and lanky. All of his T-shirts are too small when he stretches, which I welcome. "You ready?"

"Of course."

When this interview first came up, I thought it was a joke. A headhunter calling me from Wachtell, yeah right. Bella, my best friend—and the proverbial surprise-obsessed flighty blonde—must have paid someone off. But no, it was for real. Wachtell, Lipton, Rosen & Katz wanted to interview me. Today, December 15. I marked the date in my planner in Sharpie. Nothing was going to erase this.

"Don't forget we're going to dinner to celebrate tonight," David says.

"I won't know if I got the job today," I tell him. "That's not how interviews work."

"Really? Explain it to me, then." He's flirting with me. David is a great flirt. You wouldn't think it, he's so buttoned-up most of the time, but he has a great, witty mind. It's one of the things I love most about him. It was one of the things that first attracted me to him.

I raise my eyebrows at him and he downshifts. "Of course you'll get the job. It's in your plan."

"I appreciate your confidence."

I don't push him, because I know what tonight is. David is terrible with secrets, and an even worse liar. Tonight, on this, the second month of my twenty-eighth year, David Andrew Rosen is going to propose to me.

"Two Raisin Bran scoops, half a banana?" he asks. He's holding out a bowl to me.

"Big days are bagel days," I say. "Whitefish. You know that."

Before we find out about a big case, I always stop at Sarge's on Third Avenue. Their whitefish salad rivals Katz's downtown, and the wait, even with a line, is never more than four and a half minutes. I revel in their efficiency.

"Make sure you bring gum," David says, sliding in next to me. I bat my eyes and take a sip of coffee. It goes down sweet and warm.

"You're here late," I tell him. I've just realized. He should have been gone hours ago. He works market hours. It occurs to me he might not be going to the office at all today. Maybe he still has to pick up the ring.

"I thought I'd see you off." He flips his watch over. It's an Apple. I got it for him for our two-year anniversary, four months ago. "But I should jet. I was going to work out."

David never works out. He has a monthly membership to Equinox I think he's used maybe twice in two and a half years. He's naturally lean, and runs sometimes on the weekends. The wasted expense is a point of contention between us, so I don't bring it up this morning. I don't want anything to get in the way of today, and certainly not this early.

"Sure," I say. "I'm gonna get ready."

"But you have time." David pulls me toward him and threads a hand into the collar of my robe. I let it linger for one, two, three, four . . .

"I thought you were late. And I can't lose focus."

He nods. Kisses me. He gets it. "In that case, we're doubling up tonight," he says.

"Don't tease me." I pinch his biceps.

My cell phone is ringing where it sits plugged in on my nightstand in the bedroom, and I follow the noise. The screen fills with a photo of a blue-eyed, blond-haired shiksa goddess sticking her tongue sideways at the camera. Bella. I'm surprised. My best friend is only awake before noon if she's been up all night.

"Good morning," I tell her. "Where are you? Not New York."

She yawns. I imagine her stretching on some seaside terrace, a silk kimono pooling around her.

"Not New York. Paris," she says.

Well that explains her ability to speak at this hour. "I thought you were leaving this evening?" I have her flight on my phone: UA 57. Leaves Newark at 6:40 p.m.

"I went early," she says. "Dad wanted to do dinner tonight. Just to bitch about Mom, clearly." She pauses, and I hear her sneeze. "What are you doing today?"

Does she know about tonight? David would have told her, I think, but she's also bad at keeping secrets—especially from me.

"Big day for work and then we're going to dinner."

"Right. Dinner," she says. She definitely knows.

I put the phone on speaker and shake out my hair. It will take me seven minutes to blow it dry. I check the clock: 8:57 a.m. Plenty of time. The interview isn't until eleven.

"I almost tried you three hours ago."

"Well, that would have been early."

"But you'd still pick up," she says. "Lunatic."

Bella knows I leave my phone on all night.

Bella and I have been best friends since we were seven years old. Me, Nice Jewish Girl from the Main Line of Philadelphia. Her, French-Italian Princess whose parents threw her a thirteenth birthday party big enough to stop any bat mitzvah in its tracks. Bella is spoiled, mercurial, and more than a little bit magical. It's not just me. Everywhere she goes people fall at her feet. She is the easiest to love, and gives love freely. But she's fragile, too. A membrane of skin stretches so thinly over her emotions it's always threatening to burst.

Her parents' bank account is large and easily accessible, but their time and attention are not. Growing up, she practically lived at my house. It was always the two of us.

"Bells, I gotta go. I have that interview today."

"That's right! Watchman!"

"Wachtell."

"What are you going to wear?"

"Probably a black suit. I always wear a black suit." I'm already mentally thumbing through my closet, even though I've had the suit chosen since they called me.

"How thrilling," she deadpans, and I imagine her scrunching up her small pin nose like she's just smelled something unsavory.

"When are you back?" I ask.

"Probably Tuesday," she says. "But I don't know. Renaldo might meet me, in which case we'd go to the Riviera for a few days. You wouldn't think it, but it's great this time of year. No one is around. You have the whole place to yourself."

Renaldo. I haven't heard his name in a beat. I think he was before Francesco, the pianist, and after Marcus, the filmmaker. Bella is always in love, always. But her romances, while intense and dramatic, never last for more than a few months. She rarely, if ever, calls someone her boyfriend. I think the last one might have been when we were in college. And what of Jacques?

"Have fun," I say. "Text me when you land and send me pictures, especially of Renaldo, for my files, you know."

"Yes, Mom."

"Love you," I say.

"Love you more."

I blow-dry my hair and keep it down, running a flat iron over the hairline and the ends so it doesn't frizz up. I put on small pearl stud earrings my parents gave me for my college graduation, and my favorite Movado watch David bought me for Hanukkah last year. My chosen black suit, fresh from the dry cleaners, hangs on the back of my closet door. When I put it on, I add a red-and-white ruffled shirt underneath, in Bella's honor. A little spark of detail, or life, as she would say.

I come back into the kitchen and give a little spin. David's made little to no progress on getting dressed or leaving. He's definitely taking the day off. "What do we think?" I ask him.

"You're hired," he says. He puts a hand on my hip and gives me a light kiss on the cheek.

I smile at him. "That's the plan," I say.

✦

Sarge's is predictably empty at 10 a.m.—it's a morning-commute place—so it only takes two minutes and forty seconds for me to get my whitefish bagel. I eat it walking. Sometimes I stand at the counter table at the window. There are no stools, but there's usually room to stash my bag.

The city is all dressed up for the holidays. The streetlamps lit, the windows frosted. It's thirty-one degrees out, practically balmy by New York winter standards. And it hasn't snowed yet, which makes walking in heels a breeze. So far, so good.

I arrive at Wachtell's headquarters at 10:45 a.m. My stomach starts working against me, and I toss the rest of the bagel. This is it. The thing I've worked the last six years for. Well, really, the thing I've worked the last eighteen years for. Every SAT prep test, every history class, every hour studying for the LSAT. The countless 2 a.m. nights. Every time I've been chewed out by a partner for something I didn't do, every time I've been chewed out by a partner for something I did do, every single piece of effort has been leading me to, and preparing me for, this one moment.

I pop a piece of gum. I take a deep breath, and enter the building.

Fifty-one West Fifty-Second Street is giant, but I know exactly what door I need to enter, and what security desk I need to check in at (the entrance on Fifty-Second, the desk right in front). I've rehearsed this chain of events so many times in my head, like a ballet. First the door, then the pivot, then a sashay to the left and a quick succession of steps. *One two three, one two three . . .*

The elevator doors open to the thirty-third floor, and I suck in my breath. I can feel the energy, like candy to the vein, as I look around at the people moving in and out of glass-doored conference rooms like extras on the show *Suits*, hired for today—for me, for my viewing pleasure alone. The place is in full bloom. I get the feeling that you could walk in here at any hour, any day of the week, and this is what you would see. Midnight on Saturday, Sunday at 8 a.m. It's a world out of time, functioning on its own schedule.

This is what I want. This is what I've always wanted. To be somewhere that stops at nothing. To be surrounded by the pace and rhythm of greatness.

"Ms. Kohan?" A young woman greets me where I stand. She wears a Banana Republic sheath dress, no blazer. She's a receptionist. I know, because all lawyers are required to wear suits at Wachtell. "Right this way."

"Thank you so much."

She leads me around the bullpen. I spot the corners, the offices on full display. Glass and wood and chrome. The *thump thump thump* of money. She leads me into a conference room with a long mahogany table. On it sits a glass tumbler of water and three glasses. I take in this subtle and revealing piece of information. There are going to be two partners in here for the interview, not one. It's good, of course, it's fine. I know my stuff forward and backward. I could practically draw a floor plan of their offices for them. I've got this.

Two minutes stretch to five minutes stretch to ten. The receptionist is long gone. I'm contemplating pouring myself a glass of water when the door opens and in walks Miles Aldridge. First in his class at Harvard. *Yale Law Journal.* And a senior partner at Wachtell. He's a legend, and now he's in the same room as me. I inhale.

"Ms. Kohan," he says. "So glad you could make this date work."

"Naturally, Mr. Aldridge," I say. "It's a pleasure to meet you."

He raises his eyebrows at me. He's impressed I know his name sight unseen. Three points.

"Shall we?" He gestures for me to sit, and I do. He pours us each a glass of water. The other one sits there, untouched. "So," he says. "Let's begin. Tell me a little bit about yourself."

I work through the answers I've practiced, honed, and sculpted over the last few days. From Philadelphia. My father owned a lighting business, and when I was not even ten years old, I helped him with contracts in the back office. In order to sort and file to my heart's content, I had to read into them a bit, and I fell in love with the organization, the way language—the pure truth in the words—was nonnegotiable. It was like poetry, but poetry with outcome, poetry with concrete meaning—with actionable power. I knew it was what I wanted to do. I went to Columbia Law and graduated second in my class. I clerked for the Southern District of New York before accepting the reality of what I'd always known, which is that I wanted to be a corporate lawyer. I wanted to practice a kind of law that is high stakes, dynamic, incredibly competitive, and yes, offers me the opportunity to make a lot of money.

*Why?*

Because it's what I was born to do, what I have trained for, and what has led me here today, to the place I always knew I'd be. The golden gates. Their headquarters.

We go through my resume, point by point. Aldridge is surprisingly thorough, which is to my benefit, as it gives me more time to express my accomplishments. He asks me why I think I'd be a good fit, what kind of work culture I gravitate toward. I tell him that when I stepped off the elevator and saw all the endless movement, all the frenzied bustle, I felt as if I were home. It's not hyperbole, he can tell. He chuckles.

"It's aggressive," he says. "And endless, as you say. Many spin out."

I cross my hands on the table. "I can assure you," I tell him. "That won't be a problem here."

And then he asks me the proverbial question. The one you always prepare for because they always ask:

*Where do you see yourself in five years?*

I inhale, and then give him my airtight answer. Not just because I've practiced, which I have. But because it's true. I know. I always have.

I'll be working here, at Wachtell, as a senior associate. I'll be the most requested in my year on M&A cases. I'm incredibly thorough and incredibly efficient; I'm like an X-ACTO knife. I'll be up for junior partner.

*And outside of work?*

I'll be married to David. We'll be living in Gramercy Park, on the park. We'll have a kitchen we love and enough table space for two computers. We'll go to the Hamptons every summer; the Berkshires, occasionally, on weekends. When I'm not in the office, of course.

Aldridge is satisfied. I've clinched it, I can tell. We shake hands, and the receptionist is back, ushering me through the offices and to the elevators that deliver me once again to the land of the mortals. The third glass was just to throw me off. Good shot.

After the interview I go downtown, to Reformation, one of my favorite clothing stores in SoHo. I took the day off from work and it's only lunchtime. Now that the interview is over, I can turn my attention to tonight, to what is coming.

When David told me he had made a reservation at the Rainbow Room, I immediately knew what it meant. We had talked about getting engaged. I knew it would be this year, but I had thought it would have happened this past summer. The holidays are crazy, and the winter is David's busy time at work. But he knows how much I love the city in lights, so it's happening tonight.

"Welcome to Reformation," the salesgirl says. She's wearing black wide-legged pants and a tight white turtleneck. "What can I help you with?"

"I'm getting engaged tonight," I say. "And I need something to wear."

She looks confused for half a second, and then her face brightens. "How exciting!" she says. "Let's look around. What are you thinking?"

I take barrels into the dressing room. Skirts and low-backed dresses and a pair of red crepe pants with a matching loose camisole. I put the red outfit on first, and when I do, it's perfect. Dramatic but still classy. Serious but with a little edge.

I look at myself in the mirror. I hold out my hand.

*Today*, I think. *Tonight.*

# Chapter Two

The Rainbow Room is located on the sixty-fifth floor of 30 Rockefeller Plaza. It boasts one of the highest restaurant views in Manhattan, and from its magnificent windows and terraces you can see the Chrysler Building and the Empire State Building floating amongst the city skyline. David knows I'm a sucker for a view. On one of our first dates, he took me to an event at the top of the Metropolitan Museum of Art. They were showing some Richard Serra pieces on the roof, and the sunlight made the giant bronze sculptures look like they were on fire. That was two and a half years ago now, and he never forgot how much I loved it.

The Rainbow Room is usually closed for private events only, but they open their dining room during the week to select clientele. Because Tishman Speyer, where David works, owns and manages the Rainbow Room and the underlying real estate, these reservations are first made available to employees. Usually they're impossible to get, but for a proposal . . .

David greets me at Bar SixtyFive, a cocktail lounge adjacent to the restaurant. The terraces are now covered, so even though it's reaching frigid temperatures outside, people can still take advantage of the superb view.

Under the guise of David "coming from the office," we decided to meet there. He wasn't home when I came back to change, and I can only assume he was running last-minute errands, or taking a walk to ward off nerves.

David is wearing a suit, navy, with a white shirt and a pink-and-blue tie. The Rainbow Room is, of course, jacket required.

"You look very handsome," I say.

I take off my coat and hand it to him, revealing my fire-engine red ensemble. Bold, for me, in color. He whistles.

"And you look very incredible," he says. He hands my coat to a passing porter. "Would you like a drink?"

He fidgets with his tie, and I understand, of course, that he is nervous. It's endearing. Additionally, he seems to be sweating at his hairline. He definitely walked here.

"Sure," I say.

We sidle up to the bar. We order two glasses of champagne. We toast. David just stares at me, wide-eyed. "To the future," I say.

David downs half a glass. "I can't believe I didn't ask!" he says. He brushes the back of his hand against his lips. "How did it go?"

"I nailed it." I set my glass down, triumphantly. "It was honestly butter. It couldn't have gone better. Aldridge was the one who interviewed me."

"No shit. What's their time frame?"

"He said they'd let me know by Tuesday. If I get the job, I'd start after the holidays."

David takes another sip. He puts his hand on my waist and squeezes. "I'm so proud of you. One step closer."

That five-year plan I expressed to Aldridge isn't just mine, it's *ours*. We came up with it six months into dating, when it was obvious this thing between us was serious. David will transition out of investment banking and begin working at a hedge fund—more opportunity for big money, less corporate bureaucracy. We didn't even argue about where we want to live—it's always been Gramercy for both of us. The rest was a fluid negotiation. We never came to an impasse.

"Indeed."

"Mr. Rosen, your table is ready."

There is a man in white tails at our backs, ushering us out of the bar, down the hallway, and into the ballroom.

I've only ever seen the Rainbow Room in movies, but it's magnificent, truly the perfect place to get engaged. Round tables sit gracefully in tiers around a circular dance floor, where a dazzling chandelier hangs overhead. Rumors are the dance floor rotates, a spinning circle in the center of the room. Ornate floral arrangements, reminiscent of a wedding, pepper the dining room. There is a festive, old-world holiday air. Women in fur. Gloves. Diamonds. The smell of good leather.

"It's beautiful," I breathe.

David squeezes me to his side and kisses my cheek. "We're celebrating," he says.

A server holds a chair back for me. I sit. A white napkin is produced in a flourish and eased onto my lap.

The slow, smooth styles of Frank Sinatra float over the dining room. A singer croons in the corner.

"This is too much," I say. What I mean is that it's perfect. It's exactly right. He knows this. That's why he's him.

I wouldn't say I'm a romantic, exactly. But I believe in romance, which is to say, I believe in calling to inquire about a date instead of texting, and flowers after sex, and Frank Sinatra at an engagement. And New York City in December.

We order champagne again, this time a bottle. Momentarily, my chest ticks at what tonight will cost.

"Don't think about it," David says, reading me. I love that about him. That he always knows what I'm thinking, because we're always on the same page.

The bubbles arrive. Cool and sweet and crisp. Our second glasses go down easy.

"Should we dance?" David asks me.

On the floor, I see two couples swaying to "All the Way."

*Through the good or lean years, and for all the in-between years . . .*

Suddenly, I think that David may grab the mic. He may make this public. He is not a showy person, by nature, but he is confident, and unafraid of public displays. I am unnerved at this possibility. Of the ring arriving in my chocolate soufflé and his getting down on one knee for all the world to see.

"*You* want to dance?" I ask him.

David hates dancing. I have to drag him at weddings. He thinks he has no rhythm, and he's right, but so few guys have rhythm that it really doesn't matter. There are no wrong moves to "P.Y.T." except sitting down.

"Why not?" he says. "We're here."

He offers me his hand, and I take it. As we make our way down the steps to the rotunda, the song switches. "It Had to Be You."

David takes me in his arms. The two other couples—older—smile in approval.

"You know," David says, "I love you."

"I do," I say. "I mean, you'd better."

Is this it? Is this when he drops?

But he keeps just moving me, slowly around the rotating rotunda. The song ends. A few people clap. We go back to our seats. I feel, suddenly, disappointed. Could I be wrong?

We order. A simple salad. The lobster. Wine. The ring is neither perched on the lobster's claw nor drowning in a glass of Bordeaux.

We both move our food around on our plates with lovely silver forks, barely eating. David, usually chatty, has a hard time focusing. More than once he knocks and rights his water glass. *Just do it*, I want to tell him. *I'll say yes.* Perhaps I should spell it out with cherry tomatoes.

Finally, dessert arrives. Chocolate soufflé, crème brûlée, pavlova. He's ordered one of everything, but there is no ring affixed to any of their powdered tops. When I look up, David is gone. Because he is holding the box in his hands, right by my seat, where he kneels.

"David."

He shakes his head. "For once don't talk, okay? Just let me get through this."

People around us murmur and quiet. Some of the surrounding tables have phones aimed at us. Even the music lowers.

"David, there are people watching." But I'm smiling. Finally.

"Dannie, I love you. I know neither one of us is a particularly sentimental person and I don't tell you this stuff a lot, but I want you to know that our relationship isn't just part of some plan for me. I think you're extraordinary, and I want to build this life with you. Not because we're the same but because we fit, and because the more time goes on the more I cannot imagine my life taking place without you."

"Yes," I say.

He smiles. "I think maybe you should let me ask the question."

Someone close breaks out in laughter.

"I'm sorry," I say. "Please ask."

"Danielle Ashley Kohan, will you marry me?"

He opens the box and inside is a cushion-cut diamond flanked by two triangular stones set in a simple platinum band. It's modern, clean, elegant. It's exactly me.

"You can answer now," he tells me.

"Yes," I say. "Absolutely. Yes."

He reaches up and kisses me, and the dining room breaks out in applause. I hear the snaps of lenses, the *ooh*s and *aah*s of generous goodwill from surrounding patrons.

David takes the ring out of the box and slides it onto my finger. It takes a second to waddle over my knuckle—my hands are swollen from the champagne—but when it does, it sits there like it has always been there.

A waiter appears out of thin air with a bottle of something. "Compliments of the chef," he says. "Congratulations!"

David sits back down. He holds my hand across the table. I marvel at the ring, turning my palm back and forth in the candlelight.

"David," I say. "It's gorgeous."

He smiles. "It looks so good on you."

"Did you pick this out?"

"Bella helped," he says. "I was worried she was going to ruin the surprise. You know her, she's terrible at keeping anything from you."

I smile. I squeeze his hand. He's right about that, but I don't need to tell him. That is the thing about relationships: it's not necessary to say everything. "I had no idea," I say.

"I'm sorry it was so public," he says, gesturing around us. "I couldn't resist. This place is practically begging for it."

"David," I say. I look at him. My future husband. "I want you to know I'd suffer through ten more public proposals if it meant I got to marry you."

"No you wouldn't," he says. "But you can convince me of anything, and it's one of the things I love about you."

✦

Two hours later we're home. Hungry and buzzing off champagne and wine, we crouch around the computer, ordering Thai food from Spice online. This is us. Spend seven hundred dollars on dinner, come home to eat eight-dollar fried rice. I never want that to change.

I want to put on sweatpants, per usual, but something tells me not to—not tonight, not yet. If I were different, someone else—Bella, for example—I'd have lingerie to wear. I'd have bought some this week. I'd put on a matching bra and underwear and hover by the door. Fuck the pad thai. But then I probably wouldn't be engaged to David right now.

We're not big drinkers, and the champagne and wine have gotten to both of us. I edge myself farther onto the couch. I put my feet in David's lap. He squeezes the arch of my foot, kneading the tender place my heels are unkind to. I feel the buzzing in my stomach move upward to my head, until my eyes are being pulled closed like blinds. I yawn. Within a minute, I'm asleep.

# Chapter Three

I wake up slowly. How long have I been asleep? I roll over and look at the clock on the nightstand: 10:59 p.m. I stretch my legs. Did David move me to bed? The sheets feel crisp and cool around me, and I weigh just closing my eyes again and drifting back to sleep—but then I'd miss this, our engagement night, and I force them open. We still have more champagne to drink, and we need to have sex. That's a thing you should do on the night you get engaged. I yawn, blinking, and then sit up, my breath exiting my body in a rush. Because I'm not in our bed. I'm not even in our apartment. I'm wearing a formal dress, red, beaded around the neckline. And I'm somewhere I've never been before.

I could tell you I think I'm dreaming, but I don't, not really. I can feel my legs and arms and the frenetic beating of my own uneasy heart. Was I kidnapped?

I take in my surroundings. On further glance, I realize I'm in a loft apartment. The bed I'm in is flush up against floor-to-ceiling windows that appear to orient me in . . . Long Island City? I look out, desperate for some anchoring image. And then I spot the Empire State Building, rising out of the water in the distance.

I'm in Brooklyn, but where? I can see the New York City skyline across the river, and to the right, the Manhattan Bridge. Which means I'm in Dumbo; I must be. Did David take me to a hotel? I see a redbrick building across the street with a brown barn door. There's a party happening inside. I can see camera flashes and lots of flowers. A wedding, maybe.

The apartment isn't giant, but it gives the illusion of space. Two blue velvet chairs sit necking in front of a glass-and-steel coffee table. An orange dresser perches at the foot of the bed, and colorful Persian rugs make the open space feel cozy, if not a little cluttered. There are exposed pipes and wood beams and a print on the wall. It's an eye chart that reads: *I WAS YOUNG I NEEDED THE MONEY.*

Where the hell am I?

I hear him before I see him. He calls: "Are you awake?"

I freeze. Should I hide? Make a run for it? I see a large steel door, across the apartment, in the direction of where the voice is coming from. If I bolt, I might be able to get it open before—

He rounds the corner from what must be the kitchen. He's dressed in black dress pants and a blue-and-black-striped shirt, unbuttoned at the top.

My eyes go wide. I want to scream; I might.

The well-dressed stranger comes over to me, and I leap onto the other side of the bed, by the windows.

"Hey," he says. "Are you okay?"

"No!" I say. "No, I'm not."

He sighs. He does not seem surprised by my response. "You fell asleep." He runs his hand back and forth across his forehead. I notice he has a scar, crooked, over his left eye.

"What are you doing here?" I've backed myself so far into a corner I'm practically pushed up against the windows.

"C'mon," he says.

"Do you know me?"

He bends one knee onto the bed. "Dannie," he says. "Are you really asking me that?"

He knows my name. And there's something about the way he says it that makes me pause, take a breath. He says it like he's said it before.

"I don't know," I say. "I don't know where I am."

"It was a good night," he says. "Wasn't it?"

I look down at my dress. I realize, for the first time, it's one I already own. My mom and I bought it with Bella on a shopping trip three years ago. Bella has the same one in white.

"Yeah," I say, without even thinking. As if I know. As if I were there. What is happening?

And that's when I catch the TV. It has been on this whole time, the volume low. It's hanging on the wall opposite the bed and it's playing the news. On the screen is a small graphic with the date and time: December 15, 2025. A man in a blue suit is prattling on about the weather, a snow cloud swaying behind him. I try to breathe.

"What?" he says. "Do you want me to turn it off?"

I shake my head. The response is automatic, and I watch him as he walks to the coffee table and grabs the remote. As he goes, he untucks his shirt.

"Weather warning for the East Coast as a blizzard heads toward us. Possibility of six inches overnight, with continued accumulation into Tuesday."

2025. It's not possible; of course it's not. Five years . . .

This must be some kind of prank. Bella. When we were younger, she used to pull shit like this all the time. Once, for my eleventh birthday, she figured out how to get a pony into my backyard without my parents knowing. We woke up to it playing chicken with the swing set.

But even Bella couldn't get a fake date and time on national television. Could she? And who is this guy? Oh my god, David.

The man in the apartment turns around. "Hey," he says. "Are you hungry?"

At his question, my stomach rumbles. I barely ate at dinner and wherever I am, in whatever parallel universe with David, the pad thai has most certainly not yet arrived.

"No," I say.

He cocks his head to the side. "Kind of sounds like you are."

"I'm not," I insist. "I just . . . I need . . ."

"Some food," he says. He smiles. I wonder how wide the windows open.

I slowly come around the bed.

"Do you want to change first?" he asks me.

"I don't . . ." I start, but I don't know how to finish the sentence because I don't know where we are. Where I would even find clothes.

I follow him into a closet. It's a walk-in, right off the bedroom alcove. There are rows of bags and shoes and clothes hanging, organized by color. I know right away. This is my closet. Which means this is my apartment. I live here.

"I moved to Dumbo," I say, out loud.

The man laughs. And then he opens a drawer near the center of the closet and pulls out a pair of sweatpants and a T-shirt and my heart stops. They're his. He lives here, too. We're . . . together.

*David.*

I reel back and run for the bathroom. I find it to the left of the living room. I close the door and bolt it. I splash some cold water on my face. "Think, Dannie, think."

Inside the bathroom are all the products I love. Abba body cream and tea tree oil shampoo. I dab some MyChelle serum on my face, comforted by the smell, the familiarity.

On the back of the door hangs a bathrobe with my initials, one I've had forever. Also, there are a pair of drawstring black pajama pants and an old Columbia sweatshirt. I take off the dress. I put them both on.

I run some rose hip oil over my lips and unlock the door.

"We have pasta or . . . pasta!" the man calls from the kitchen.

First things first, I need to find out this guy's name.

His wallet.

David and I have a sixty-forty split when it comes to our finances, based on the income discrepancy between us. We decided this after we moved in together and haven't changed it since. I have never once looked inside his wallet except for one unfortunate incident involving a new knife and his insurance card.

"Pasta sounds good," I say.

I go back near the bed, to where his pants hang half off a chair, trailing to the floor. I glance toward the kitchen and check the pockets. I pull out his wallet. Old leather, indistinguishable brand. I riffle through it.

He doesn't look up from filling a pot with water.

I pull out two business cards. One to a dry cleaner. The other a Stumptown punch card.

Then I find his license. Aaron Gregory, thirty-three years old. His license is New York State, and he's six-foot and has green eyes.

I put everything back where I found it.

"Do you want red sauce or pesto?" he asks from the kitchen.

"Aaron?" I try.

He smiles. "Yes?"

"Pesto," I say.

I walk toward the kitchen. It's 2025, a man I've never met is my boyfriend, and I live in Brooklyn.

"Pesto is what I wanted, too."

I sit down at the counter. There are cherrywood stools with wire-framed backs I don't recognize and don't particularly like.

I take him in. He's blond, with green eyes and a jaw that makes him look like one of the superhero Chrises. He's hot. Too hot for me, to be totally honest with you, and evidently, based on his looks and his name, not Jewish. I feel my stomach twist. This is what becomes of me in five years? I'm dating a golden Adonis in an artist's loft? Oh god, does my mother know?

The water boils, and he pours the pasta into the pot. Steam rises up and he steps back, wiping his forehead.

"Am I still a lawyer?" I ask suddenly.

Aaron looks at me and laughs. "Of course," he says. "Wine?"

I nod, exhaling a sigh of relief. So some things have gotten off track, but not all. I can work with this. I just have to find David, figure out what happened there, and we'll be back in business. Still a lawyer. Hallelujah.

When the noodles are cooked, he drains them and tosses them back into the pot with the pesto and Parmesan, and all of a sudden I'm dizzy with hunger. All I can think about right now is the food.

Aaron takes two wineglasses down from a cabinet, moving expertly around the kitchen. My kitchen. Our kitchen.

He pours me a glass of red and hands it over the counter. It's big and bold. A Brunello, maybe. Not something I'd usually buy.

"Dinner is served."

Aaron hands me a giant steaming bowl of spaghetti and pesto, and before he even comes back around the counter, I'm shoveling a forkful into my mouth. It occurs to me, mid-bite, that this could all be some kind of government science play and he could be poisoning me, but I'm too hungry to stop or care.

The pasta is delicious—warm and salty—and I don't look up for another five minutes. When I do, he's staring at me.

I wipe my mouth with my napkin. "Sorry," I say. "I feel like I haven't eaten in years."

He nods and pushes back his plate. "So now we have two choices. We can just get drunk, or we can get drunk and play Scattergories."

I love board games, which, of course, he would know. David is more of a card guy. He taught me how to play Bridge and Rummy. He thinks board games are childish, and that if we're playing something we should be strengthening our brain pathways, which both Bridge and Rummy do.

"Get drunk," I say.

Aaron gives my arm an affectionate squeeze. I feel like his hand is still there when he lets go. There is something strange here. Some strange pull. Some emotion that begins to expand in the room, fill up the corners.

Aaron tops off our wineglasses. We leave our plates where they sit on the counter. Now what? And then I realize he's going to want to get into bed. This boyfriend of mine, he's going to want to touch me. I can just feel it.

I make a beeline for one of the blue velvet chairs and take a seat. He looks at me sideways. *Huh.*

All at once something occurs to me. I look down at my hand, panicked. There, on my finger, is an engagement ring. It's a solitaire canary diamond with tiny stones around it. It's vintage and whimsical. Not the ring David gave me tonight. It's not anything I'd ever pick out. Yet here it is, on my finger.

*Shit. Shit. Shit. Shit.*

I bolt up from the chair. I pace the apartment. Should I leave? Where would I go? To my old place? Maybe David is still there. But what are the odds? He's probably living in Gramercy with some non-insane wife. Maybe if I tell him what's going on he'll know how to fix it. He'll forgive me for whatever I did to get us here—me in this apartment with a stranger and him on the other side of the bridge. He's the best problem solver. He'll figure it out.

I get up and head toward the door. I need to get out of here. To escape whatever feeling is flooding this room. Where do I keep my coats?

"Hey," Aaron says. "Where are you going?"

Think fast. "Just the deli," I say.

"The deli?"

Aaron gets up and comes over to me. Then he puts his hands on my face. Right up against either cheek. His hands are cool, and for a moment the temperature change and motion shocks me and I make a move to reel back, but he holds me in place.

"Stay. Please don't leave right now."

He looks at me and his eyes are liquid, open. So this is what this guy has on me. This feeling. It's . . . it's new and familiar all at once. It's heavy, weighted. It sits all around us. And, despite myself, I want to . . . I want to stay.

"Okay," I whisper. Because his skin is still on mine and his eyes are still looking at me, and while I don't understand why I've committed to spend my life with this man, I do know that the bed we share gets a lot of action, because . . . this is big. I feel its resonance in my body, the reverberations of some kind of seismic tidal wave. Outside, the sky turns.

He heads toward the bed, holding my hand, and I follow. The wine has started to make me feel languid. I want to stretch out.

I perch on the edge of the bed.

"Five years," I mutter.

Aaron just looks at me. He sits back against the pillows. "Hey," he says. "Can you come here?"

But it's not a question, not really, not insofar as it only has one, rhetorical, answer.

He holds his arms open and out, and I ease onto the bed. I can feel it, this tug on my limbs, like I'm a marionette being pulled unevenly forward, toward him.

God help me, I let him hold me. He pulls me to him, and I feel his breath warm near my cheek.

His face hovers close. Here we go, he's going to kiss me. Am I going to let him? I think about it, about David, and about this Aaron's muscled arms. But before I can weigh the pros and cons and come to a solid conclusion, his lips are on mine.

They land gently and he holds them there, delicately—as if he knows, as if he's letting me get used to him. And then he uses his tongue to open my mouth slowly.

Oh my god.

I'm melting. I've never felt anything like this. Not with David, not with Ben, the only other guy I dated seriously, not even with Anthony, the study abroad fling I had in Florence. This is something else entirely. He kisses and touches like he's inside my brain. I mean, I'm in the future, maybe he is.

"You sure you're okay?" he asks me, and I respond by pulling him closer.

He threads his hands under my sweatshirt and then it's off

before I even realize it, the cool air hitting my bare skin. Am I not wearing a bra? I am not wearing a bra. He bends and takes one of my nipples into his mouth.

This is insane. I'm insane. I've lost my mind.

It feels so good.

The rest of the clothes come off. From somewhere—a different stratosphere—I hear a car horn honk, a train rumble, the city carry on.

He kisses me harder. We get horizontal quickly. Everything feels incredible. His hands tracing the curves of my stomach, his mouth on my neck. I've never had a one-night stand up until this point—but this has to count, right? We met barely an hour ago and now we're about to have sex.

I can't wait to tell Bella about this. She'll love it. She'll . . . But what if I never make it back? What if this guy is just my fiancé now and not a stranger and I can't even share the details of this wild and . . .

He presses his thumb down into the crease of my hip, and all thoughts of time and space escape through the slightly cracked window.

"Aaron," I say.

"Yes."

He rolls on top of me, and then my hands are finding the muscles in his back, the crevices of his bones, like terrain—knotted and wooden and peaceful. I arch against him, this man who is a stranger but somehow something else entirely. His hands cup my face, they run down my neck, they wrap around my rib cage. His mouth is urgent and seeking against mine. My fingers grip his shoulders. Slowly, and then all at once, I forget where I am. All I'm aware of are Aaron's arms wrapped tightly around me.

# Chapter Four

I wake up with a jolt, grasping at my chest.

"Hey, hey," a familiar voice says. "You're awake."

I look up to see David standing over me, a bowl of popcorn in one hand. He's also holding a bottle of water—not exactly the wine I was just drinking. Just drinking? I look down at my body, still fully clothed in my red Reformation ensemble. What the hell just happened?

I scramble up to sitting. I'm back on the couch. David is now in his chess team tournament sweatshirt and black sweatpants. We're in our apartment.

"I thought you might be down for the count," David says. "And miss our big night. I knew that second bottle would do us in. I already took two Advil, do you want some?" He sets the popcorn and water down and leans over to kiss me. "Should we call our parents now or tomorrow? You know they're all losing it. I told everyone beforehand."

I parse through what he's saying. I'm frozen. It must have been a dream, but it . . . how could it be? I was, just three minutes ago, in bed with someone named Aaron. We were kissing, and his hands were on me, and we were having the most intense sex of my life. Dream me slept with a stranger. I feel the need to touch my body, to confirm my physical reality. I put a hand on each elbow and hold my arms to my chest.

"You okay?" David asks. He's pulled himself out of the jovial moment and is looking at me intently.

"How long was I out for?" I ask him.

"About an hour," he says. Something dawns on him. He leans closer to me. The proximity of his body feels like an intrusion. "Hey, listen, you're going to get that job. I can tell you're stressed about it and maybe this was too much to have happen in one day, but there's no way they don't hire you. You're the perfect candidate, Dannie."

I feel like asking him *what job?*

"The food came," he says, sitting back. "I stuck it in the fridge. I'll get plates."

I shake my head. "I'm not hungry."

David looks at me with shock and awe. "How is that possible? You told me you were weak with hunger, like an hour ago." He stands up and goes into the kitchen, ignoring me. He opens the refrigerator and starts pulling out containers. Pad thai. Chicken curry. Fried rice. "All your favorites," he says. "Hot or cold?"

"Cold," I say. I pull the blanket closer around me.

David comes back balancing the containers on plates. He starts taking off tops, and I smell the sweet and sour and tangy spices.

"I had the craziest dream," I tell him. Maybe if I talk about it it'll make sense. Maybe if I lay it all out here, outside of my brain. "I just . . . I can't shake it. Was I talking in my sleep?"

David piles some noodles onto a plate and grabs a fork. "Nope. Don't think so. I showered for a little, so maybe?" He jams a giant bite of pad thai into his mouth and chews. Some stray noodles migrate to the floor. "Was it a nightmare?"

I think about Aaron. "No," I say. "I mean, not exactly."

David swallows. "Good. Your mom called twice. I'm not sure how long we can hold her off." David puts his fork down and threads his arm around me. "But I had some plans for us alone tonight."

My eyes dart to my hand. The ring, the right one, is back on my finger. I exhale.

My phone starts buzzing.

"Bella again," David says, somewhat wearily.

I'm already off the couch, snatching the phone and taking it with me into the bedroom.

"I'm gonna flip on the news," David calls after me.

I close the door behind me and pick up the call. "Bells."

"I waited up!" It's loud where she is, the sound of people fills the phone—she's out partying. She laughs, her voice a cascade of music. "You're engaged! Congratulations! Do you like the ring? Tell me everything!"

"Are you still in Paris?" I ask her.

"Yes!" she says.

"When are you coming home?"

"I'm not sure," she says. "Jacques wants to go to Sardinia for a few days."

Ah, Jacques. Jacques is back. If Bella woke up five years in the future in a different apartment, she probably wouldn't even blink.

"In December?"

"It's supposed to be quiet and romantic."

"I thought you were going to the Riviera with Renaldo."

"Well, he bailed, and then Jacques texted that he was in town and voilà. New plans!"

I sit down on my bed. I look around. The tufted gray chairs I bought with my first paycheck at Clarknell, the oak dresser that was a hand-me-down from my parents' place. The Bakelite lamps David brought with him from his Turtle Bay bachelor pad.

I see the expanse of that loft in Dumbo. The blue velvet chairs.

"Hey," I say. "I have to tell you something kind of crazy."

"Tell me everything!" she hollers through the phone, and I imagine her spinning out in the middle of a dance floor, on the roof of some Parisian hotel, Jacques tugging at her waist.

"I'm not sure how to explain it. I fell asleep, and . . . I wasn't dreaming. I swear I was in this apartment and this guy was there. It was so real. Like I really went there. Has anything like that ever happened to you?"

"No, darling, we're going to the Marais!"

"What?"

"Sorry, everyone in the crowd is absolutely starving, and it's practically light out. We've been partying for decades. So wait, it was like a dream? Did he do it on the terrace or in the restaurant?" I hear an explosion of sound and then a door shut, a retreat to silence.

"Oh, the restaurant," I say. "I'll tell you everything when you're back."

"I'm here, I'm here!" she says.

"You're not," I say, smiling. "Be safe, okay?"

I can see her rolling her eyes. "Do you know that the French don't even have a word for safety?"

"That is not even remotely true," I say. "*Beaucoup.*" It's pretty much one of the only French words I know.

"Even so," she says. "I wish you had more fun."

"I have fun," I say.

"Let me guess. David is now watching CNN Live and you're wearing a face mask. You just got *engaged*!"

I touch my fingers to my cheek. "Only dry skin here."

"How was the job interview?" she asks. "I didn't forget, I just temporarily forgot."

"It was great, honestly. I think I got it."

"Of course you got it. You not getting it would require a rip in the universe that I'm not sure is scientifically possible."

I feel my stomach tighten.

"Boozy brunch when I'm back," she says. The door opens again and sound rushes back in through the phone. I hear her kiss someone twice.

"You know I hate brunch," I say.

"But you love me."

She hangs up in a whirlwind of noise.

David comes into the bedroom, his hair rumpled. He takes off his glasses and rubs the bridge of his nose.

"You tired?" he asks me.

"Not really," I say.

"Yeah, me neither." He climbs into bed. He reaches for me. But I can't. Not right now.

"I'm just going to get some water," I say. "Too much champagne. Do you want some water, too?"

"Sure." He yawns. "Do me a favor and get the light?"

I get up and flip the light switch. I walk back into the living room. But instead of pouring a glass of water, I go to the windows. The TV is off and it's dark, but the streets are flooded with light. I look down. Third Avenue is busy even now, well past midnight. There are people out—laughing and screaming. Heading to the bars of our youth: Joshua Tree, Mercury Bar. They'll dance to nineties music they're too young to really know, well into the morning. I stand there for a long time. Hours seem to pass. The streets quiet down to a New York whisper. By the time I go back into the bedroom, David is fast asleep.

# Chapter Five

I get the job; of course I do. They call me a week later and offer it, a fraction below my current salary. I argue them up, and by January 8 I'm giving my two weeks' notice. David and I move to Gramercy. It happens a year later, almost down to the day. We find a great unfurnished sublet in the building we've always admired. "We'll stay until something opens to buy," David tells me. A year later something opens to buy, and we buy it.

David begins working at a hedge fund started by his ex-boss at Tishman. I get promoted to senior associate.

Four and a half years pass. Winters and falls and summers. Everything goes according to plan. Everything. Except that David and I don't get married. We never set a date. We say we're busy, which we are. We say we don't need to until we want kids. We say we want to travel. We say we'll do it when the time is right—and it never is. His dad has heart trouble one year, we move the next. There are always reasons, and good ones, too, but none of them are why. The truth is that every time we get close, I think about that night, that hour, that dream, that man. And the memory of it stops me before I've started.

After that night, I went to therapy. I couldn't stop thinking about that hour. The memory was real, like I had, in fact, lived it. I felt like I was going crazy and because of that, I didn't want to talk to anyone, not even Bella. What would I say? I woke up in the future? Where I had sex with a stranger? The worst thing is, Bella would probably believe me.

I know that therapists are supposed to help you figure out whatever insanity is lingering in your brain, and then help you get rid of it. So the following week I went to someone on the Upper West Side. Highly recommended. In New York, all the best shrinks are on the Upper West Side.

Her office was bright and friendly, if not a little sterile. There was one giant plant. I couldn't figure out if it was fake or not. I never touched it. It was on the other side of the sofa, behind her chair, and it would have been impossible to get to.

Dr. Christine. One of those professionals who uses their first name with their title to seem more relatable. She didn't. She wore swaths of Eileen Fisher—linens and silks and cottons spun so excessively I had no idea what her shape even was. She was sixty, maybe.

"What brings you in today?" she asked me.

I had been in therapy once, after my brother died. A fatal drunk driving accident fifteen years ago that had the police show up at our house at 1:37 in the morning. He wasn't the one at the wheel. He was in the passenger seat. What I heard first were my mother's screams.

My therapist had me talk about him, our relationship, and then draw what I thought the accident might have looked like, which seemed condescending for a twelve-year-old. I went for a month, maybe more. I don't remember much, except that afterward my mom and I would stop for ice cream, like I was seven and not nearly thirteen. I often didn't want any, but I always got two scoops of mint chocolate chip. It felt important to play along then, and for a long time after.

"I had a strange dream," I said. "I mean, something strange happened to me."

She nodded. Some of the silk slipped. "Would you like to tell me about it?"

I did. I expressed to her that David and I had gotten engaged, that I'd had too much champagne, that I'd fallen asleep, and that I'd woken up in 2025 in a strange apartment with a man I'd never met before. I left out that I slept with him.

She looked at me for a long time once I stopped talking. It made me uncomfortable.

"Tell me more about your fiancé."

I was immediately relieved. I knew where she was headed with this. I was unsure about David, and therefore my subconscious was projecting a kind of alternative reality where I was not subject to the burdens of what I had just committed to in getting engaged.

"He's great," I said. "We've been together for over two years. He's very driven and kind. He's a good match."

She smiled then, Dr. Christine. "That's wonderful," she said. "What do you think he'd say about this experience you're describing?"

I didn't tell David. I couldn't, obviously. What would I possibly say? He'd think I was crazy, and he'd be right.

"He'd say it was a dream and that I'm stressed out about work."

"Would that be true?"

"I don't know," I said. "That's why I'm here."

"It seems to me," she said, "that you're unwilling to say this was just a dream, but you're not sure what it would mean if it wasn't."

"What else could it possibly be?" I genuinely wanted to know where she was going with this.

She sat back in her chair. "A premonition, maybe. A psychosomatic trip."

"Those are just other words for dreams."

She laughed. She had a nice one. The silk slipped again. "Sometimes unexplainable things happen."

"Like what?"

She looked at me. Our time was up.

After our session, I felt strangely better. Like in going in there I could see the whole thing for what it was: crazy. I could give the whole weird dream to her. It was her problem now. Not mine. She could file it with all her divorces, sexual incompatibilities, and mother issues. And for four and a half years, I left it there.

# Chapter Six

It's a Saturday in June, and I'm going to meet Bella for brunch. We haven't seen each other in almost two months, which is the longest we've ever gone, including her London sojourn of 2015, when she "moved" to Notting Hill for six weeks to paint. I've been buried in work. The job is great, and impossible. Not hard, impossible. There is a week's worth of work in every day. I'm always behind. I see David for five minutes, maybe, every day when one of us wakes up sleepily to greet the other. At least we're on the same schedule. We're both working toward a life we want, and will have. Thank god we understand each other.

Today it's raining. It's been a wet spring, this one of 2025, so this is not out of the ordinary, but I ordered some new dresses and I was hoping to wear one. Bella is always calling my style "conservative," because 90 percent of the time I'm in a suit, and I thought I'd surprise her with something unexpected today. No luck. Instead, I tug on jeans, a white Madewell T-shirt, and my Burberry trench and ankle rain boots. Temperature says sixty-five degrees. Enough to sweat with a top layer but be freezing without one.

We're meeting at Buvette, a tiny French café in the West Village we've been going to for years. They have the best eggs and croque monsieur on the planet—and their coffee is strong and rich. Right now, I need a quart.

Also, it's one of Bella's favorite spots. She knows all the waiters. When we were in our twenties, she'd go there to sketch.

I end up taking a cab because I don't want to be late, even though I know Bella will be running fifteen minutes behind. Bella is chronically fifteen to twenty minutes late everywhere she goes.

But when I arrive she's already there, seated in the window at the two-top.

She's dressed in a long, flowing floral dress that's wet at the edges—at five-foot-three she's not tall enough for it—and a crimson velvet blazer. Her hair is down and falls around her in tufts, like spools of wool. She's beautiful. Every time I see her I'm reminded just how much.

"This cannot possibly be happening," I say. "You beat me here?"

She shrugs, her gold hoops bouncing against her neck. "I couldn't wait to see you." She gets out of her chair and pulls me into a tight hug. She smells like her. Tea tree and lavender, a hint of cinnamon.

"I'm wet," I yelp, but I don't let go. It feels good. "I missed you, too."

I tuck my umbrella under my chair and loop my raincoat over the back. Inside it's chillier than I thought it would be. I rub my hands together.

"You look older," she says.

"Gee, thanks."

"That's not what I mean. Coffee?"

I nod.

She holds her cup up to the waiter. She comes here far more often than I do. Her place is three blocks away, on the corner of Bleecker and Charles, a floor-through level of a brownstone her dad bought for her two years ago. It's three bedrooms, impeccably decorated in her colorful, bohemian, I-didn't-even-think-about-this-but-it-looks-gorgeous style.

"What's darling Dave up to this morning?" she asks.

"He went to the gym," I say, opening my napkin.

"The gym?"

I shrug. "That's what he said."

Bella opens her mouth to say something, but closes it again. She likes David. Or at least, I think she does. I suspect she'd like me to be with someone more adventurous, someone who maybe pushed me outside my comfort zone a little bit more. But what she doesn't realize, or what she conveniently forgets, is that she and I are not the same person. David is right for me, and the things I want for my life.

"So," I say. "Tell me everything. How is work coming at the gallery? How was Europe?"

Five years ago, Bella did a show of her artwork at a small gallery in Chelsea named Oliander. The show sold out, and she did another. Then two years ago, Oliander, the owner, wanted to sell the place and came to her. She used her trust fund to buy it. She paints less than she used to, but I like that she has some stability in her life. The gallery has meant that she can't disappear anymore—at least not for weeks at a time.

"We nearly sold out the Depreche show," she says. "I'm so bummed you missed it. It was spectacular. My favorite by far." Bella says that about every single artist she shows. It's always the best, the greatest, the most fun she's ever had. Life is an upward escalator. "Business is so good I'm thinking about hiring another Chloe."

Chloe has been her assistant for the last three years, and runs the logistics at Oliander. She's kissed Bella twice, which has not seemed to complicate their business relationship.

"You should do it."

"Might give me time to actually sculpt or paint again. It has been months."

"Sometimes you have to sacrifice to achieve your dreams."

She smiles sideways at me. The coffee comes. I pour some cream into it and take a slow, heady sip.

When I look up, she's still smiling at me. "What?" I ask.

"Nothing. You're just so . . . 'sacrifice to achieve your dreams.' Who talks like that?"

"Business leaders. Heads of companies. CEOs."

Bella rolls her eyes. "When did you get like this?"

"Do you ever remember my being any different?"

Bella puts her hand to her chin. She looks straight at me. "I don't know," she says.

I know what she means, but I never really want to talk about it. Was I different as a child? Before my brother died? Was I spontaneous, carefree? Did I begin to plan my life so that no one would ever show up at my door and throw the whole thing off a cliff? Probably. But there isn't much to be done about it now. I am who I am.

The waiter circles back to us, and Bella raises her eyebrows at me as if to ask *you ready?*

"You order," I say.

She speaks to him entirely in French, pointing out items on the menu and discussing them. I love watching her speak French. She's so natural, so vibrant. She tried to teach me once in our early twenties, but it just didn't stick. They say that languages come better to people who are right-brained, but I'm not so sure. I think you need a certain looseness, a certain fluidity, to speak another language. To take all the words in your brain and turn them over, one by one, like stones—and find something else scrolled on the underside.

We spent four days together in Paris once. We were twenty-four. Bella was there for the summer, taking an art course and falling in love with a waiter in the Fourteenth arrondissement. I came to visit. We stayed at her parents' flat, right on Rue de Rivoli. Bella hated it. "Tourist location," she told me, although the whole city seemed for the French, and the French alone.

We spent the entire four days on the outskirts. Eating dinner at cafés on the fringes of Montmartre. During the day we wandered in and out of galleries in the Marais. It was a magical trip, made all the more so by the fact that the only time I'd been out of the country was a trip to London with my parents and David and my annual pilgrimage to Turks and Caicos with his parents. This was something else. Foreign, ancient, a different world. And Bella fit right in.

Maybe I should have felt disconnected from her. Here was this girl, my best friend, who fit this faraway place like a hand to a glove. I didn't, and yet she still took me with her. She was always taking me with her, wanting me to be a part of her wide, open life. How could I feel anything but lucky?

"To get back to the prior discussion," Bella says when the waiter is gone, "I think sacrifice is in direct opposition to manifestation. If you want your dreams you should look for abundance, not scarcity."

I take a sip of coffee. Bella lives in a world I do not understand, populated by phrases and philosophies that apply only to people like her. People, maybe, who do not yet know tragedy. No one who has lost a sibling at twelve can say with a straight face: *everything happens for a reason.*

"Let's agree to disagree," I tell her. "It has been too long since I've seen you. I want to be bored senseless hearing all about Jacques."

She smiles. It sneaks up her cheeks until it's practically at her ears.

"*What?*"

"I have something to tell you," she says. She reaches across the table and takes my hand.

Instantly, I'm flooded with a familiar sensation of pulling, like there's a tiny string inside of me that only she can find and thread. She's going to tell me she met someone. She's falling in love. I know the drill so well I wish we could go through all the steps right here at this table, with our coffee. Intrigue. Obsession. Distaste. Desperation. Apathy.

"What's his name?" I ask.

She rolls her eyes. "Come on," she says. "Am I that transparent?"

"Only to me."

She takes a sip of her sparkling water. "His name is Greg." She lands hard on the one syllable. "He's an architect. We met on Bumble."

I nearly drop my coffee. "You have Bumble?"

"Yes. I know you think I can meet someone buying milk at the deli, but, I don't know, lately I've been wanting something different and nothing has been that interesting in a while."

I think about Bella's love life over the last few months. There was the photographer, Steven Mills, but that was last summer, almost a year ago.

"Except Annabelle and Mario," I say. The collectors she had a brief fling with. A couple.

She bats her eyes at me. "Naturally," she says.

"So what's the deal?" I ask.

"It has been like three weeks," she says. "But, Dannie, he's wonderful. Really wonderful. He's really nice and smart and—I think you're really going to like him."

"Nice and smart," I repeat. "Greg?"

She nods, and just then our food appears in a cloud of smoke. There are eggs and caviar on crispy French bread, avocado toast, and a plate of delicate crepes dusted with powdered sugar. My mouth waters.

"More coffee?" Our waiter asks.

I nod.

"Yum," I say. "This is perfect." I immediately cut into the avocado toast. The poached egg on top oozes out yolk, and I scoop a segment onto my plate. I make a vaguely pornographic noise through a mouthful.

Bella watches me and laughs. "You're so deprived," she says.

I throw her a disgruntled look as I make my way to the crepes. "I have a job."

"Yes, how is that going?" She tilts her head to the side.

"It's great," I say. I want to add *some of us have to work for a living*, but I don't. I learned a long time ago there is a difference with Bella, and our relationship, between judgmental and unkind. I try not to stray over the line. "I think it's going to be another year, and then partner."

Bella does a little shimmy in her chair. Her sweater slips from where it sits on her shoulders and I'm met with a slice of collarbone. Bella has always had a zaftig figure, glorious in its curvature, but she looks slimmer to me today. Once, during the month of Isaac, she lost twelve pounds.

Greg. I already have a bad feeling.

"I think we should all go to dinner," Bella says.

"Who?"

She gives me a look. "Greg," she says. She sucks her bottom lip in, lets it pop back out. Her blue eyes find mine. "Dannie, I'm telling you, you don't have to believe me, but this one is different. It *feels* different."

"They always do."

She narrows her eyes at me and I can tell I've crossed it. I sigh. I can never quite say no to her. "Okay," I say. "Dinner. Pick any Saturday two weeks from now and it's yours."

I watch Bella as she loads up her plate—first eggs, then a crepe—and feel my stomach start to relax as she eats with gusto. The sky changes from rain to clouds to sunshine. When we leave the streets are almost entirely dry.

# Chapter Seven

"What happened to the blue shirt?"

David comes out of our bedroom in a black button-down and dark jeans. We're already running late. We're supposed to be at Rubirosa in SoHo in ten minutes and it will take us at least twenty to get downtown. Bella may always be late, but I still like beating her places. It's how we've always done things. Brunch was enough change for one week.

"You don't like this?" David hunches down and surveys himself in the mirror above the sofa.

"It's fine. I just thought you were wearing the blue one."

He heads back into the bedroom, and I check my lipstick in the same mirror. I'm wearing a black sleeveless turtleneck and a blue silk skirt with heels. The weather says sixty-seven degrees, low of sixty-three, and I'm trying to decide whether to bring a jacket.

He comes back in, buttoning the blue one. "Happy?"

"Very," I say. "Will you call a car?"

David busies himself with his phone, and I check to make sure I have our keys, my cell phone, and Bella's gold-beaded bracelet. I borrowed it six months ago and never gave it back.

"Two minutes."

When we get to the restaurant, Bella is standing outside. My first instinct is confusion—she beat me, again. My second is that it's already over with Greg and we're going to be having dinner alone. This has happened twice before (Gallery Daniel and, I think, Bartender Daniel). I feel a wave of irritation, followed by one of sympathy and inevitability. Here we go again. Always the same thing.

I get out of the car first. "I'm sorry," I start, just as the restaurant door opens and out onto the pavement walks Greg. Except he's not Greg. He's Aaron.

Aaron.

Aaron, whose face and name have been running in my head, on a loop, for the last four and a half years. The center of so many questions and daydreams and forced replays made manifest on the sidewalk now.

It wasn't a dream. Of course it wasn't. He's standing here now, and there is no one else he could be. Not a man I've spotted at the movies, not an associate I once traded work jabs with. Not someone I shared a plane ride seated next to. He is only the man from the apartment.

I reel back. I do not know whether to scream or run. Instead, I'm cemented. My feet have merged with the pavement. The answer: my best friend's boyfriend.

"Babe, this is my best friend, Dannie. Dannie, this is Greg!" She snuggles into him, her arms looping around his shoulders.

"Hey," he says. "I've heard a lot about you."

He picks up my hand to shake it. I search his face for any sign of recognition, but, of course, I come up empty. Whatever has happened between us . . . hasn't yet.

David extends his hand. I'm just standing there, my mouth hanging open, neglecting to introduce him.

"This is David," I sputter. David in the blue shirt shakes Aaron in the white shirt's hand. Bella smiles. I feel as if all the air on the sidewalk has been sucked back into the sky. We're going to suffocate out here.

"Shall we?"

I follow Greg/Aaron up the steps and into the crowded restaurant. "Aaron Gregory," he says to the hostess. Aaron Gregory. I flash on his license in my hand. Of course.

"Aaron?"

"Oh, yeah. My last name is Gregory. Greg just kind of stuck." He gives me a small smile. It feels too familiar. I don't like it.

I feel like I'm sinking. Like I'm falling through the floor, or maybe the floor is falling, too, except no one else is moving. It's just me, catapulting through space.

Time.

"Aaron."

He looks at me. Dead on. I hear David behind us laugh at something Bella has said. I smell her perfume—French rose. The kind you can only buy at the drugstores in Paris. "I'm not one of the bad ones," he tells me. "Just because I know you think I am."

I exhale. I feel dizzy. "I do?"

"You do," he says. We start following the hostess. We snake around the bar, in between the two-top tables with couples bent together over pizza and deep glasses of red. "I can tell by the way you're looking at me. And what Bella has said."

"What has she said?"

We pass through an archway and Aaron hangs back, holding his arm out to let me pass. My shoulder brushes his hand. This isn't happening.

"That she has dated some guys who maybe didn't treat her right, and that you're an amazing friend, and you're always there to pick up the pieces. And that I should be warned you'll probably hate me at first."

We've arrived at the table. It's in the back room, pushed up against the left-hand wall. David and Bella are upon us.

"I'll slide in the corner," Bella says. She shoves herself in first and pulls me down next to her. David and Aaron sit across from us.

"What's good here?" Aaron asks. He gives Bella a wide smile and reaches across the table for her hand. He strokes her knuckles.

I don't need to look at the menu, but I do anyway. The arugula pizza and Rubirosa salad are what we always get.

"Everything," Bella says. She squeezes and releases his hand and shimmies her torso. She's wearing a short black ruffled dress with roses on it that I bought with her on a shopping trip to The Kooples. She has neon-green suede heels tucked under her, and dangly green plastic earrings clank against her cheeks.

I need to avoid Aaron's face. His entire person—him—seated twelve inches across the table from me.

"Bella tells us you're an architect," David says, and my heart squeezes with affection for him. He always knows the things you're supposed to ask—how you're supposed to behave. He always remembers the protocol.

"Indeed," Aaron says.

"I thought architects didn't really exist," I say. I'm keeping my eyes on the menu.

Aaron laughs. I glance up at him. He points to his chest. "Real. Pretty sure."

"She's talking about this article Mindy Kaling wrote like a million years ago. She says that architects only exist in romantic comedies." Bella rolls her eyes at me.

"She does?" Aaron points to me.

"No, Mindy," Bella says. "Mindy says that."

I think it was in the *Times*. Titled something like: "Types of Women in Romantic Comedies Who Are Not Real." The architect thing was anecdotal. Incidentally, Mindy also said that a workaholic and an ethereal dream girl were not believable stereotypes, either, yet here we are.

"No handsome architects," I say. "To clarify."

Bella laughs. She leans across the table and touches Aaron's hand. "That's about as close to a compliment as you're going to get, so enjoy it."

"Well then, thank you."

"My dad is an architect," David says, but no one responds. We're now busying ourselves with the menu.

"Do you guys want red or white?" Bella asks.

"Red," David and I say at the same time. We never drink white. Rosé, occasionally, in the summer, which it isn't yet.

When the waiter comes over, Bella orders a Barolo. When we were in high school, we all took shots of Smirnoff while Bella poured Cabernet into a decanter.

I've never been a big drinker. In school it affected my ability to get up early and study or run before class, and now it does the same for work—only worse. Since I turned thirty, even a glass of wine makes me groggy. And after the accident no one was allowed to drink in our house, not even a thimbleful of wine. Completely dry. My parents still are, to this day.

"I'm in the mood for some meat," David says. We've never ordered anything other than the arugula or classic pizza here. Meat?

"I'd split a sausage with you," Aaron says.

David smiles and looks at me. "I never get sausage. I like this guy."

I've been preoccupied, possessed, since I saw him on the sidewalk. For the first time, I consider the reality that this man is Bella's boyfriend. Not the guy from the premonition—but the one sitting across from her now. For one thing, he seems good and solid. Funny and accommodating. It's usually like pulling teeth to get one of her boyfriends to make eye contact.

If he were anyone else, I might be thrilled for her. But he isn't.

"Where do you live?" I ask Aaron.

I see flashes of the apartment. Those big, open walls. The bed that overlooked the city skyline.

"Midtown," he says.

"Midtown?"

He shrugs. "It's close to my office."

"Excuse me," I say.

I get up from the table and wind my way to the bathroom, which exits off a little hallway.

"What's going on?" It's David on my heels. "That was weird. Are you okay?"

I shake my head. "I don't feel well."

"What happened?"

I look at him. His face is studying me with concern and . . . something else. Surprise? It's close cousins with annoyance. But this is unusual behavior for me, and so I'm not sure.

"Yeah, it just hit me. Can we go?"

He glances back into the restaurant, as if his gaze will reach the table where Bella and Aaron sit, no doubt just as baffled.

"Are you going to throw up?"

"Maybe."

This does it. He springs into action, placing a hand on my lower back. "I'll let them know. Meet me outside; I'll call a car."

I nod. I head outside. The temperature has dropped markedly since we arrived. I should have brought a jacket.

David comes out with my bag, and Bella.

"You hate him," she says. She crosses her arms in front of her chest.

"What? No. I don't feel well."

"It was pretty spontaneous. I know you. You once muscled through the full-blown flu to fly to Tokyo."

"That was work," I say. I'm clutching my stomach. I'm actually going to vomit. It's all going to come out on her green suede shoes.

"I like him," David says. He looks to me. "Dannie does, too. She had a fever earlier. We just didn't want to cancel."

I feel a wave of affection for him, for this lie.

"I'll call you tomorrow," I tell her. "Go enjoy your dinner."

Bella doesn't budge from her place on the sidewalk, but our car comes and David holds the door open for me. I dive inside. He walks around and then we're off down Mulberry, Bella disappearing behind us.

"Do you think it's food poisoning? What did you eat?" David asks.

"Yeah, maybe." I lean my head against the window, and David squeezes my shoulder before taking out his phone. When we get home, I change into sweats and crawl into bed.

He comes and perches on the edge. "Can I do anything?" he asks me. He smoothes down the comforter, and I grab his hand before he lifts it off.

"Lay down with me," I say.

"You're probably contagious," he says. He puts the back of his hand on my cheek. "I'm going to make you some tea."

I look at him. His brown eyes. The slight tufts of his hair. He never uses product, no matter how many times I tell him everyone needs it.

"Go to sleep," he says. "You'll feel better in the morning."

He's wrong, I think. I won't. But I fall asleep anyway. When I dream, I'm back in that apartment. The one with the windows and the blue chairs. Aaron isn't there. Instead, it's Bella. She finds his sweatpants in the top drawer of the dresser. She holds them up and shakes them at me. *What are these doing here?* she wants to know. I don't have an answer. But she keeps demanding one. She walks closer and closer to me. *What are these doing here? Tell me, Dannie. Tell me the truth.* When I go to speak, I realize the entire apartment is filled with water and I'm choking on everything I cannot say.

# Chapter Eight

"It's nice to see you again," Dr. Christine says.

The plant is still there. I assume, now, that it's fake. Too much time has passed.

"Yes, well," I say. "I don't really know who else to tell."

"Tell what?"

The truth of what I have learned. That what I saw in that apartment is from the future. It will occur in exactly five months and nineteen days, on December 15. I graduated as valedictorian of Harriton High, magna cum laude from Yale, and top of my law class at Columbia. I'm not gullible, nor am I a fool. What happened wasn't a dream; it was a premonition—a prophecy sketched to life—and now I need to know how and why it happened, so I can make sure it never does.

"I met the man," I tell her. "From the dream."

She swallows. It could be my imagination, but it seems like it's taking some effort. I want to skip this part, the part where we have to determine what it is and how it happened, the process. The part where she thinks I'm maybe a little bit crazy. Hallucinating, possibly. Working out past trauma, etc. I'm only interested in prevention now.

"How do you know it was him?"

I give her a look. "I didn't tell you we slept together."

"Oh." She leans forward in her brown leather chair. Unlike the plant, it's new. "That seems an important part. Why do you think you left it out?"

"Because I'm engaged," I tell her. "Obviously."

She leans forward. "Not to me."

"I don't know," I say. "I just didn't. But I know it's him, and he's now dating my best friend."

Dr. Christine looks at her notes. "Bella."

I nod, although I don't remember talking about her. I must have.

"She's very important to you."

"Yes."

"And you feel guilty now."

"Well, technically, I haven't done anything wrong."

She squints at me. I put a fist to my forehead and hold it there.

"You mentioned you're engaged," she says. "To the same man you were with when we last spoke?"

"Yes."

"It has been over four years since I saw you. Do you have plans to get married?"

"Some couples decide not to."

She nods. "Is that what you and David have decided?"

"Look," I say. "I just want to make sure this doesn't happen again, or happen at all. That's why I'm here."

Dr. Christine sits back as if creating more space between us. A pathway to the door, maybe.

"Dannie," she says. "I think something is going on that you don't understand, and that is frightening to you, as someone whose actual job it is to discover and prove causality."

"Causality," I repeat.

"If I do this, I'll get this result." She holds out her hands like a weighted Grecian scale. "This experience does not fit in your life, you have not taken any steps to have it, and yet here it is."

"Well, right," I say. "That's why I need it to not be."

"And how do you propose you do that?"

"I don't know," I say. "That's kind of why I'm here."

Predictably, our time is up.

✦

I decide I need to go in search of the apartment. I need something concrete, some form of evidence.

Sunday, David heads into the office and I tell him I'm going for a run. I used to run all the time in my twenties. Long runs. Down the West Side Highway and through the Financial District, between the tall buildings and across the cobblestones. I've run the loop in Central Park, around the reservoir, watching the leaves change from green to yellow to amber, the water reflecting the seasons. I've run two marathons and half a dozen halfs. Running does all the things for me it does for everyone else—clears my head, gives me time to think, makes my body feel good and loose. But it also has the added benefit of taking me places. When I first moved to the city I could only afford to live in Hell's Kitchen, but I wanted to be everywhere. So I ran.

In the early days of our relationship I used to try to get David to come with me, but he'd want to stop after a few blocks and get bagels so I started leaving him at home. Running is better alone anyway. More space to think.

It's 9 a.m. by the time I cross the Brooklyn Bridge, but it's Sunday, early, so there aren't that many tourists out yet. Just bikers and other joggers. I keep my head high, shoulders back, focusing on my core pulling forward. My breathing is ragged. It has been too long since I've been on a long run, and I feel my lungs rebelling against the exertion.

I never saw the outside of the building. But from the view I'd have to place it somewhere close to the water, maybe near Plymouth. I get over the bridge and slow to a walk as I make my way down Washington Street toward the river. The sun has started to burn off the haze of the morning, and the water reflects in sparkles. I take off my sweatshirt and tie it around my waist.

Dumbo, short for Down Under the Manhattan Bridge Overpass, used to be a ferry landing and still has an industrial feel. Large warehouse buildings mix with overpriced grocer markets and all-glass apartment buildings. As my breathing slows, I realize I should have done a search before I came down. Apartment views, open listings. I could have made a spreadsheet and gone through it—why didn't I think of that?

I stop in front of Brooklyn Bridge Park, in front of a brick-and-glass building that takes up the entire block. Not it.

I pull out my phone. Did I (do I?) buy this apartment? I make good money, more than most of my peers, but a two-million-dollar one-bedroom loft seems out of my price range. At least in the next six months. And it doesn't make any logistical sense. We have our dream place in Gramercy, big enough to put a kid in, someday. Why would I want to be here?

My stomach starts to rumble, and I walk west to see if I can find somewhere to grab an apple or a bagel, and think. I turn up Bridge Street and after a few blocks I find a deli with a black awning—Bridge Coffee Shop. It's a tiny place, with a counter deli and a board menu. There's a police officer there; that's how you know it's good. A woman with a wide smile stands behind the counter and converses in Spanish with a young mother with a sleeping baby. When they spot me, they wave goodbye to each other and the woman wheels her baby out. I hold the door open for her.

I order a bagel with whitefish salad, my usual. The woman behind the counter nods in solidarity with my order.

A man comes in and pays for a coffee. Two teenagers get bagels with cream cheese. Everyone here is a regular. Everyone says hello.

My bagel sandwich comes up for pickup. I take the white paper bag, thank the woman, and make my way back down toward the water. Brooklyn Bridge Park is less a park and more a stretch of grass. The benches are full, and I pop down on a rock, right by the water's edge. I open up my sandwich and take a bite. It's good, really good. Surprisingly close to Sarge's.

I look out over the water—I've always loved the water. I've had little of it over the course of my life, but when I was younger, we used to spend July Fourth week at the Jersey Shore in Margate, a beach town that is practically an extended suburb of Philadelphia if you go by population. My parents would rent a condo, and for seven blissful days we'd eat shaved ice and run the crowded shore with hundreds of other kids, our parents happily situated in their beach chairs, watching from the sand. There was the night in Ocean City, on the rides, spinning on the Sizzler or riding the bumper cars. The dinner at Mack & Manco Pizza and cheese hoagies from Sack O' Subs, dripping in oil and red wine vinegar, opened in paper at the beach.

Michael, my brother, gave me my first cigarette there, smoked under the boardwalk, nothing but the taste of freedom between us and our fingertips.

We stopped going after we lost him. I'm not sure why, except that everything that felt familial, that seemed to tie us together, was intolerable. Like our joy or unity was a betrayal of him, his life.

"Dannie?"

I close my eyes and open them again. When I look up, I see him standing above me in a bike helmet, half on his seat. Aaron. You've got to be kidding me.

# Chapter Nine

"Hi. Wow." I scramble to my feet, shoving my sandwich back into the bag. "What are you doing down here?"

He's wearing a blue T-shirt and khaki pants, a brown leather messenger bag slung over his chest.

"It's my weekend bike route." He gestures to his bag, shakes his head. "No, Bella actually sent me on an errand this morning."

"Oh yeah?"

Aaron unclips his helmet. The line of his hair is wet and matted down with sweat. "You seem to be feeling better."

I put my hands on my hips. "I am."

He smiles. "Good. You want to come?"

"Where?"

He scoots himself closer. "I'm looking at an apartment."

Of course he is. I didn't need a Google search. I just needed Aaron to show up, right now, and lead me there.

"Let me guess," I say. "Plymouth Street?"

"Close," he says. "Bridge."

This is insane. This is not happening. "Yes," I say. "I'll come."

"Great."

He loops his helmet over his handlebars and we start walking.

"You're a runner?" he asks me.

"I used to be," I say. I can feel the sting in my left knee and hip as we walk, a product of not enough stretching, and no squats before taking off.

"I know. I don't get on my bike as much as I'd like anymore, either."

"Why isn't Bella here?" I ask.

"She had to go into the gallery," he says. "She asked me to check it out. You'll get it when you see it, I think. Hang on." We're at a crosswalk and he holds his hand back as two bikers speed by. "Try not to die on my watch, huh?"

I blink back at him in the sunlight. I should have worn sunglasses.

"Okay, now we can go."

We cross the street and then we're making our way up Plymouth until we get right to where it meets Bridge, running perpendicular. Just where I came from. And then I see it. I missed it on my walk just now, blinded by my search for a sandwich. It's the redbrick event space with the barn door. I recognize it now. But not just from that night. I was at a wedding here three years ago. David's friends Brianne and Andrea from Wharton Business School. It's the old Galapagos Art Space, and it's what I saw out the window that night, four and a half years ago. And behind me, across the street, at 37 Bridge, is the building Aaron is about to lead me into.

"Watch your step," he says, as we cross the street and make our way to the door. Sure enough, I'm right. It's a brick-and-concrete building, less industrial than some surrounding it.

There's no lobby, just a buzzer and a padlock, and Aaron takes a ring of keys from his messenger bag and begins trying them. The first two don't work, and then on the third the lock swings open, the chain coming undone in his hands. The steel door swings open to reveal the side of a freight elevator. Aaron uses a second key to call it down for us—this time on the first try.

"They're expecting you?" I ask.

Aaron nods. "A buddy of mine is a broker and gave me the keys. Said we could check it out today."

We. Bella.

The elevator lumbers down. Aaron holds the door open and I step inside, then he wheels his bike in after us. He hits the button for the fourth floor and we're making our way upward, the mechanics of the freight heaving and sputtering as we go.

"This building doesn't seem up to code," I say, crossing my arms. Aaron smiles.

"I like that you and Bella are best friends. It's fun."

"What?" I cough twice into my closed fist. "What do you mean?"

"You're so different."

But I don't have time to respond because the doors are opening, delivering us straight into the apartment from four and a half years ago. I know immediately, without having to take a step inside, that it's the one. Of course it is. Where else did I think this morning would deposit me?

But the apartment isn't at all what it was—or will be. It's a construction site. Old wood beams sit piled in a corner. Plumbing and wires hang unfinished from outlets. There's a wall where I do not remember one being. No appliances. No running water. The space is raw—open, honest—not a stitch of makeup on.

"Job for an architect," I say. "I get it now."

But Aaron hasn't heard me. He's busy leaning his bike up against a wall—where I remember the kitchen being—and stepping back to survey the place. I watch him cross the apartment, walk over to the windows. He turns around, taking in the long view.

"Bella wants to live here?" I ask. Her apartment is perfect, an actual dream. She bought it before it even came to market, fully renovated. She has three bedrooms, floor-to-ceiling windows, and a galley kitchen. I can't understand her wanting to move. She decorated that place for two full years. She still claims to not be done.

But Bella has always been one for a project. She loves potential, possibility, an unknown terrain such as this one. The only trouble is she rarely, if ever, sees anything through. I've seen her spend obscene amounts of money on projects and renovations that never ultimately come together. There was the Paris apartment, the LA loft, the jewelry line, the Thai silk scarf company, the shared artists space in Greenpoint. The list is long.

"She does," Aaron says. "Or at least see if she can." He's speaking quietly. His attention isn't on his words but instead on his surroundings. I can see him sketching, drawing, molding this place to life in his head.

They've only been together two months. Eight weeks. Granted, that's two weeks longer than Bella's longest relationship, but still—David didn't even know my middle name at the end of two months. The fact that Aaron is here—looking at a place for Bella to live? That he's tapping the walls and stomping the floorboards—it gives me pause. Whatever level they're at, this quickly, isn't good.

"Seems like a big project," I say.

"Not too big," he says. "There are good bones here. And Bella tells me she likes a project."

"I know that," I say.

At this, he looks at me. He turns his entire attention toward me—my lone figure, standing in this swampy, sweaty space, clad in black running pants and an old camp T-shirt, while the potential of the future hangs around us like storm clouds.

"I know you do," he says. It's softer than I imagined whatever he'd say would be. "I'm sorry if I misspoke." He takes a step closer to me. I inhale. "The truth is I saw you go into the deli. I circled around and followed you back to the water." He rubs a hand over his forehead. "I wasn't sure if I should say hi, but I really—I really do want you to like me. I feel like we got off on the wrong foot and I'm wondering if there's anything I can do to change that."

I back away. "No," I say. "It's not—"

"No, no, it's okay." He gives me another lopsided smile, but this one looks hesitant, almost embarrassed. "Look, I don't need to be loved by everyone. But it would be nice if my girlfriend's best friend could stand to be in the same room as me, you know?"

This room. This apartment. This unfulfilled space.

I nod. "Yeah," I say. "I know."

He brightens at this. "We can take things slow. No meals for a while. Maybe just start with some sparkling water? Work our way up to a coffee?"

I try for a smile. To anyone else, that would have been funny. "Sounds good," I say. It feels physically impossible to say something interesting.

"Great." He holds my gaze for a beat. "Bella's gonna flip when I tell her I ran into you. What are the odds?"

"In a city of nine million? Less than zero."

He goes over to where wires hang unaccompanied off walls. "What do you think of putting the—"

"Kitchen?" I offer.

He smiles. "Exactly. And you could do the bedroom back

there." He points toward the windows. "I bet we could get a sick walk-in closet."

We walk through the apartment for another five minutes. Aaron takes some photos as he goes. When we head back down the elevator, my cell phone is ringing. It's Bella.

"Greg texted me. How crazy is that? What were you even doing down there? You never run in Brooklyn. What did you think of the place?" She stops, and I can hear her breathing—shallow and expectant through the phone.

"It's nice, I guess," I say. "But your place is perfect. Why would you want to move?"

"You hate it?"

I think about lying to her. About telling her I don't like it. That the windows have the wrong view, that it smells like trash, that it's too far. I've never lied to Bella, and I do not want to, but she also can't buy this place. She can't move here. It's for her protection as well as my own.

"It just seems like a lot of work," I tell her. "And kind of far."

She exhales. I can feel her annoyance. "From what?" she says. "No one lives in Manhattan anymore. It's so stuffy, I can't believe I do. You need to be a little more open-minded."

"Well," I say. "I don't really have to be anything. I'm not going to be the one living there."

# Chapter Ten

"David, we need to get married."

It's the following Friday, and David and I are on the couch trying to decide what to order for dinner. It's past 10 p.m. We had a reservation for two hours ago, but one of us had to work later and then the other decided to do the same. We got home ten minutes ago and collapsed jointly onto the sofa.

"Now?" David asks. He takes off his glasses and looks around. He never uses the bottom of his T-shirt because he thinks it smudges the lenses more. He makes a move to get up and go in search of a cleaner when I grab his hand.

"No. I'm serious."

"Me, too."

David sits back down. "Dannie, I've asked you before to set a date. We've talked about it. You never think it's the right time."

"That's not fair," I say. "We've both felt that way."

David sighs. "Do you really want to talk about this?"

I nod.

"Life has been busy, yes. But it's not true to say postponing things has come from us equally. I've been okay with waiting, because it's what you want."

David has been patient. We've never spoken about it, not in so many words, but I know he's wondered, *Why hasn't it happened?* Why do we never talk about it, not in specifics? Life got busy, and it was easy for me to pretend he didn't think about it a lot, and maybe he didn't. David has always been fine with my being in the driver's seat when it comes to our relationship. He knows it's where I feel comfortable, and he's happy to let me have it. It's one of the reasons we work so well.

"You're right," I say. I take both of his hands in mine now. The glasses dangle awkwardly from his pointer finger—an unfortunate third wheel. "But I'm saying it's time now. Let's do it."

David squints at me. He understands now that I'm serious. "You've been acting really weird lately," he says.

"I'm proposing here."

"We're already engaged."

"David," I say. "Come on."

At this, he stops. "Proposing?" he says. "I took you to the Rainbow Room. This is pretty lame."

"You're right."

Still holding his hands, I slide down off the couch until I'm on one knee. His eyes widen in amusement.

"David Rosen. From the first minute I saw you—at Ten Bells in that blue blazer with your headphones in—I knew you were the one."

I have a flash of him: young professional, hair cut too short, smiling awkwardly at me.

"I wasn't wearing headphones."

"Yes you were. You told me it was too loud in there."

"It is too loud in there," David says.

"I know," I say, shaking his hands. His glasses fall. I pick them up and put them on the sofa next to him. "It *is* too loud in there. I love that we both know that, and that we agree that movies should be twenty minutes shorter. I love that we both hate slow-walkers and that you think watching reruns is a waste of time value. I love that you use the term *time value*!"

"To be fair, that's—"

"David," I say. I drop his hands and place both my palms on either side of his face. "Marry me. Let's do it. For real this time. I love you."

He looks at me. His naked brown eyes look into mine. I feel my breath suspend. One, two—

"Okay," he says.

"Okay?"

"Okay." He laughs, and reaches for me. My lips meet his, and then we're in a tangle of limbs making our way to the floor. David sits up and bangs into the coffee table. "Shit. Ow." It's wood with a glass top and tends to come off its hinges unless you move the whole thing in one piece.

We stop what we're doing to attend to the table.

"Watch the corners," I say. We pick it up and set it back down, nudging the top into formation on the base. Once it's done, we stare at each other from either end of the table, breathing hard.

"Dannie," he says. "Why now?"

I don't tell him what I can't, of course. What Dr. Christine accused me of withholding. That the reason I've been avoiding our forever is the same reason it needs to happen now—without delay. That in forging one path, I am, in fact, ensuring another never comes to fruition.

Instead, I say this:

"It's time, David. We fit together. I love you. What more do you need? I'm ready, and I'm sorry it took me so long."

And that's true, too. As true as anything is.

"Just that," he says. His face looks happier than I've seen it in years.

He takes my hand and, despite the three feet now between the couch and the coffee table, he leads me deliberately, slowly, into the bedroom. He nudges me back gently until I'm just perched on the bed.

"I love you, too," he says. "In case it wasn't obvious."

"It is," I say. "I know."

He undresses me with an intention that hasn't been there in a long time. Usually when we have sex, we don't do a lot of mood-setting. We're not particularly imaginative, and we're always pressed for time. The sex David and I have is good—great, even. It always has been. We work well together. We communicated early and often and we know what works. David is thoughtful and generous and, although I'm not sure I'd call us ambitious, there is a certain competitive edge to our lovemaking that never lets it feel stale or boring.

But tonight is different.

With his right hand, he reaches forward and begins to unbutton my shirt. His knuckles are cool, and I shiver against him. My shirt is an old, white button-down J.Crew. Boring. Predictable. He'll be met with a nude bra underneath. Same old. But what's happening here tonight feels anything but.

He keeps unbuttoning. He takes his time, threading the silk knobs through their eye slits until the whole thing comes undone at the waist. I shimmy my shoulders until it's off and falls to the floor.

David puts one hand on my stomach, and with the other he

threads a thumb into the seam of my skirt. He holds me in place as he unzips it. This is less of a slow burn. It comes off in one swoop, falling into a puddle at my feet. I stand up and step out of it. My bra and underwear don't match. They're both Natori, although the bra is nude cotton and the underwear is black silk. I dispense with both and then push him down onto the bed. I lean forward over him, my breast grazing the side of his face. He reaches out and bites it.

"Ow!" I say.

"Ow?" He puts both hands on my back and runs them down slowly. "That hurt?"

"Yes. Since when are you a biter?"

"Since never," he says. "Sorry."

He reaches out and kisses me. It's a slow and deep kiss, meant to recenter us. It works.

David is working on his shirt—his hands on the buttons. I put mine over his and stop him.

"What?" he asks. He's out of breath, his chest straining.

I don't say anything. When he tries to stand, I put my hands on his shoulders and nudge him back down.

"Dannie?" he whispers.

I answer by guiding his hand to my stomach and then down, down until I feel that concave spot that makes me inhale. I hold his hand there. He looks at me—first confusion, then recognition dawning as I press his hand back and then forward, back and then forward. I take my hand away from his and grab on to his shoulders. He's breathing along with me—and I close my eyes against the rhythm, his hand, the incoming collapse that is mine, and mine alone.

✦

Afterward, we lie in bed together. We're both on our phones, looking up venues.

"Should we tell people?" David asks.

I pause, but what I say is: "Of course. We're getting married."

He looks at me. "Right. When do you want to do it?"

"Soon," I say. "We've waited so long already. Next month?"

David laughs. It's a sincere laugh, guttural—the kind I love from him. "You're funny," he says.

I put down my phone and roll to him. "What?"

"Oh, you're serious? Dannie, you're not serious."

"Of course I am."

He shakes his head. "Not even *you* could plan and execute a wedding in a month."

"Who says we have to have a wedding?"

He raises his eyebrows at me, then squints them together. "Your mother, mine. Come on, Dannie. This is ridiculous. We've waited four and a half years, we can't just elope now. Are you kidding? Because I really can't tell."

"I just want to get it done."

"How romantic," he deadpans.

"You know what I mean."

David sets his phone down. He looks at me. "I don't, actually. You love planning. That's like . . . your whole thing. You once planned a Thanksgiving down to pee breaks."

"Yeah, well . . ."

"Dannie, I want to get married, too. But let's do it the right way. Let's do it *our* way. Okay?"

He looks at me, waiting for an answer. But I can't give him one, not the one he wants. I don't have time for our way. I don't have time to plan. We have five months. Five months until I'm living in an apartment my best friend wants to buy, with the boyfriend she wants to buy it with. I need to stop this. I need to do whatever I can to make sure it never comes true.

"I'll be a planning machine," I say. "It's all I'm going to focus on. How does December sound? We can have a holiday wedding to match our holiday proposal. It'll be festive."

"We're Jews," David says. He's back on his phone.

"Maybe it will snow," I say, ignoring him. "David? December? I don't want to wait."

This makes him stop. He shakes his head, leans over, and kisses my shoulder blade. I know I've won. "December?"

I nod.

"Okay," he says. "December it is."

# Chapter Eleven

I have a giant case dropped in my lap on Thursday. One of our biggest clients—let's just say they revolutionized the health-food store—wants to announce an acquisition of a delivery service company on Monday, before the markets open. David and I were supposed to go home to Philadelphia and tell my parents the December plan in person, but it's never going to happen this weekend.

I call him at eight, while crouched over piles of documents in the conference room. There are twelve other associates and four partners barking orders and containers of empty Chinese food surrounding me. It's a war zone. I love it.

"I'm not getting out of here this weekend," I tell him. "Even to come home to sleep. Forget Philly."

I hear the TV on behind him. "What happened?"

"Can't say, but it's a big one."

"No shit," he says. "Whol—"

I clear my throat. "I'm going to be sleeping here for the next three days. Can we do next weekend?"

"I have Pat's bachelor party."

"Right. Arizona." They're going to drink beer and practice target shooting—neither of which David has any interest in. I'm not even sure why he's going. He barely sees Pat anymore.

"It's fine," he says. "We'll just call and fill them in. They'll be thrilled either way. I think your mom was starting to give up on me."

My parents love David. Of course they do. He's a lot like my brother, or what I imagine he'd have turned out to be. Smart, calm, even-tempered. Michael never got in trouble. He was the one making chore charts when we were kids, and he did model UN before he even learned to drive. He and David would be friends, I know they would. And it still stings me that he's not here. That he won't ever be here. That he didn't see me graduate or accept my first job, hasn't been to our apartment, and won't get to watch me get married.

My parents bugged David and me incessantly during the first two years of our engagement to set a date, but less so now. I know how much they want this for me, and themselves. David's wrong—at this point, they'd probably be fine with City Hall.

"Okay. My dad might be in the city next week."

"Thursday," David says. "I'm already taking him to lunch."

"You're the best."

He makes a noncommittal noise through the phone. Just then, Aldridge walks into the room. I hang up on David without saying goodbye. He'll understand. He used to do the same thing to me all the time at Tishman.

"How's it looking?" Aldridge asks.

Normally a managing partner would not ask a senior associate how an acquisition of this magnitude was "looking." He'd go directly to a senior partner in the room. But since Aldridge hired me, we've developed a real rapport. From time to time, he calls me into his office to talk about cases, or offer me guidance. I know the other associates notice, and I know they don't like it, and it feels great. There are a few ways to get ahead at a corporate law firm, and being the managing partner's favorite is definitely one of them.

Most corporate lawyers are sharks. But I've never heard Aldridge so much as raise his voice. And he somehow manages to have a personal life. He's been married to his husband, Josh, for twelve years. They have a daughter, Sonja, who is eight. His office is peppered with photos of her, them. Vacations, school pictures, Christmas cards. A real life outside those four walls.

"We're still in due diligence but should have some documents up for signature on Sunday," I say.

"Saturday," Aldridge hits back. He looks at me, an eyebrow raised.

"That's what I meant."

"Did everyone order food?" Aldridge announces to the room. In addition to the Chinese food cartons on the conference table, there are burger wrappers from The Palm and chopped salad containers from Quality Italian, but in the middle of a big deal like this, food is a *constant* necessity.

Immediately, all fifteen lawyers look up, eyes blinking. Sherry, the senior partner managing the case, answers for the room. "We're fine, Miles," she says.

"Mitch!" Aldridge calls for his assistant who is never more than ten feet away. "Let's order some Levain. Get these fine people a little caffeine and sugar."

"We've got it covered, really—" Sherry starts.

"These people look hungry," he says.

He strolls out of the conference room. I catch Sherry's eyes narrowing before she dives back into the document that's in front of her. Sometimes kindness under pressure can feel like a slight, and I don't blame Sherry for reacting that way. She doesn't have time to console us with cookies—that's a privilege for the very high up.

The thing many people don't realize about corporate lawyers is that they are nothing like what you see on TV shows. Sherry, Aldridge, and I will never step foot in a courtroom. We'll never argue a case. We do deals; we're not litigators. We prepare documents and review every piece of paperwork for a merger or an acquisition. Or to take a company public. On *Suits*, Harvey does both paperwork and crushes it in court. In reality, the lawyers at our firm who argue cases don't have a clue what we do in these conference rooms. Most of them haven't prepared a document in a decade.

People think our form of corporate law is the less ambitious of the two, and while in many ways it's less glamorous—no closing arguments, no media interviews—nothing compares to the power of the paper. At the end of the day, law comes down to what is written, and we do the writing.

I love the order of deal making, the clarity of language—how there is little room for interpretation and none for error. I love the black-and-white terms. I love that in the final stages of closing a deal—particularly those of the magnitude Wachtell takes on—seemingly insurmountable obstacles arise. Apocalyptic scenarios, disagreements, and details that threaten to topple it all. It seems impossible we'll ever get both parties on the same page, but somehow we do. Somehow, contracts get agreed upon and signed. Somehow, deals get done. And when it finally happens, it's exhilarating. Better than any day in court. It's written. Binding. Anyone can bend a judge's or jury's will with bravado, but to do it on paper—in black and white—that takes a particular kind of artistry. It's truth in poetry.

I come home once on Saturday just to shower and change, and on Sunday I drag myself home well past midnight. When I get there David is asleep, but there's a note on the counter and takeout pasta in the fridge: cacio e pepe from L'Artusi, my favorite. David is always really thoughtful like this—having my favorite takeout in the fridge, leaving the chocolate I like on the counter. He spent the weekend at the office as well, but since he moved to the fund he has more autonomy over his time than I do. I'm still at the mercy of the partners, the clients, and the whims of the market. For David, it's mostly just the market, and since much of the money his company handles is longer-term investment, it takes a lot of the harried day-to-day pressure off. As David likes to say: "No one ever runs into my office."

I have two missed calls and three texts from Bella, whom I've ignored all weekend, and, in fact, all of last week. She doesn't know David and I got reengaged on the living room floor, and that we are officially planning a wedding for December—or we will be anyway when we have a second free.

I text her back: *Just getting in from an all-weekender. Call you tomorrow.*

Despite the fact that I haven't slept in close to seventy-two hours, I don't feel tired. We got the signatures. Tomorrow—or today, actually—our clients will announce that they have acquired a billion-dollar company. They're expanding their global reach and will revolutionize the way people shop for groceries.

I feel like I always do after we close a big case: high. I haven't done cocaine, except for one ill-advised night in college, but it's the same sensation. My heart races, my pupils dilate. I feel like I could run a marathon. We won.

There's an open bottle of Chianti on the counter, and I pour myself a glass. Our apartment has a big kitchen window that looks out over Gramercy Park. I sit down at the kitchen table and gaze out the window. It's dark out, but the city lights illuminate the trees and sidewalk. When I first moved to New York, I used to walk by the park and think that someday I'd live near it. Now, David and I have a key. We can go inside the park anytime we want. But we don't, of course. We're busy. We went the day we got the key, with a bottle of champagne, stayed long enough to open it and make a toast, but haven't been back since. It's pretty to look at through the window, though. And the location is convenient. Very central. I promise myself that David and I will take some iced coffees in there and do some wedding planning soon.

It's a beautiful apartment. It has two bedrooms and high ceilings, a full kitchen and dining area, a TV and couch alcove. We decorated it in all grays and whites. It's calming, serene. It looks like the kind of apartment that gets photographed. It's everything I ever wanted.

I look down at my hand, still wearing that engagement ring. And now, soon, a band. I finish my wine, brush my teeth, wash my face, and crawl into bed. I take the ring off and set it in the little bowl on my nightstand. It sparkles back at me, a promise. I vow that first thing tomorrow, I'll call a wedding planner.

# Chapter Twelve

I leave work at seven on Monday, a full hour before I should, and meet Bella at Snack Taverna in the West Village. It's this tiny bistro, the best Greek food in the city, and we've been going there since we moved to New York—way before I could afford to.

Bella is back to being fifteen minutes late. I order us fava beans drenched in olive oil and garlic—her favorite. They're on the table when she arrives.

She texted me back this morning and demanded we have dinner tonight. *It has been too long,* she said. *I feel like you're avoiding me.*

I rarely leave work early, if ever. When David and I make dinner reservations they're always for eight-thirty or nine. But now it's a little past seven, still light out, and I'm sitting here. Bella has always been the only person in my life who can talk me out of my norm.

"It's so hot out there," she says when she arrives. She's wearing a white brocade-and-lace dress from Zimmermann and gold lace-up sandals. Her hair is up in a topknot, some loose strands dangling down her neck.

"It's a swamp. Summer always happens so suddenly." I lean over the table and kiss her on the cheek. I've sweated through my silk shirt and pencil skirt. I own basically no summer clothes. Luckily the air-conditioning is on full blast in here.

"How was the weekend?" she asks. "Did you sleep at all?"

I smile. "No."

She shakes her head. "You loved it."

"Maybe." I scoop some beans onto her plate. I have to know: "Did you guys hear anything more about the apartment?"

She looks at me and frowns, and then her face dawns recognition. "Oh, right! There's this other one I think I want. It's this totally savage place in Meatpacking. I honestly didn't know they had anything like that left there. Everything is so generic now."

"You don't like the Dumbo loft?"

She shrugs. "I'm just not sure I want to live there. There's only one grocery store, and it must be freezing in the winter. All of those wide streets that close to the water? It seems kind of isolated."

"It's close to every train," I say. "And the view is spectacular. There's so much light, Bella. I can see you painting there."

Bella squints at me. "What's going on? You hated that place. You told me I shouldn't even consider it."

I wave her off. She's right, though. What am I doing? The words keep tumbling out, like I have no control over them. "I don't know," I say. "What do I know? I've lived within ten blocks for the last decade."

Bella leans forward. Her face splits into a sly smile. "You love that place."

It's raw space, but I have to admit it's beautiful. Somehow industrial and energetic and peaceful, all at once.

"No," I say. Firm. Definitive. "It's a pile of plywood. I'm just playing devil's advocate."

Bella crosses her arms. "You love it," she says.

I don't know why I can't just condemn it. Tell her she's right—it's freezing and too far and absurd—then drop it. I should be thrilled that she has forgotten about it. I want her to forget about it. I want that apartment to disappear into the atmosphere. So far I'm doing a good job at preventing that fateful hour. If the apartment disappears, so does what happened there.

"No, it's true," I say. "Dumbo is far. And Aaron said it would need a ton of work." The last part is a little bit of a lie.

Bella opens her mouth to say something but closes it again.

"So things are good with you guys?" I venture.

Bella sighs. "He said you had a nice time at the apartment. Like maybe you liked him a little better? He said you seemed friendly, which is entirely out of character."

"Hey."

"You're many things," Bella says, "but friendly never really comes to mind."

I have a flash of Bella and me, newly minted New Yorkers, in line for some ludicrously expensive club in the Meatpacking District. Bella had lent me one of her dresses, something short and bright, and it was cold, although I don't remember the season—late fall, early winter? We were without coats, as we usually were in the years surrounding twenty.

In this slice of memory, Bella is flirting with the door guy, a club promoter named Scoot or Hinds, some sound not word, someone who liked when hot girls showed up, liked when Bella did. She's telling him she just has a few more friends she wants to bring in.

"They like you?" he asks.

"No one is," Bella says. She shakes her hair off her neck.

"Her?" Scoot points to me. He's less than impressed, this I can tell. Being Bella's friend has always felt a little bit like standing in her shadow. It used to make me insecure, maybe it still does, but over time we found our things, our shared ground, our complimenting balance. Standing in front of that club maybe we hadn't, yet.

Bella leans forward and whispers something into Scoot's ear. I don't hear, but I can imagine what it is: *She's a princess, you know. She's royalty. Fifth in line to the Dutch throne. A Vanderbilt.*

It used to embarrass me that Bella had to do this. It embarrasses me that night in Meatpacking, too. But I never tell her. Her proximity is my gift; my silence is hers. I make her life smooth and solid. She makes mine bright and dazzling. This seems fair. A good trade.

"Come on in, ladies," Scoot says. We do. We enter Twitch or Slice or Markd. Whatever it was called, it's gone now. We dance. Men buy us drinks. I feel pretty in her dress, although it is a little too short on me, a little loose in the chest. It hugs in the wrong spots.

At a certain point, two men come up to hit on us. I am not interested. I have a boyfriend. He's in law school at Yale. We've been together for eight months. I'm faithful to him. I think, maybe, I'll marry him, but it is a passing thought.

Everywhere we go Bella flirts. She does not like that I don't. She thinks I am withholding, that I do not know how to have a good time. She's right, but only sometimes. This form of fun does not come naturally to me, and therefore feels impossible to engage in. I am constantly trying to learn the rules, only to realize that the people who win don't seem to follow any.

One of the men makes a comment. Everyone laughs. I roll my eyes.

"You're so friendly," he says. It sticks.

At the restaurant now, I scoop a fava bean onto a small piece of crispbread. It's hot, and the garlic pops in my mouth.

"Morgan and Ariel met Greg on Saturday," Bella says. "*They* loved him."

Morgan and Ariel are a couple Bella met through the gallery scene four-ish years ago. Since then, they've become more David's and my friends than Bella's—mostly because we're better at making dinner reservations and staying in the country. Morgan is a photographer who does popular cityscapes and had a coffee table book called *On High* come out last year to much fanfare. Ariel works in private equity.

"Oh?"

"Yeah," Bella says. "I honestly thought you would, too." She continues while I chew. "I'm not mad, it's just . . . you're always wanting me to be more serious, and be with someone who cares. Like, you never stop talking about that. And he does. And it doesn't seem to matter to you."

"It matters," I tell her. I do not want to keep talking about this.

"You have a weird way of showing it."

She's annoyed, her voice edgy, her arms outstretched. I sit back.

"I know," I say. I swallow. "I mean, I can see that, that he cares. And I'm happy for you."

"You are?" she says.

"I am," I say. "He seems like a good guy."

"A good guy? Come on, Dannie, that's pathetic." She's petulant, angry. I don't really blame her. I'm giving her nothing. "I'm really crazy about him," she says. "I've never felt this way before, and I know I've said this a lot, and I know you don't believe me—"

"I believe you," I say.

Bella sticks her elbows on the table and leans forward. All the way. "What is it?" she says. "It's me, Dannie. You can say anything. You know that. What do you not like about him?"

All at once my eyes sting up with tears. It is an unusual reaction for me, and I blink, more in surprise than in an effort to stop it. Bella looks so hopeful sitting across from me. Naïve, even. So full of the possibility she purports to feel. And I have a giant secret I cannot tell her. Something profound, terrible, and strange has happened in my life, and she doesn't get to know.

"I guess I've had you all to myself for a really long time," I say. "It's not fair, but the idea of you being with someone for real makes me feel, I don't know." I swallow. "Jealous, maybe?"

She sits back, satisfied. Thank god I came up with something. Bless me for being a lawyer. She buys it. This makes sense to her. She knows I have always wanted the space closest to her, front position, and she has given it to me.

"But you have David, and it's fine," she says.

"Yeah. It's just always been that way, so it feels different."

She nods.

"But you're right," I say. "It's dumb. I guess emotions aren't always rational."

Bella laughs. "I genuinely never thought I'd hear you say those words." She reaches across the table and squeezes my hand. "Nothing is going to change, I promise you. Or if it does, it'll be for the better. You'll see me even more. You'll see me so much you'll be sick of me."

"Well then, cheers—I look forward to being sick of you."

Bella smiles. We clink glasses. Then she waves a hand back and forth in front of her face. "So you like him, sorta. Maybe. You're jealous. We'll leave it there. Okay?"

I shake my head. "Sure."

"But he really is—" she starts, and her voice trails off, her gaze with it. "I don't know how to describe it. It's like I finally get it, you know? What everyone always talks about."

"Bella," I say. "That's wonderful."

Bella wiggles her nose. "What's new with you?"

I take a deep breath. I blow some air out through my lips. "David and I got engaged," I say.

She picks up her water glass. "Dannie. That's decades-old news."

"Four and a half years."

"Right."

"No. I mean, we're going to get married this time. For real. In December."

Bella's eyes widen. Then they flit down to my hand and back up again. "Holy shit. For real?"

"For real. It's time. We're both just so busy and there's always a reason not to, but I realized there's a really big reason to do it. So we will."

The waiter comes over, and Bella turns to him abruptly. "A bottle of champagne and ten minutes," she says. He leaves.

"He's been asking me to set a date for a long time."

"I'm aware," Bella says. "But you always say no."

"It's not that I say no," I say. "It's just that I haven't said yes."

"What changed?"

I look at her. Bella. My Bella. She looks so radiant, so high on love. How can I tell her that it's her? That she's the reason.

"I guess I just finally know the future I want," I say.

She nods. "Did you tell Meryl and Alan?"

My parents. "We called them. They're thrilled. They asked if we wanted to do it at The Rittenhouse."

"Do you? In Philly? It's so generic." Bella wiggles her nose. "I always saw you doing something very Manhattan."

"I'm generic, though. You always forget that."

She smiles.

"But no Philly," I say. "It's just inconvenient. We'll see what's available in the city. "

The champagne comes, and our glasses are filled. Bella holds hers to mine. "To good men," she says. "May we know them, may we love them, may we love each other's."

I swallow down some bubbles.

"I'm starving," I say. "I'm ordering."

Bella lets me. I get a Greek salad, lamb souvlaki, spanakopita, and roasted eggplant with tahini.

We sink into the food like a bath.

"Do you remember the first time we came here?" Bella asks me. We rarely make it through a meal without her repurposing some memory. She is so sentimental. Sometimes I think about our old age and it seems intolerable to have to sift through that much history. We have twenty-five years now, and there's already too much to pull from, too much to make her weepy. Old age is going to be brutal.

"No," I say. "It's a restaurant. We've come here a lot."

Bella rolls her eyes. "You had just moved down from Columbia, and we were celebrating your job with Clarknell."

I shake my head. "We celebrated Clarknell at Daddy-O." The bar off Seventh we used to frequent at all hours of the night for the first three years we lived in the city.

"No," Bella says. "We met Carl and Berg there before we came here, just you and me."

She's right, we did. I remember the tables all had candles on them, and there was a bowl of Jordan almonds by the door. I scooped two handfuls into the pouch in my purse on the way out. They don't keep them stocked anymore, probably because of customers like me.

"Maybe we did," I say.

Bella shakes her head. "You can never be wrong."

"It's actually part of my job description," I say. "But I seem to remember a night in late two thousand fourteen."

"Way before David," Bella says.

"Yeah."

"You love him?" she says. It's a strange thing to ask and it's not lost on either one of us, this question, and that she's asked it.

"I do," I say. "We want so many of the same things, we have the same plans. It fits, you know?"

Bella cuts a slice of feta and spears a tomato on top. "So you know what it's like, then," she says.

"What?"

"To feel like you've met your person."

Bella holds my gaze, and I feel something sharp prick my stomach from the inside out. It's like she put the pin there.

"I'm sorry," I say. "I'm sorry if I was weird with Aaron. I really do like him, and I'll love him if and whenever you do. Just take it slow," I say.

She puts the bite into her mouth and chews. "Impossible," she says.

"I know," I say. "But I'm your best friend. I have to say it anyway."

# Chapter Thirteen

The swamp of July meets us with a heavy, cloying inevitability: the weather is going to get worse before it gets better. We still have to get through August. David asks me to meet him for lunch in Bryant Park one Wednesday toward the end of the month.

In the summer, Bryant Park sets up café tables around the perimeter and corporates in suits take their lunches outside. David's office is in the thirties and mine in the fifties, so Forty-Second and Sixth Avenue is our magic midway zone. We rarely meet for lunch, but when we do, it's usually Bryant Park.

David is waiting with two Nicoise salads from Pret and my favorite Arnold Palmer from Le Pain Quotidien. Both establishments are in walking distance and have indoor seating so we can eat there in the colder months. We're not fancy lunch people. I'd be happy with a deli salad for two meals out of three most days. In fact, one of our first dates was to this very park with these very salads. We sat outside even though it was too cold, and when David noticed me shivering, he unwrapped his scarf and put it around me, then he jumped up to get me a hot coffee from the cart on the corner. It was a small gesture, but so indicative of who he was—

who he is. He's always been willing to put my happiness before his comfort.

I take a car down to meet him, but I'm still drenched when I arrive.

"It's a hundred degrees," I say, folding myself into the seat across from him. My heels are rubbing blisters into the backs of my feet. I need talcum powder and a pedicure, immediately. I can't remember the last time I stopped to get my nails done.

"Actually, it's ninety-six but feels like one oh two," David says, reading off his phone.

I blink at him.

"Sorry," he says. "But I understand the point."

"Why are we outside?" I reach for my drink. It's miraculously still cold, even though the ice has almost melted entirely.

"Because we never get any fresh air."

"This is hardly fresh," I say. "Do the summers keep getting worse?"

"Yes."

"I'm too hot to even eat."

"Good," he says. "Because the food was a ruse."

He drops a calendar book down on the table between us.

"What is this?"

"It's a planner," he says. "Dates, times, numbers. We need to start getting organized about this thing."

"The wedding?"

"Yes," he says. "The wedding. Unless we start making phone calls, everything is going to be booked. They are already. We're too tired at night to talk about it, and this is how we got four years down the line."

"And a half," I remind him.

"Right," he says. "And a half."

He bites his bottom lip and shakes his head at me.

"We need a human planner," I say.

"Yes, but we needed to plan to even get a planner. A lot of the top people book up two years in advance."

"I know," I say. "I know."

"I'm not saying this is like, your area," David says. "But I think we should do it together. I'd like that. If you want."

"Of course," I say. "I'd love that."

This is how badly David wants to marry me. He'll take his lunch hour to look over *Brides*.

"No cheesy shit," he says.

"I'm offended at the suggestion," I say.

"And I don't think we should have a wedding party," he says. "Too much work, and I don't want a bachelor party."

Pat's, in Arizona, didn't exactly go according to plan. They booked the wrong hotel and ended up getting delayed at the airport for nine and a half hours. Everyone got drunk on beers and Bloody Marys, and David was hungover the rest of the weekend.

"I'm with you. Bella can hold our rings, or something."

"Fine."

"And white flowers only."

"Works for me."

"Heavy cocktail hour, who cares about dinner?"

"Exactly."

"And open bar."

"But no shots."

David smiles. "No special wedding shot? All right, then." He flips over his wrist. "Nice progress. I gotta go."

"That's it?" I say. "Planner and run?"

"You want to have lunch now?"

I look at my phone. Seven missed calls and thirty-two new emails. "No. I was late when I got here."

David stands and hands me my salad. I take it.

"We'll get it done," I tell him.

"I know we will."

I imagine David wearing a sweater and a gold band on his ring finger, opening wine in our kitchen on a cozy winter night. A sense of sustained comfort. The materials of a warm life.

"I'm happy," I tell him.

"I'm glad," he says. "Because either way, you're stuck with me."

# Chapter Fourteen

It's now the end of August. Long ago in January, David and I booked a summer share in Amagansett for Labor Day weekend with Bella and our friends Morgan and Ariel.

Bella and Aaron are still together, and unsurprisingly, Aaron is joining us on this trip, turning the weekend into a triple date, which is fine by me. Historically, Bella and I are on opposite schedules at the beach. She sleeps late and parties late. I wake up at dawn and go for a run, cook us breakfast, and fit in a few hours of work before heading down to the water.

David rented us a Zipcar, which is proving problematic in transporting us, our luggage, and Morgan, who is meant to be driving with us. Ariel is taking the jitney later after work.

"This thing looks like it belongs on a Monopoly board," Morgan says. She's in her forties, which you'd never know except for the salt-and-pepper hair she sports. She has a baby face, no wrinkles, not even the tiny lines around her eyes. It's wild. I've been sneaking Botox since I was twenty-nine, although David would murder me if he ever found out.

"They said it fits four." David is shoving my weekend bag

over our suitcase, jamming his shoulder into the trunk and pushing.

"Four tiny people and their tiny-people purses."

I laugh. We haven't even tried to fit Morgan's backpack or roller bag in yet.

Two hours later, we're on our way in an SUV David rented last minute from Hertz. We leave the Zipcar parked illegally on our street with the promise from a manager of imminent pickup.

Morgan sits up front with David while I balance my computer on my knees in the back. It's Thursday, and although this week is sanctioned vacation, there is still work to be done.

They're singing along to Lionel Richie. "Endless Love."

*And I, I want to share all my love, with you. No one else will do.*

"This reminds me," I yell forward. "We need a list of do-not-plays for the wedding."

Morgan turns the music down. "How is planning going?"

David shrugs. "Cautiously optimistic."

"He's lying," I say. "We're totally behind."

"How did you guys do it?" David asks.

Morgan and Ariel were married three years ago in an epic weekend in the Catskills. They rented out this themed inn called The Roxbury, and the whole wedding took place in various structures on a neighboring farm. They brought in everything: tables, chairs, chandeliers. They arranged artful bales of hay to separate the lounge area from the dance floor. There was a cheese-and-whisky bar, and every table had the most gorgeous arrangement of wildflowers you'd ever seen. Photos from their wedding were on *The Cut* and *Vogue* online.

"It was easy," Morgan says.

"We're not on their level, babe," I say. "Our entire apartment is white."

Morgan laughs. "Please. You know it's what I love to do. We had fun with it." She fiddles with the dial on the radio. "So Greg is coming?"

"I think so. Is he?"

David looks back at me.

"Yep."

"He seems great, right?" Morgan asks.

"Really nice," David says. "We've only met him, what? Once? It's been a crazy summer. I can't believe it's over." He glances at me in the rearview.

"Almost over," Morgan says.

I make a noncommittal noise in the backseat.

"He seems stable, though, like he has a real job and isn't constantly trying to get her to leave the country on her parents' credit card," David continues.

"Not like us zany freeloader artists," Morgan teases.

"Hey," David says. "You're more successful than any of us."

It's true. Morgan sells out every show she puts on. Her photos go for fifty thousand dollars. She gets more for a twenty-four-hour editorial job than I make in two months.

"We had a great time with him at dinner a few weeks ago," Morgan says. "She seems different. I went by the gallery last week, too, and thought so again. Like more grounded or something."

"I agree," I volunteer. "She does."

The truth is that since that day in the park, since David and I started talking about the wedding seriously, I've thought about my vision less and less. We're building the right future now, the one that we've been working toward. All evidence is on our side that that version will be the one we're living come December. I'm not worried.

"Her longest relationship by a mile already," Morgan says. "You think this one will stick?"

I hit save on an email draft. "Seems that way."

We turn off the main highway, and I close my computer. We're nearly there.

The house is the one we've rented for this same week the last five summers in a row. It's in Amagansett, down Beach Road. It's old. The shingles are falling off and the furniture is mildew-y, and yet it's perfect because it's right on the water. There's nothing separating us from the ocean but a sand dune. I love it. As soon as we pass the Stargazer and turn onto 27, I lower the window to let in the thick, salty air. I immediately start to relax. I love the massive old trees lining the lanes and stretching down to that wide expanse of beach—big sky, big ocean, and air. Room.

When we pull up to the house it's already late in the afternoon, and Bella and Aaron are there. She rented a yellow convertible, and it's parked out front, a chipper greeting. The door to the house is flung open, as if they've just arrived, although I know they haven't. Bella texted me they were there hours ago.

My first instinct is to be annoyed—how many summers, how many times, have I told her to keep the doors closed so we don't get bugs? But I check myself. This is *our* house, after all. Not just mine. And I want all of us to have a nice weekend.

I help David unload the trunk, handing Morgan her roller as Bella comes out of the house. She has on a pale blue linen dress, the bottom of which has paint splotches on it. This fills me with a very particular kind of joy. To my knowledge she hasn't painted all year, and the sight of her—hair wild in the wind, the atmosphere of creation hanging around her like mist—is wonderful to witness.

"You made it!" She throws her arms around Morgan and gives me a big kiss on the side of my head.

"I told Ariel we'd pick her up at the east station in like twenty minutes. David, can you grab her? I can't figure out how to put the top up." She gestures toward the perky convertible.

"I can do it," Morgan says.

"It's no problem." This from David, even though traffic was horrific and we'd been in the car for nearly five hours. "Let me just drop our stuff."

Bella kisses me on both cheeks. "Come on in," she says to Morgan. "I did room assignments."

David raises his eyebrows at me as we follow the two of them inside.

The house is decorated in part like an old farmhouse and in part like a college girl's first shabby-chic apartment. Old wooden boxes and furniture intermix with white oversize couches and Laura Ashley pillows.

"You two are downstairs again," Bella says to David and me. The downstairs bedroom is ours, and has been since we first rented the house, the summer Francesco came and he and Bella fought loudly in the kitchen for thirty-six hours before he pulled away in the middle of the night—with the one and only car we'd rented for the weekend.

"Morgan and Ariel are upstairs with us."

"You know we don't swing straight," Morgan says, already on the stairs.

"I'm not straight," Bella says.

"Yeah, but your boyfriend is."

David and I set our suitcases down in the bedroom. I sit on the bed, which is wicker, as is the dresser and rocking chair, and I'm hit with a nostalgia I don't usually experience or entertain.

"They got new sheets this year," David says.

I look down, and he's right. They're white when they're usually some mix of paisley.

David leans down and brushes his lips to my forehead. "I'm gonna jet. You need anything?"

I shake my head. "I'll unpack for us."

He stretches, bending over and grabbing onto opposite elbows with his hands. I stand up and rub the spot on his lower back that I know pinches. He winces.

"Do you want me to drive?" I ask. "I can go. You just drove for five hours."

"No," David says, still folded in half. "I forgot to put you on the rental agreement."

He lifts himself, and I hear his vertebrae crack on the way up.

"Bye." He kisses me and leaves, grabbing the keys out of his pocket.

I open the closet to find a hanging rod, but no hangers—as usual, Bella has stolen them all and taken them upstairs.

I plod into the hallway in search of the coat closet and find Aaron in the kitchen.

"Hey," he says. "You guys made it. Sorry, I went for a swim."

He's dressed in board shorts with a towel draped over his shoulders like a cape.

"David went to town to get Ariel," I say.

Aaron nods. "That was really nice of him. I would have been happy to go."

"David loves the car, it's no problem," I say.

He smiles.

"Morgan is upstairs with Bella." I point toward the ceiling with my index finger. I hear their feet moving on the floorboards above us.

"You hungry?" he asks me.

He goes to the refrigerator and takes out three avocados. I'm struck by his ease, his belonging here.

"Right, you cook," I say.

He cocks his head at me.

"I just mean, Bella said."

He nods in response.

What Bella actually said was that he made butternut squash and sage risotto, but before she could have one little bite they'd had sex on the counter, right there in the kitchen. I blink away the image and run my hands down my face, shaking my head.

"So is that a no on guacamole?"

"What? No, yes, definitely. I'm starving," I say.

"You have interesting ways, Ms. Kohan."

He starts piling ingredients onto the counter: onions, cilantro, jalapeños, and a variety of vegetables.

"Can I help?" I ask.

"You can open that tequila," he says.

He gestures with his head to the countertop, where our booze for the weekend is artfully displayed. I find the tequila.

"Ice?" I ask. "I'll pour."

"Thanks."

I take two small tumbler glasses down from the cabinet and pour a finger of tequila in each one. I pull out the ice tray, careful to hold the bottom drawer of the freezer when I do—another quirk of the house.

"Heads-up." Aaron tosses me a lime. I miss, and it rolls out of the room. I'm chasing it on my hands and knees when Bella comes floating down the stairs, still in her blue tunic, hair now up.

"Rogue lime," I say, snatching it before it scurries under the sofa.

"I'm starving," she says. "What do we have?"

"Aaron is making guacamole."

"Who?"

I shake my head. "Greg. Sorry."

"What do you guys want to do for dinner?" Bella asks us. I follow her into the kitchen and she snakes her arms around Aaron's waist, kissing him on the back of the neck. He offers her up his tequila. She shakes her head.

I know, of course, that they've gotten closer. That while I've been at work all summer, Bella has been falling for this man. That they've been to museums and outdoor concerts and cool, tiny wine bars. That they've walked the West Side Highway at dusk and the High Line at sunrise and had sex on every single piece of furniture in her brownstone. Almost. She's told me all of it. But seeing them now, I'm met with a prick in my chest that I'm not entirely sure how to identify.

I take a seat at the counter and pick a tortilla chip out of the bag that Aaron has set out. He scoops some diced onions onto the back of a knife and dusts them into the guacamole bowl.

"Where did you learn to cook?" I ask. Anyone with knife skills impresses me. I like to believe it's the one thing that prevents me from being a good cook.

"I'm kind of self-taught," he says. He nudges Bella to the side and opens the oven. In goes an array of sliced peppers, onions, and potatoes. "But I grew up around food. My mom was a cook."

I know what that means. It's not the words themselves, although they are markers, but the way he says it—with a slight bewildered edge. Like he can't quite believe it, either.

"I'm sorry," I say.

He looks back at me. "Thank you. It was a long time ago."

"Dinner?" Bella asks. Her hands are on her hips, and Aaron loops his arms through hers, pulling her in and kissing her on the side of her face. "Whatever you want," he says. "I've got snacks covered."

"Tonight we have reservations at the Grill, or we can walk to Hampton Chutney if we're not in the mood for something serious," I say.

I'm always in charge of dinner reservations. Bella is always in charge of choosing which ones we use.

"I thought the Grill was tomorrow night."

I grab my phone and pull up our reservations document. Huh. "You're right," I say. "It is tomorrow night."

"Good," Bella says. "I wanted to stay in anyway." She snuggles closer to Aaron, who loops an arm around her.

"We can call David, ask him to stop at the store?"

"No need," Aaron says. "We came loaded. I have plenty to cook." He goes to the fridge and yanks it open. I peer over the counter. I see rainbows of vegetables and fruits, paper-wrapped cheeses, fresh parsley and mint, containers of oily olives, some rolling lemons and limes, and a large wedge of Parmesan. We are supremely stocked.

"You got all of this?" I ask.

In prior years, I'd be lucky to show up to a stick of butter. There is never anything in Bella's fridge but mossy lemons and vodka.

"What do you think?" she asks me.

"That I can't believe you went grocery shopping."

She beams.

I head out onto the back patio, which overlooks the ocean. It's cloudy today, and I shiver a little in my T-shirt and shorts. I need to grab a sweatshirt. I breathe in the fresh air, salty and tangy, and I exhale out the drive, the week, Aaron in the kitchen.

I open my eyes to the slow, melodic stylings of Frank Sinatra. "All the Way" wafts outside. I'm instantly reminded of the Rainbow Room, of twirling slowly under that rotating ceiling.

I turn around. Through the window I can see Aaron, his arms

around Bella, moving her to the beat. Her head is on his shoulder and there is a slight smile on her face. I wish I could take a picture. I've known her for twenty-five years and I've never seen her this relaxed with anyone, this herself. And I've never seen her close her eyes against a man.

I wait to go back inside until I hear the crunch of David's car returning on the gravel. By that time, the sun has already almost entirely set. There is just the fading of light, a slight blue on the disappearing horizon.

# Chapter Fifteen

When Bella and I were in high school, we used to play a game we called Stop. We'd see how far we could get in describing the grossest, nastiest thing before the other would be so revolted they'd have to yell out "Stop!" It started with an unfortunate piece of forgotten freezer meat and carried on from there. There were anthills, poison ivy welts, the intestines of a cow, and the microenvironment at the bottom of the community swimming pool.

This game comes to mind the next morning when I come upon a dead seagull on my run. Its head is bent at an impossible angle and its wings are shredded, the meaty portion, or what's left of it, being feasted on by flies. A piece of its red spine sits disconnected from its body.

I remember reading once that when a seagull dies it falls out of the sky on the spot. You could be just sitting on the beach, enjoying an orange ice pop, and wham, seagull to the head.

The fog is thick—a hazy mist that hangs over sand like a blanket. If I could see for a mile, which I can't, I might spot a fellow morning jogger, out training for the fall marathon. But as far as my eye can see, it's just me here now.

I bend down closer to the seagull. I don't think it has been dead a long time. But here, out in nature, things evolve quickly.

I snap a picture to show Bella.

No one was awake when I got up. David was like a log next to me, and the upstairs was still, but then it was barely six. Sometimes Ariel gets up to do work. I tried last summer to get her to jog with me, but there were so many excuses and it took so long that this year I vowed to invite no one.

I've never been a late sleeper, but these days anything past seven feels like noon. I need the morning. There's something about being the first one awake that feels precious, rare. I feel accomplished before I've even had my first cup of coffee. The whole day is better.

The return is short, no more than two miles, and when I get back the house is still asleep. I take the gray-shingled stairs to the kitchen and edge the sliding door open. My shirt is damp from my run—a combination of sweat and sea mist. I take it off, toss it over the back of a chair, and head toward the coffeepot, just in my sports bra.

Lid up, filter in, four giant scoops and an extra for the pot. It's a full house. I'm leaning forward, elbows on the counter, waiting for the first drips of caffeine, when I hear Bella's feet on the stairs. I can always tell it's her. I know the way her body sounds. I can hear the way she walks, honed from decades of sleepovers, her cushioned feet padding around the kitchen for late-night snacks. If I were blind, I think, I'd be able to tell every time she entered a room.

"You're up early," I say.

"I didn't drink last night." I hear her slide onto a stool, and I take a second mug down from the cabinet. "Did you sleep well?"

David is a silent sleeper. No snoring, no movement. Being in bed with him is like being alone. "I love waking up to the ocean," I say.

"It reminds me of when your parents had that place at the shore, remember?"

The coffee starts to descend in a sputtering fit. I turn toward Bella. Her hair is down and tangled around her, and she's wearing a white lace nightgown with a long terrycloth bathrobe, opened, over it.

"You came there?" I ask.

She looks at me like I'm crazy. "Yeah. You guys had it until we were like fourteen."

I shake my head. "We got rid of it after Michael—" I say. Still, all these years later, I can't bring myself to use the word.

"No, you didn't," she says. "You kept it for like four more summers. The place in Margate. The one with the blue awning?"

I take the pot out. It hisses in anger—it's not time—and I pour her half a cup, setting it down on the counter in front of her. "That wasn't ours."

"No, it was," Bella says. "It was on the ocean block. That little white house with the blue awning. The blue awning!"

"There was no awning," I say. I go to the refrigerator and take out almond milk and hazelnut Coffee mate. Bella remembered and picked it up for me.

"Yes there was," she says. "It was two blocks from the Wawa, and you guys kept bikes down there and we'd lock them up at the condos with the blue awnings!"

I hand her the almond milk. She shakes and pours.

"There was a dead seagull on the beach today," I say.

"Gross. Rotting carcass? Snapped spine into bone-popping shreds? Fly-eaten eyes pecked down to hollow sockets?"

"Stop." I slide her my phone, and she looks.

"I've seen worse."

"You know they fall out of the sky when they die?" I say.

"Yeah? What else would you expect them to do?"

The coffee machine downshifts into maintenance, and I pour myself a full cup, adding a hefty portion of creamer.

I go to sit next to Bella at the counter.

"Doesn't look like a beach day," she says. She swivels on her stool and looks outside.

"It'll burn off."

She shrugs, takes a sip, makes a face.

"I don't know how you drink that almond water," I say. "Why suffer? Do you know how good this is?" I hold my cup out to her.

"It's milk," she says.

"It's really not."

"It's me," she says. "I've just been feeling funky all week."

"Are you sick?"

She swallows. I feel something catch in my throat.

"I'm pregnant," she says. "I mean, I'm pretty sure."

I look at her. Her whole face is shining. It's like staring at the sun.

"You think or you know?"

"Think," she says. "Know?"

"Bella."

"I know. It's crazy. I started feeling strange last week, though."

"Have you taken a test?"

She shakes her head.

Bella was pregnant once before. A guy named Markus, whom she loved as much as he loved cocaine. She never told him. We were twenty-two, maybe twenty-three. Our first stumbling, dazzling year in New York.

"I missed my period," she says. "I sort of thought maybe I'd get it, but I haven't. My stomach feels weird, my boobs feel weird. I've been putting it off, but I think . . ." She trails off.

"Did you tell Aaron?"

She shakes her head. "I wasn't sure there'd be anything to tell."

"How long ago was your missed period?"

She takes another sip. She looks at me. "Eleven days ago."

✦

We go to the store as we are—she in the nightgown with a sweatshirt thrown over, me in my running clothes. There is no one at the small-town drugstore but the woman who works there, and she smiles when we hand over the test. It always surprises me that we're old enough to receive smiles now, have these moments be blessings, not curses.

When we get back, the house is still quiet, asleep. We crouch in the downstairs bathroom, just the two of us, sitting nervously on the edge of the tub, stealing glances at the counter.

The timer dings.

"You look," she says. "You tell me. I can't do it."

Two pink lines.

"It's positive," I say.

Her face falls into a sea of relief so powerful I have no choice. My eyes fill with tears.

"Bella," I say. Stunned.

"A baby," she mouths.

We close the space between us, and she is in my arms—my Bella. She smells like talcum powder and lavender and all things dewy and precious and young. I feel so protective over these two beating hearts in my arms that I can barely breathe.

We pull apart, misty-eyed and incredulous and laughing.

"Do you think he'll be mad?" she asks me suddenly.

All at once, she's in the driver's seat of her silver Range Rover and we're listening to "Anna Begins" with the windows down. It's summer, and it's late. We were supposed to be home hours ago, but no one is at Bella's house. Her mother is in New York for the opening of a restaurant and her father is traveling for work.

We're coming from Josh's house—or is it Trey's? They both have pools. We're still wearing our bathing suits, but they're dry now. The air is hot and sticky, and I have this sense in me—born of youth and vodka and the Counting Crows—that we are invincible. I look over at Bella, sitting back at the wheel, mouth open, singing, and I think that I never want to be without her—and then, that I never want to share her. That she belongs to me. That we belong to each other.

"I don't know," I say. "But it doesn't matter. This is our baby."

She giggles. "I love him," she says. "I know it sounds crazy. I know you think I'm crazy. But I really, really do." She puts a hand on her belly, right on top of her nightgown.

"I don't think you're crazy," I say. "I trust you."

"That's a first," she says. Her hand is still resting there on her belly. I see it growing, floating out in front of her like an inflatable balloon.

"Well," I say. "Then it's about time."

# Chapter Sixteen

Bella says she doesn't want to tell anyone. Not this weekend, not until she's back in the city with Aaron. Let's just enjoy the beach, she says. And we do.

We bring coolers, chairs, and blankets to the beach and stay there, swimming and eating salty chips and dripping watermelon, drinking beers and lemonade until the sun slips into the horizon.

Ariel and Morgan go for a walk in between swim sessions. I see them down the beach, clad in matching board shorts, holding hands. David and Aaron toss a Frisbee for a little while. Bella and I lounge under an umbrella. It's idyllic, and I have a flash of years forward—all of us here, together, and her baby, toddling by the shore.

"Want to go for a walk?" I ask David when he comes back. He plops down on the blanket next to me. His shirt is wet at the chest, and his sunglasses hang down by his nose. I take them off and see that the skin around his eyes is sunburned—rimmed. We love it out here, but neither of us was made for the sun.

"I was hoping for a nap," he says. He kisses my cheek. His face is sweaty, and I feel the moisture on my skin. I hand him the sunblock.

"I'll go."

I look up to see Aaron dripping over me, a beach towel flung over his right shoulder.

"Oh." I look to my side, to where Bella is fast asleep on a beach blanket, her mouth slightly ajar, her foot dangling softly in the sand like a limp puppet.

I look to David. "Problem solved," he says.

"Okay," I say to Aaron.

I stand up and brush myself off. I'm wearing board shorts, a bikini top, and a wide-brimmed hat I got at a resort in Turks and Caicos on a trip with David's family three years ago. I tighten the string.

"East or west?" he asks me.

"I actually think it's north or south."

He's not wearing sunglasses and he squints at me, his face scrunching against the sun.

"Left," I say.

The Amagansett beach is wide and long, one of the many reasons I love it so much. You can walk for miles uninterrupted, and many stretches are nearly deserted, even in the summer months.

We start walking. Aaron loops his towel around his neck and pulls with each hand at the edges. Neither one of us speaks for a minute. I'm struck, not by the silence but by the crash of the ocean—the sense of peace I feel in nature, I feel here. I don't think I realize, living in New York, how much light and noise pollution affect my day-to-day life. I tell him this now.

"It's true," he says. "I really miss Colorado."

"Is that where you're from?"

He shakes his head. "It's where I lived after college. I just moved to New York like ten months ago."

"Really?"

He laughs. "Am I that jaded already?"

I shake my head. "No, I'm just surprised whenever someone has spent a good portion of their adult life somewhere else. Weird, I know."

"Not weird," he says. "I get it. New York kind of makes you feel like it's the only place in existence."

I kick up a shell. "That's because it is. Says its insanely biased inhabitants."

Aaron threads his fingers together and stretches upward. I keep my eyes on the sand.

"David's great," he says. "It's been nice to spend some time with him this weekend."

I look down at my left hand. The ring catches the summer light in sudden, brilliant bursts. I should have taken it off today. I could lose it in the water.

"Yeah," I say. "He's great."

"I'm jealous of your relationship with Bella. I don't have that many friends from high school I'm still that close with."

"We've been friends since we were seven years old," I say. "I barely have a childhood memory she's not a part of."

"You're protective of her," he says. It's not a question.

"Yes. She's my family."

"I'm glad someone is looking out for her. You know, besides me." He tries for a smile.

"I know you are," I say. "It wasn't you. She's just dated people who didn't really put her first. She falls in love quickly."

"I don't," he says. He clears his throat. The moment stretches out to the horizon. "I mean, I haven't, in the past."

I know what he's saying—what he's hesitant to say now, even to me. He's in love with her. My best friend. I look over at him, and his eyes are fixed out on the ocean.

"Do you surf?" he asks me.

"Really?"

He turns back to me. He wears a sheepish expression. "I thought I might be embarrassing you with this bleeding heart."

"You weren't," I say. "I think I brought it up." I walk a few paces down to the water's edge. Aaron joins me. "No," I say. "I don't surf." There are no surfers out there right now, but it's late. The real ones are usually gone by 9 a.m. "Do you?"

"No, but I always wanted to. I didn't grow up around the ocean. I was sixteen before I went to the beach for the first time."

"Really? Where are you from?"

"Wisconsin," he says. "My parents weren't big travelers, but when we went on vacation it was always to the lake. We rented this house on Lake Michigan every summer. We'd stay there for a week and just live on the water."

"Sounds nice," I say.

"I'm trying to convince Bella to go with me in the fall. It's still one of my favorite places."

"She's not much of a lake girl," I say.

"I think she'd like it."

He clears his throat. "Hey," he says. "Thanks for earlier. I don't really ever talk about my mom."

I look down at my feet. "It's okay," I say. "I get it."

The water comes up to greet us.

Aaron jumps back. "Shit, that's cold," he says.

"It's not that bad; it's August. You don't even want to know what it feels like in May."

He hops around for another moment and then stops, staring at me. All at once, he kicks up the retreating water. It lands on me in a cascade, the icy droplets dotting my body like chicken pox.

"Not cool," I say.

I splash him back, and he holds up his towel in defense. But then we're running farther into the ocean, gathering more and more water in our attacks until we're both soaking wet, his towel nothing more than a dripping deadweight.

I duck my head under the water and let the shock of cold cool my head. I don't bother taking off my hat. When I come back up, Aaron is a foot from me. He stares at me so intently I have the instinct to look behind me but don't.

"What?"

"Nothing," he says. "I just . . ." He shrugs. "I like you."

Instantly, I'm not in the Atlantic anymore; we're not here on this beach but instead in that apartment, in that bed. His hands, devoid of the sopping towel, are on me. His mouth on my neck, his body moving slowly, deliberately over mine—asking, kneading, pressing. The pulse of the blood in my veins pumping to a rhythm of *yes*.

I close my eyes. *Stop. Stop. Stop.*

"Race you back," I say.

I kick up some water and take off. I know I'm faster than him—I'm faster than most people, and he's weighed down by ten pounds of towel. I'll beat him in a flash. When I get back to the blanket, Bella is awake. She rolls over, sleepily, shielding her eyes from the sun.

"Where did you go?" she asks.

I'm breathing too hard to answer.

# Chapter Seventeen

September is busy season at work. If everyone agrees to take a collective breath at the end of August, then September is a full-on sprint. I come back from the beach to a pile of documents and don't look up from them until Friday. Bella calls me on Wednesday, gasping with laughter.

"I told him!" she says. She squeals, and I hear Aaron there next to her. I imagine his arms around her, around her chest, careful with her, with this life now between them.

"And?"

"Dannie says 'and,'" Bella says.

I hear static, and then Aaron is on the line. "Dannie. Hey."

"Hi," I say. "Congratulations."

"Yeah. Thanks."

"Are you happy?"

He pauses. I feel my stomach tighten. But then, when I hear him speak, it's the purest, most obvious resonance of joy. It fills up the phone. "You know," he says. "I really, really am."

On Saturday, Bella and I pick up coffees at Le Pain Quotidien on Broadway because she wants to go shopping. I expect we'll hit up the stores on lower Fifth, maybe pop into Anthropologie, J.Crew, or Zara. But instead I find myself, Americano in hand, standing outside of Jacadi, the French baby store on Broadway.

"We have to go in," she says. "Everything is too adorable." I follow her.

There are rows of tiny onesies with matching cotton hats, knit sweaters, tiny overalls. It is a shrunken department store—full of petite Mary Janes and patent-leather loafers, all in minute, pocketable sizes. Bella is wearing a pink silk slip dress with an oversize white cotton sweater tied at the waist. Her hair is wild. She is glowing. She looks beautiful, radiant. Like a goddess.

It's not that I don't want kids, but I've just never felt particularly drawn to motherhood. Babies don't make me coo and weaken, and I've never experienced any sort of biological clock about my reproductive window. I think David would be a good father, and that we'll probably go ahead and have kids one day, but when I think about that future picture, us with a child, I often come up blank.

"When is your doctor's appointment?" I ask her.

Bella holds up a little yellow-and-white-polka-dot jumper. "Do you think this is gender neutral?"

I shrug.

"The baby will be here in the spring, so we'll need some long-sleeved stuff." She hands me the jumper and pulls two off-white cable-knit sweaters from the table in different sizes.

"How is Aaron?" I ask.

She smiles dreamily. "He's great; he's excited. I mean it's sudden, of course, but he seems really happy. We're not twenty-five anymore."

"Right," I say. "Are you guys going to get married?"

Bella rolls her eyes and hands me a pair of socks with tiny anchors on them. "Don't be so obvious," she says.

"You're having a baby; it's a legitimate question."

She turns to me. Her whole body focused now. "We haven't even discussed it. This seems like enough for now."

"So when's the doctor?" I ask, switching gears. "I want to see that sonogram pic."

Bella smiles. "Next week. They said not to rush coming in. When it's this early, there isn't much to do anyway."

"But shop," I say. My arms are full of small items now. I shuffle toward the register counter.

"I think it's a girl," Bella says.

I have an image of her, sitting in a rocking chair, holding an infant wrapped in a soft pink blanket.

"A girl would be great," I say.

She pulls me in and tucks me to her side. "Now you have to get started, too," she says.

I imagine being pregnant. Shopping in this store for my own tiny creation. It makes me want a cocktail.

✦

On Sunday, I go over to her apartment. I ring the bell twice. When the door finally opens Aaron is there, or at least his head is. He pulls the door back, and I'm met with at least a dozen packages—boxes and baskets and all sorts of gifts—littering the entryway.

"Did you guys rob a department store?" I ask.

Aaron shrugs. "She's excited," he says. "So she's shopping?" I watch his face closely, looking for signs of judgment or hesitation, but I find none, only a little amusement. He's dressed in jeans and a white T-shirt, no socks. I wonder if he's moved some stuff in yet. If he will. They'll have to live together, won't they?

He kicks a box to the side and the door swings open. I enter and close it behind me. "Congratulations," I say.

"Oh, yeah, thanks." He's stacking a garment bag on top of an Amazon delivery. He stops. He stands, tucks his hands into his pockets. "I know it's pretty soon."

"Bella has always been impatient," I say. "So it doesn't totally surprise me."

He laughs, but it seems more for my benefit. "I just want you to know I really am happy. She's the best thing that has ever happened to me."

He looks right at me when he says it, the same way he did at the beach. I blink away.

"Good," I say. "I'm glad."

Just then Bella's voice floats in from the other room. "Dannie? Are you here?"

Aaron smiles and steps to the side, holding his arm out for me to pass.

I follow the sound of her voice down the hallway, past the kitchen and her bedroom and into the guest room. The bed has been pushed to the side, the dresser placed in the center of the room, and Bella, in overalls and a head scarf, is painting white marshmallow clouds on the walls.

"Bells," I say. "What's going on?"

She looks at me. "Baby's room," she says. "What do you think?"

She stands back, putting her hands on her hips and surveying her work.

"I think you're ahead of the curve for the first time in your life," I say. "And it's freaking me out. Isn't the nursery usually a month-seven project?"

She laughs, her back to me. "It's fun," she says. "I haven't really painted in a long time."

"I know." I go to stand next to her and lob an arm over her shoulder. She leans into me. The clouds are off-white and the sky a pale salmon color with shades of baby blue and lavender. It's a masterpiece.

"You really want this," I say, but it's not really to her. It's to the wall. To whatever beyond has brought forth this reality. For a moment, I don't remember the future I once saw. I am overcome by the one that is solidly, undeniably present here.

# Chapter Eighteen

David and I are supposed to meet with the wedding planner next Saturday morning. It's now mid-September, and I've been told, in no uncertain terms, that if I do not choose flowers now I will be using dead leaves as centerpieces.

The week is crazy at work—we get hit with a ton of due diligence on two time-sensitive cases Monday, and I barely make it home except to sleep all week. I take out my phone as I walk to the elevators the following Friday night to tell David we may need to push the meeting—I'm desperate for some sleep—when I see I have four missed calls from an unknown number.

Scam calls have been rampant lately, but they're usually marked. I check my voicemail on my way downstairs, hanging up and retrying when I get down to the lobby. I'm just passing through the glass doors when I hear the message.

"Dannie, it's Aaron. We went to the doctor today and— Can you call me? I think you need to come down here."

My heart plummets to my feet as I hit call back immediately with shaking hands. Something is wrong. Something is wrong with the baby. Bella had her doctor's appointment today. They were going to hear the heartbeat for the first time. I should have protected her. I should have stopped her from buying all those clothes, making all those plans. It was too soon.

"Dannie?" Aaron's voice is hoarse through the phone.

"Hey. Hi. Sorry. I was . . . Where is she?"

"Here," he says. "Dannie, it's not good."

"Is something wrong with the baby?"

Aaron pauses. When his voice comes through, it breaks at the onset. "There's no baby."

✦

I toss my heels into my bag, pull on my slides, and get on the subway down to Tribeca. I always wondered how people who had just been delivered tragic news and had to fly on airplanes did it. Every plane must carry someone who is going to their dying mother's bedside, their friend's car accident, the sight of their burned home. Those minutes on the subway are the longest of my life.

Aaron answers the door. He's wearing jeans and a button-down, half untucked. He looks stunned, his eyes red-rimmed. My heart sinks again. It's through the floorboards, now.

"Where is she?" I ask him.

He doesn't answer, just points. I follow his finger into the bedroom, to where Bella is crouched in the fetal position in bed, dwarfed by pillows, a hoodie up and sweatpants on. I snap my shoes off and go to her, getting right in around her.

"Bells," I say. "Hey. I'm here." I drop my lips down and kiss the top of her sweatshirt-covered head. She doesn't move. I look at Aaron by the door. He stands there, his hands hanging helplessly at his sides.

"Bells," I try again. I rub a hand down her back. "Come on. Sit up."

She shifts. She looks up at me. She looks confused, frightened. She looks the way she did on my trundle bed decades ago when she'd wake up from a bad dream.

"Did he tell you?" she asks me.

I nod. "He said you lost the baby," I say. I feel sick at the words. I think about her, just last week, painting, preparing. "Bells, I'm so sorry. I—"

She sits up. She puts a hand over her mouth. I think she might be sick.

"No," she says. "I was wrong. I wasn't pregnant."

I search her face. I look to Aaron, who is still in the doorway. "What are you talking about?"

"Dannie," she says. She looks straight at me. Her eyes are wet, wide. I see something in them I've only ever seen once before, a long time ago at a door in Philadelphia. "They think I have ovarian cancer."

# Chapter Nineteen

She says a lot of things then. About how ovarian cancer, in very rare cases, can cause a false positive. About how the symptoms sometimes mimic pregnancy. Missed period, bloated abdomen, nausea, low energy. But all I hear is a humming, a buzz in my ears that gets louder and louder the more she talks until it's impossible to hear her. Her mouth is opening and all that's coming out are a thousand bees, zinging and stinging their way to my face until my eyes are swollen shut.

"Who told you this?"

"The doctor," she says. "We went for a scan today."

"They did a CT scan." It's Aaron, at the door. "And a blood test."

"We need a second opinion," I say.

"I said the same thing," Aaron says. "There's a great—"

I cut him off with my hand. "Where are your parents?"

Bella looks from Aaron to me. "My dad is in France, I think. Mom is home."

"Did you call them?"

She shakes her head.

"Okay. I'm going to call Frederick and ask him for a roster of his friends at Sinai. He's on the board of cardiac, right?"

Bella nods.

"Okay. We'll make an appointment with the top oncologist." I swallow the word down. It tastes like darkness.

But this is what I know how to do; this is what I'm good at. The more I talk, the more the buzzing dims. Facts. Documents. Who knows what crack-brained doctor they went to? An ob-gyn is not an oncologist. We don't know anything yet. He's probably mistaken. He must be.

"Bella," I say. I take her hands in mine. "It's going to be fine, okay? Whatever it is, we'll figure it out. You're going to be fine."

✦

On Monday morning, we're at the office of Dr. Finky—the best oncologist in New York City. I meet Bella at the Ninety-Eighth Street entrance to Mount Sinai. She gets out of the car, and Aaron is with her. I'm surprised to see him. I didn't think he was coming. Now that she's not pregnant, now that we're faced with this, the biggest of all news, I don't know that I expected him to stick around. They've spent one summer together.

Dr. Finky's office is on the fourth floor. In the elevator ride up, we're met with a dewy pregnant mother. I feel Bella turn inward, behind me, toward Aaron. I hit the floor key harder.

The waiting room is nice. Cheerful. Yellow-striped wallpaper, potted sunflowers, and a variety of magazines. The good ones. *Vanity Fair, The New Yorker, Vogue.* There are only two people waiting, an elderly couple who seem to be FaceTiming their grandchild. They wave at the camera, *ooh*ing and *aah*ing. Bella cringes.

"We have a nine a.m. appointment. Bella Gold?"

The receptionist nods and hands me a clipboard full of papers. "Are you the patient?"

I look behind me to where Bella stands. "No," Bella says. "I am."

The woman smiles at her. She wears two braids down her back and a nametag that reads "Brenda."

"Hi, Bella," she says. "Can I ask you to fill out these forms?"

She speaks in a soothing, motherly tone, and I know that is why she is here. To soften the blow of whatever happens when patients disappear behind those doors.

"Yes," Bella says. "Thank you."

"And can I make a copy of your insurance card?"

Bella riffles in her bag and pulls out her wallet. She hands a Blue Cross card over. I wasn't sure Bella had insurance or kept a card on her. I'm impressed at the number of steps she'd needed to go through to get there. Does she buy it through the gallery? Who set that up for her?

"Blue Cross?" I say when we're walking back to the waiting chairs.

"They have good out-of-network," she says.

I raise my eyebrows at her, and she smiles. The first moment of levity we've experienced since Friday.

I called her dad on Friday. He didn't pick up. On Saturday, I left him a voicemail: *It's about Bella's health. You need to call me immediately.*

Bella has often said her parents were too young to have a child, and I understand what she's saying but I don't think that's it, at least not entirely. It's that they never had any interest in being parents. They had Bella because having children was a thing they thought you should do, but they didn't want to raise her, not really.

Mine were always around—for both Michael and me. They signed us up for soccer and went to all the games—jumping at things like snack duty and uniforms. They were protective and strict. They expected things from me: good grades, excellent scores, impeccable manners. And I gave them all of that, especially after Michael, because he would have, and had. I didn't want them to miss out any more than they were. But they loved me through the downturns, too—the B minus in calc, the rejection from Brown. I knew that they knew that I was more than a resume.

Bella was smart in school, but disinterested. She floated through English and history with the ease of someone who knows it doesn't really matter. And it didn't. She was a great writer—still is. But it was art where she really found her stride. We went to a public school and funding was nonexistent, but the parent participation was hefty, and we were granted a studio with oil paints, canvases, and an instructor dedicated to our creative achievement.

Bella would always draw when we were kids, and her sketches were good—preternaturally good. But in studio she started producing work that was extraordinary. Students and teachers would come from different classrooms just to see. A landscape, a self-portrait, a bowl of rotting fruit on the counter. Once she did a painting of Irving, a nerdy sophomore from Cherry Hill. After she drew him, his entire reputation changed. He was elusive, compelling. People saw him as she'd sketched him. It was like she had this ability to uncork whatever was inside and let it spill out joyfully, excessively, messily.

Her father, Frederick, called me Saturday afternoon, from Paris. I told him what we knew: Bella had thought she was pregnant, she went in for an ultrasound to confirm, they did some tests, and she left with an ovarian cancer diagnosis.

I was met with stunned silence. And then a call to arms.

"I'll call Dr. Finky," he said. "I'll tell him we need an appointment first thing Monday. Stand by."

"Thank you," I said, which felt natural but shouldn't have.

"Will you call her mother?" he asked me.

"Yes," I said.

Bella's mother started sobbing instantly on the phone, I knew she would. Jill has always had a flair for the dramatic.

"I'm getting on the next flight," she said, even though, presumably, she was in Philadelphia and could drive here in just under double the time it would take to get to the airport.

"We're getting an appointment for Monday morning," I said. "Would you like me to send you the details?"

"I'm calling Bella," she said, and hung up.

Last I heard Jill had a boyfriend our age. She was married once more, after Bella's father, to a Greek shipping heir who cheated on her rampantly and publicly. She's never made good choices. If I'm honest, she's modeled Bella's romantic history—but hopefully not anymore, not with Aaron.

Monday morning, sitting in the office filling out papers, I don't ask about Jill because I don't have to. I know what happened. She lost the paper with the time, or she had a massage she couldn't cancel, or she forgot to buy a train ticket and figured she'd come tomorrow. It's always a million different reasons that all say the same thing.

Bella makes her way through the paperwork, and Aaron and I sit stonily, flanking her. I see him pop his foot over his leg, jiggling it nervously. He rubs a hand over his forehead.

Bella is wearing jeans and an orange sweater even though it's too hot outside for either of those things. Summer will not quit, even though we're now nearing the end of September.

"Ms. Gold?"

A young male nurse or physician assistant wearing wire-rimmed glasses appears in front of a glass door.

Bella shifts the paperwork nervously in her lap. "I didn't finish," she says.

Brenda at the desk smiles. "It's okay. We can get to it after." She looks from me to Aaron. "Are both of you headed back?"

"Yes," Aaron answers.

The nurse, Benji, chats happily to us as we move down the hallway. Again, with the cheer. You would think we were walking to an ice cream parlor or waiting in line for the Ferris wheel.

"Right this way."

He holds his arm across a doorway to a white room, and the three of us enter in the same formation: me, Bella, Aaron. There are two seats in the corner and an examining chair. I stand.

"We'll just do some quick stats while we wait for Dr. Finky."

Benji takes Bella's vitals—her pulse, her temperature—and looks inside her throat and ears. He has her get on the scale and takes her weight and height. Aaron doesn't sit, either, and, with the two chairs and us standing, the room seems small, almost claustrophobic. I'm not sure how we're going to fit another person in there.

Finally, the door opens.

"Bella, I haven't seen you since you were ten years old. Hello."

Dr. Finky is a short man—round and plump—who moves with a precise and almost dart-like speed.

"Hi," Bella says. She extends her hand, and he takes it.

"Who are these people?"

"This is my boyfriend, Greg." Aaron extends his hand. Finky shakes it. "And my best friend, Dannie." We do the same.

"You have a good support system; that's nice," he says. I feel my stomach clench and release. He shouldn't have said that. I don't like it.

"So you came to the doctor thinking you were pregnant? How about you explain how you arrived in my office today?"

Finky puts on his glasses, takes out his notebook, and starts nodding and writing. Bella explains it all, again: The missed period. The bloating. The false positive on the pregnancy test. Going to the doctor. The CT scan. The blood test results.

"We need to run some additional tests," he says. "I don't want to say anything yet."

"Can we do that today?" I ask. I've been taking notes, writing down everything that comes out of his mouth in my book, the one that's supposed to be functioning as a wedding planner.

"Yes," he says. "I'm going to have the nurse come back in to get you started."

"What's your opinion?" I ask him.

He takes off his glasses. He looks at Bella. "I think we need to run some additional tests," he tells her.

He doesn't have to say anything more. I'm a lawyer. I know what words mean, what silences mean, what repetition means. And I know, there in black and white, what he thinks. What he suspects. Maybe, even, what he already knows. They were right.

# Chapter Twenty

Here is the thing no one tells you about cancer: they ease you into it. After the initial shock, after the diagnosis and the terror, they put you on the slow conveyor belt. They start you off nice and easy. You want some lemon water with that chemo? You got it. Radiation? No problem, everyone does it, it's practically weed. We'll serve you those chemicals with a smile. You'll love them, you'll see.

Bella does indeed have ovarian cancer. They suspect stage three, which means it has spread to nearby lymph nodes but not to surrounding organs. It's treatable, we're told. There is recourse. So many times, with ovarian cancer, there isn't. You find it too late. It's not too late.

I ask for the statistics, but Bella doesn't want them. "Information like that gets in your head," she says. "It'll have a higher probability of affecting the outcome. I don't want to know."

"It's numbers," I say. "It'll affect the outcome anyway. Hard data doesn't move. We should know what we're dealing with."

"We get to determine what we're dealing with."

She puts an embargo on Google, but I search anyway: 47

percent. That is the survival rate of ovarian cancer patients over five years. Less than fifty-fifty.

David finds me on the tile floor of the shower.

"Fifty is good odds," he tells me. He crouches down. He holds my hand through the glass door. "That's half." But he's a terrible liar. I know he would never make a bet on those odds, not even drunk at a table in Vegas.

✦

Five days later, I'm back at an appointment with Bella. We've been referred to a gynecological oncologist who will sort and determine the course of surgery and treatment. This time, it's just the two of us. Bella asked Aaron to stay behind. I wasn't there for that conversation. I do not know what it looked like. Whether he fought. Whether he was relieved.

We're introduced to Dr. Shaw in his office on Park Avenue, between Sixty-Second and Sixty-Third. It's so civilized when we pull up, I think we've been given the wrong address—are we headed to a luncheon?

His office is subtler, more subdued—inside there are patients who are suffering. You can tell. Dr. Finky's office is the first stop—the new and freshly washed train, full of steam. Dr. Shaw is where you go for the remaining miles.

Once the nurse takes us back, Dr. Shaw comes in to greet us quickly. Immediately I like his friendly face—it's open, even a little earnest. He smiles often. I can tell Bella likes him, too.

"Where are you from?" she asks him.

"Florida, actually," he says. "Sunshine state."

"It's always been strange to me that Florida is the sunshine state," Bella says. "It should be California."

"You know," Dr. Shaw says, "I agree."

He's tall, and when he folds himself onto his small rolling stool his knees nearly come up to his elbows.

"All right," he says. "Here's what we're going to do."

Dr. Shaw presents the plan. Surgery to "debulk" the tumor, followed by four rounds of chemo over two months. He warns us that it will be brutal. I find myself, more than once in Dr. Shaw's office, wishing I could trade places with Bella. It should be me. I'm strong. I can handle it. I'm not sure Bella can.

The surgery is scheduled for Tuesday, back at Sinai hospital. It includes a full hysterectomy, and they're also removing both her ovaries and her fallopian tubes. Something called a bilateral salpingo-oophorectomy. I find myself Googling medical terms in the car, on the subway, in the bathroom at work. She'll no longer produce eggs. Or have a place where they could, one day, develop.

At this revelation, Bella starts to cry.

"Can I freeze my eggs first?" she asks.

"There are fertility options," Dr. Shaw tells her, gently. "But I wouldn't recommend them, or waiting. The hormones can sometimes exacerbate the cancer. I think it's critical we get you into surgery as soon as possible."

"How is this happening?" Bella asks. She drops her face into her hands. I feel nauseous. Bile rises to my throat and threatens to spill out onto the floor of this Park Avenue office.

Dr. Shaw rolls forward. He puts a hand on her knee. "I know it's hard," he says. "But you're in the best hands. And we're going to do everything we can for you."

"It's not fair," she says.

Dr. Shaw looks to me, but for the first time I feel at a loss for words. Cancer. No children. I have to focus on inhaling.

"It's not," he says. "You're right. But your attitude matters a lot. I'm going to fight for you, but I need you in here with me."

She looks up at him, her face streaked with tears. "Will you be there?" she asks him. "For the surgery."

"You bet," he says. "I'll be the one performing it."

Bella looks to me. "What do you think?" she asks me.

I think about the beach in Amagansett. How was it only three weeks ago that she was blushing over a pregnancy test—glowing with expectation?

"I think we need to do the surgery now," I say.

Bella nods. "Okay," she says.

"It's the right decision," Dr. Shaw says. He slides over to his computer. "And if you have any questions, here is my direct cell number." He hands us both a business card. I copy the number down in my notebook.

"Let's talk through what to expect now," he says.

There is more talk then. About lymph nodes and cancer cells and abdominal incisions. I take precise notes, but it is hard—it is impossible—for even me to follow everything. It sounds as if Dr. Shaw is speaking in a different language—something harsh. Russian, maybe Czech. I have the feeling that I do not want to understand; I just want him to cease speaking. If he stops speaking, none of it is true.

We leave the office and stand on the corner of Sixty-Third and Park. Inexplicably, impossibly, it is a perfect day. September is glorious in New York, belied even further by the knowledge that the fall will not hold—and today is banner. The wind is gentle, the sun is fierce. Everywhere I look, people are smiling and talking and greeting one another.

I look to Bella. I do not have a clue what to say.

It is unbelievable that right now there is something deadly

growing inside of her. It seems impossible. Look at her. Look. She is the picture of health. She is rosy-cheeked and full and radiant. She is an impressionist painting. She is life incarnate.

What would happen if we just pretended we'd never heard? Would the cancer catch up? Or would it take the hint and screw off? Is it receptive? Is it listening? Do we have the power to change it?

"I have to call Greg," she says.

"Okay."

Not for the first time this morning, I feel my cell phone vibrate fiercely in my bag. It's past ten, and I was due in the office two hours ago. I'm sure I have a hundred emails.

"Do you want me to get you a car?" I ask.

She shakes her head. "No, I want to walk."

"Okay," I say. "We'll walk."

She takes out her phone. She doesn't lift her eyes. "I'd rather be alone."

When we were in high school, Bella used to sleep at my house more than she slept at her own. She hated being alone, and her parents traveled all the time. They were away at least 60 percent of each month. So she lived with us. I had a pullout trundle bed beneath mine, and we'd lie awake at night, rolling from my bed to hers and then climbing back up again, counting the stick-on stars on my ceiling. It was impossible, of course, because who could tell them apart? We'd fall asleep amidst a jumble of numbers.

"Bells—"

"Please," she says. "I promise I will call you later."

I feel her words bite through me. It's bad enough as it is, but now why would we face it alone? We need to stop down. We need to get coffee. We need to talk about this.

She starts walking and, instinctively, I follow her, but she knows I'm behind her and she turns around, her hand signaling—*Be gone.*

My phone buzzes again. This time I pull it out and answer.

"It's Dannie," I say.

"Where the hell are you?" I hear my case partner Sanji's voice through the phone. She's twenty-nine and graduated from MIT at sixteen. She's been working professionally for ten years. I've never heard her use a word that wasn't absolutely necessary. The fact that she added "hell" speaks volumes.

"I'm sorry, I got caught up. I'm on my way."

"Don't hang up," she says. "We have a problem with CIT and corporate. There are gaps in their financials."

We were supposed to complete our due diligence on CIT, a company our client, Epson, a giant tech corporation, is acquiring. If we don't have a complete financial report, the partner is going to lose it.

"I'm going down to their offices," I say. "Hang tight."

Sanji hangs up without saying goodbye, and I book it down to the Financial District where CIT has their headquarters. It's a company specializing in website coding. I've been there a little too often for my liking lately.

We've been in constant contact with their in-house counsel for over six months, and I know how they work extremely well now. Hopefully, this is an oversight. There are tax reports and statements for a full eight months that are missing.

When I arrive, I'm let up immediately, and Darlene, the receptionist, shows me to the associate general counsel's office.

Beth is at her desk and looks up, blinking once at me. She's a woman in her mid-to-late fifties and has been at the company since its inception twelve years ago. Her office resembles her in its stoicism, not a single photo on her desk, and she doesn't wear a ring. We're cordial, even friendly, but we never speak about anything personal, and it's impossible to tell what greets her at home when she leaves these office walls.

"Dannie," she says. "To what do I owe this displeasure?"

I was in her office yesterday.

"We're still missing financials," I say.

She does not stand up, or gesture for me to sit. "I'll have my team review," she says.

Her team consists of one other lawyer, Davis Brewster, with whom I went to Columbia. He is smart. I have no idea how he ended up as a midsize company's legal counsel.

"This afternoon," I tell her.

She shakes her head. "You must really love your job," she says.

"No more or less than any of us," I say.

She laughs. She looks back at her computer. "Not quite."

✦

At 5 p.m., more documents come through from CIT. I'm going to be here until at least nine parsing through them. Sanji paces the conference room like she's figuring out an attack strategy. I text Bella: *Check in with me.* No response.

It's 10 p.m. before I leave. Still nothing from Bella. Everything in my body feels crunched, like I've been ground down to an inch over the course of today. As I walk, I feel myself stretching back up. I don't have sneakers with me, and after about five blocks my pump-clad feet begin to hurt, but I keep walking. As the blocks go on—down Fifth, rolling through the forties like the subway—I begin to pick up the pace. By the time I get to East Thirty-Eighth Street, I'm running.

I arrive at our Gramercy apartment gasping and sweating. My

top is nearly soaked through and my feet throb with numb disconnection. I'm afraid to look down at them. I think if I do, I'll see pools of blood seeping out from the soles.

I open the door. David is at the table, a glass of wine next to him, his computer open. He jumps up when he sees me.

"Hey," he says. He takes me in, his eyes narrow as he scans my face. "What happened to you?"

I bend down to take off my shoes. But the first won't come off. It seems stitched to my foot. I scream out in pain.

"Hey," David says. "Woah. Okay. Sit down." I collapse onto the little bench we have in the hallway and he crouches down. "Jesus, Dannie, what did you do? Run home?"

He looks up at me and, in that moment, I feel myself falling. I'm not sure if I'm going to faint or combust. The fire in my feet rises, threatening to engulf me whole.

"She's really sick," I say. "She needs surgery next week. Stage three. Four rounds of chemo."

David hugs me. I want to feel the comfort of his arms. I want to fold into him. But I can't. It's too big. Nothing will help, nothing will obscure it.

"Did they give you some data?" David asks, grasping. "The new doctor? What did he say?" He releases me and puts a hand gently on my knee.

I shake my head. "She'll never be able to have kids. They're taking out her entire uterus, both ovaries . . ."

David winces. "Damn," he says. "Damn, Dannie, I'm so sorry."

I close my eyes against the rising tide of pain from my feet, the knives that are now burying themselves into my heels.

"Take them off," I tell him. I'm practically panting.

"Okay," he says. "Hang on."

He goes to the bathroom and comes back with baby powder.

He shakes the bottle and a cloud of white dust descends on my foot. He wiggles the heel of my shoe. I feel nauseous with pain.

Then it's off. I look down at my foot—it's raw and bleeding but looks better than I thought it would. He dumps some more powder on it.

"Let me see the other one," he says.

I give him my other foot. He shakes the bottle, wiggles the heel, performs the same ritual.

"You need to soak them," David says. "Come on."

He puts an arm around me and leads me, wincing and groaning, into the bathroom. We have a tub, although it's not a claw-foot. It's always been a dream of mine to have one, but our bathroom was already built. It's so stupid, impossible even, that my brain still relays this information to me now, still notes it—the missing feet of a porcelain tub. As if it matters.

David begins to run the water for me. "I'm going to put some Epsom salt in it," he says. "You'll feel better."

I grab his arm as he turns to go. I cling to it—hold it against my chest like a child with their stuffed animal.

"It's going to be okay," he tells me. But, of course, the words mean nothing. No one knows that. Not him. Not Dr. Shaw. Not even me.

# Chapter Twenty-One

Bella will not return my calls or texts, so finally, on Saturday night, I dial Aaron.

He picks up on the second ring. "Dannie," he says. He's whispering. "Hey."

"Yeah. Hi."

I'm in the bedroom of our apartment, my bandaged feet kneading the soft carpet. "Is Bella there?"

There's a pause on the other end of the line.

"Come on, Aaron. She won't return my phone calls."

"She's actually sleeping," he says.

"Oh." It's barely 8 p.m.

"What are you doing?"

I look down at my sweatpants. "Nothing," I say. "I should probably get back to work. Will you tell her I called?"

"Yeah, of course," he says.

All at once I feel irrationally angry. Aaron, this stranger. This man, who she has known for less than four months, is the one in her apartment. He's the one she's turning to. He doesn't even know her. And me, her best friend, her family—

"She needs to call me," I say. My tone has changed. It bears the fire of my thumping thoughts.

"I know," Aaron says. His voice is low. "It's just been—"

"I don't care what it has been. With all due respect, I don't know you. My best friend needs surgery on Tuesday. She needs to call me."

Aaron clears his throat. "Do you want to take a walk?" he asks me.

"What?"

"A walk," he says. "I could use some air. It kind of sounds like you could, too."

I'm not sure what to say. I want to tell him I have too much work, and it's true—I've been distracted all week trying to prepare the documents we need for signature. We still don't have everything from CIT, and Epson is getting anxious; they want to announce next week. But I don't say no. I need to talk to Aaron. To explain to him that I have this, that he can go back to whatever life he was living last spring.

"Fine," I say. "The corner of Perry and Washington. Twenty minutes."

✦

He's waiting on the curb when my taxi pulls up. It's still light out, although it will fade soon. October hangs a whisper away—the promise of only more darkness. Aaron is wearing jeans and a green sweater, and so am I, and for a minute, the visual as I pay the driver and get out of the cab—two matching people meeting each other—almost makes me laugh.

"And to think I almost brought my orange bag," he says. He

gestures to the leather Tod's crossbody Bella gave me for my twenty-fifth birthday.

We start to walk. Slowly. My feet are still sore and raw. Down Perry toward the West Side Highway. "I used to live down here," he says, filling the silence. "Before I moved to Midtown. Just for six months; it was my first apartment. My building was a block over, on Hudson. I liked the West Village, but it was kind of impossible to get anywhere on public transport."

"There's West Fourth," I say.

He moves his face in a sign of recognition. "We were above this pizza place that closed," he says. "I remember everything I owned smelled like Italian food. My clothes, sheets, everything."

I surprise myself by laughing. "When I first moved to the city, I lived in Hell's Kitchen. My entire apartment smelled like curry. I can't even look at the stuff now."

"Oh, see," he says, "I just always crave pizza."

"How long have you been an architect?" I ask him.

"Since the beginning," he says. "I think I was born one. I went to school for it. For a little while I thought maybe I'd be an engineer, but I wasn't smart enough."

"I doubt that."

"You shouldn't. It's the truth."

We walk in silence for a moment.

"Did you ever think about being a litigator?" he asks me, so suddenly I'm caught off guard.

"Excuse me?"

"I mean, I know you practice deal law. I'm wondering if you ever thought about being one of those lawyers who goes to court. I bet you'd crush at it." He gives me a one-eyed smile. "You seem like you'd be good at winning an argument."

"No," I say. "Litigating isn't for me."

"How come?"

I sidestep around a puddle of liquid on the sidewalk. In New York you never know what is water and what is urine.

"Litigating is bending the law to your will, it's deception, it's all about perception. Can you convince a jury? Can you make people feel? In deal making, nothing is above the law. The written words are what matters. Everything is there in black and white."

"Fascinating," he says.

"I think so."

Aaron lifts his hands from his sides and rubs them together. "So listen," he says. "How are you?"

The question makes me stop walking.

So does he.

I turn slightly inward, and he mirrors me. "Not good," I say, honestly.

"Yeah," he says. "I figured. I can't imagine how hard this must be for you."

I look at him. His eyes meet mine.

"She's—" I start, but I can't finish it. The wind picks up, dancing the leaves and trash into a veritable ballet. I start to cry.

"It's okay," he says. He makes a move forward, but I take one back and we stand on the street like that, not quite meeting, until the river quiets.

"It's not," I say.

"Yeah," he says. "I know."

I swallow what remains of my tears. I look across at him. I feel anger hit my bloodstream like alcohol. "You don't," I say. "You have no idea."

"Dan—"

"You don't have to do this, you know. No one would blame you."

He peers at me. "What do you mean?" He seems to genuinely not understand.

"I mean, this isn't what you signed up for. You met a pretty girl, she was healthy, she's not anymore."

"Dannie," Aaron says, like he's choosing his words very carefully. "It's important that you know that I'm not going anywhere."

"Why?" I ask him.

A jogger passes by and, sensing the tension of the moment, crosses the street. A car horn honks. A siren whirls somewhere down Hudson.

"Because I love her," he says.

I ignore the confession. I've heard it before. "You don't even know her."

I start walking again. A kid zooms past us with a basketball, his mother sprinting after him. The city. Full and buzzy and unaware that somewhere, fifteen blocks south, tiny cells are multiplying in a plot to destroy the whole world.

"Dannie. Stop."

I don't. And then I feel Aaron's hand on my arm. He yanks and turns me around.

"Ow!" I say. "What the hell." I rub my upper arm. I am, all at once, overcome with the urge to slap him, to punch him in the eye and leave him, crumpled and bleeding, on the corner of Perry Street.

"Sorry," he says. His eyebrows are knit together. He has a dimple in the space above his nose. "But you need to listen to me. I love her. That's the long and short of it. I don't think I could live with myself if I bailed now, but that's not even relevant because, like I said, I love her. This isn't like anything I've ever had before. This is real. I'm here."

His chest rises and falls like it's taking physical effort to be upright. That I understand.

"It's going to be more painful if you leave later," I say. I feel my lip quiver again. I demand it to stop.

Aaron reaches out to me. He takes both my elbows in his palms. His chest is so close I can smell him.

"I promise," he says.

We must walk back. I must call a car. We must say goodnight. I must come home and tell David. I must, at some point, fall asleep. But later I don't remember. All I remember is his promise. I take it. I hold it in my heart like proof.

# Chapter Twenty-Two

On Tuesday, October 4, I arrive at Mount Sinai on East One Hundred First Street an hour before the scheduled surgery. I still haven't spoken to Bella, but I come to her pre-op room to find both her father and mother there. I don't think they've been in the same room in over a decade.

The room is loud, even boisterous. Jill, impeccably dressed in a Saint Laurent suit and with her hair blown out, chats with the nurses as if she's preparing to host a luncheon, not for her daughter's reproductive organs to be removed.

Frederick chats with Dr. Shaw. They both stand at the foot of Bella's bed, arms crossed, gesturing amicably.

This isn't happening.

"Hi," I say. I knock on the side door that is obviously already open.

"Hey," Bella says. "Look who made it." She gestures to her father, who turns around and gives me a sideways wave.

"I see that," I say. I put my bag down on a chair and go to Bella's bedside. "How are you?"

"Fine," she says, and I see it right there—the indignant stubbornness that has been avoiding me for the past week. Her hair is already in a cap, and she's wearing a hospital gown. How long has she been here?

"What did Dr. Shaw say?"

Bella shrugs. "Ask him yourself."

I take a few steps down. "Dr. Shaw," I say. "Dannie."

"Of course," he says. "Notepad woman."

"Right. So how is everything looking?"

Dr. Shaw gives me a small smile. "Okay," he says. "I was just explaining to Bella and her folks here that surgery will take about five or six hours."

"I thought it was three," I say. I've done extensive research. I've barely left Google. Filing statistics. Researching these procedures, recovery times, added benefits of taking out both ovaries instead of one.

"It could be," he says. "It depends on what we find when we get in there. A full hysterectomy is usually three, but because we're also removing the fallopian tubes we may need more time."

"Are you performing an omentectomy today?" I ask.

Dr. Shaw looks at me with a mixture of respect and surprise. "We're going to do a biopsy of the omentum for staging. But we will not be removing it today."

"I read that a complete removal increases survival odds."

To his credit, Dr. Shaw does not look away. He does not clear his throat and look to Jill or Bella. Instead, he says, "It's really a case by case."

My stomach turns. I look to Jill, who is up by Bella's head, smoothing her cap-covered hair.

A memory. Bella. Age eleven. Crawling up into my bed from the trundle because she'd had a nightmare. *It was snowing and I couldn't find you.*

"Where were you?"

"Alaska, maybe."

"Why Alaska?"

"I don't know."

But I did. Her mother had been there for a month. Some kind of two-and-a-half-week cruise followed by a specialized spa.

"Well, I'm right here," I said. "You'll always be able to find me, even in snow."

How dare Jill show up. How dare she claim ownership and offer comfort now. It's too late. It has been too late for over twenty years. I know I'd hate Bella's parents even more if they didn't show today, but I still want them gone. They don't get the place by her side, especially not now.

Just then Aaron walks through the door. He's holding one of those carry trays full of Starbucks cups and starts handing them out.

"None for you," Dr. Shaw says, pointing to Bella.

She laughs. "That's the worst part about this. No coffee."

Dr. Shaw smiles. "I'll see you in there. You're in great hands."

"I know," she says.

Frederick shakes Dr. Shaw's hand. "Thank you for everything. Finky speaks very highly of you."

"He taught me a lot of what I know. Excuse me." He makes a move toward the door and stops when he reaches me. "Could I speak to you in the hall?"

"Of course."

The room has descended into caffeinated chaos, and no one notices Dr. Shaw's request or my exit.

"We're going to try our best to get all of the tumor. We've categorized Bella's cancer at a stage three, but we really won't know definitely until we take tissue samples of the surrounding organs.

And I know you raised a concern about an omentectomy. We're just not sure how far it has spread yet."

"I understand," I say. I feel a deep, wet cold creep from the hospital floor, up my legs, and settle in my stomach.

"It's possible we may need to remove a portion of Bella's colon as well." Dr. Shaw looks to Bella's door and back at me. "You are aware that you are listed as Bella's next of kin?"

"I am?"

"You are," he says. "I know her parents are here, but I wanted you to be made aware, too."

"Thank you."

Dr. Shaw nods. He turns to leave.

"How bad is it?" I ask him. "I know you can't tell me that. But if you could—how bad is it?"

He looks at me. He looks like he really would like to answer. "We're going to do everything we can," he says. And then he's striding toward the operating room doors.

✦

They wheel Bella into surgery with little fanfare. She is stoic. She kisses Jill and Frederick and Aaron, who Jill has clearly taken to. A little too much. She keeps finding excuses to grab his forearm. Once, Bella looks at me and rolls her eyes. It feels like a candle in the darkness.

"You're going to be great," I tell her. I bend over her. I kiss her forehead. She reaches up and grabs my hand. And then lets go just as abruptly.

When she's gone, we're moved into the big waiting room, the one filled with people. They have sandwiches and board games. Some chat on cell phones. A few have blankets. There is laughing.

Yet, every time the double doors open, the entire room stops and looks up in anticipation.

"I'm sorry I didn't get you a coffee," Aaron says. We choose seats by the window. Jill and Frederick pace a few feet away talking on their phones.

"It's fine," I say. "I'll go down to the cafeteria or something."

"Yeah. It's going to be a while."

"Had you met her parents before?" I ask Aaron. Bella never mentioned it, but now I'm not so sure.

"Just this morning," he says. "Jill came and picked us up. They're kind of a trip."

I snort.

"That bad, huh?" he asks me.

"You have no idea."

Jill saunters over. I realize she's wearing heels.

"I'm putting in an order to Scarpetta," she says. "I think we could all use some comfort food. What can I get you two?"

It's barely 9 a.m.

"I'll probably just go down to the cafeteria," I say. "But thank you."

"Nonsense," she says. "I'll order some pasta and salad. Greg, do you like pasta?"

He looks to me for the answer. "Yes?"

My cell phone rings then. David.

"Excuse me," I tell the group, which now includes Frederick, who is looking over Jill's shoulder at her phone.

"Hey," I say. "God, David, this is a nightmare."

"I imagine. How was she this morning?"

"Her parents are here."

"Jill and Maurice?"

"Frederick, yes."

"Wow," he says. "Good for them, I guess. Better they be there than not, right?"

I don't respond, and David tries again. "Do you want me to come sit with you?"

"No," I say. "I told you. One of us has to keep our job."

"The firm understands," David says, even though we both know that's not true. I didn't tell anyone about Bella's illness, but even if I did, they would be supportive as long as it didn't get in the way of my work. Wachtell isn't a charity.

"I brought a ton of work with me. I just told them I'm working remotely today."

"I'll come by at lunch."

"Call me," I say, and we hang up.

I sit back down in my chair. "There's a free latte," Aaron says, handing me a Starbucks. "I forgot to make Jill's nonfat."

"How could you," I say in mock horror, and Aaron chuckles. It feels wrong here, that sound of joy.

"I guess I was a little focused on my girlfriend's cancer." He gives me an exaggerated headshake. "How dare I."

Now I'm the one to laugh.

"Do you think this counts as blowing it with her parents?"

"There's always the chemo," I say. And now we're both in hysterics. A woman knitting a few chairs over from us looks up, annoyed. I can't help it, though. It feels nearly impossible to get any air, that's how hard we're laughing.

"Radiation," he says, gasping.

"Third time's a charm."

It's Frederick's stern look that sends us up and out of our seats, sprinting toward the door.

When we're in the hallway, I take big, gulping breaths. It feels like I haven't had air in a week.

"We're going outside," he says. "You have your cell phone?"

I nod.

"Good. Yours is the update phone. I made sure on the chart."

We head down in the elevators and the double doors spit us out onto the street. There's a park across the way. Small children dangle from swings, surrounded by planted trees. Nannies and parents bark into their cell phones.

We're on the sidewalk, the length of Fifth Avenue splayed out before us. Cars push one another forward, egging the others on. The city inhales and inhales and inhales.

"Where are we going?" I ask him. My bones feel tired. I lift my leg up, testing.

"It's a surprise," he says.

"I don't like those."

Aaron laughs. "You're gonna be fine," he says.

He grabs my hand, and we're turning up Fifth Avenue.

# Chapter Twenty-Three

"We can't go far," I say. I'm practically running to keep up, he's moving so quickly.

"We're not," he tells me. "Just up. Here."

We're at the back entrance of a doorman building on One Hundred First Street. He takes an ID out of his wallet and swipes the key fob. The door opens.

"Are we breaking and entering?"

He laughs. "Just entering."

We're in what appears to be a basement storage unit, and I follow Aaron through rows of bikes and giant plastic storage containers with out-of-season items into an elevator in the back.

I check my phone to make sure I still have service. Four bars.

It's a freight elevator, old and lumbering, and we shuffle our way to the rooftop. When we step off, we're greeted by a tiny stretch of grass surrounded by a concrete terrace and beyond that, the city splayed out before us. There's a glass dome behind us, some kind of party venue.

"I just thought you could probably use a little bit of space," he says.

I walk tentatively toward the terrace, run my hand along the marbled concrete. "How do you have access to this place?"

"It's a building I'm working on," he says. He comes to stand beside me. "I like it because it's so high. Usually buildings on the East Side are pretty squat."

I look at the hospital, dwarfed below us, imagining Bella lying on a table, her body splayed open somewhere inside. My grip on the concrete tightens.

"I've screamed up here before," Aaron tells me. "I wouldn't judge if you wanted to."

I hiccup. "That's okay," I say.

I turn to him. His eyes are focused below us. I wonder what he's thinking, if he sees Bella the way I do.

"What do you love about her?" I ask him. "Will you tell me?"

He smiles immediately. He doesn't lift his eyes. "Her warmth," he says. "She's so damn warm. Do you know what I mean?"

"I do," I say.

"She's beautiful, obviously."

"Boring," I say.

He smiles. "Stubborn, too. I think you guys have that in common."

I laugh. "You're probably not wrong."

"And she's spontaneous in the way people aren't anymore. She lives for now."

A ping of recognition in my chest. I look to Aaron. His eyebrows are knit. He looks, all at once, like it's just occurred to him, what that really means. The possibility ahead. *Ding ding ding.* And then I realize it's my cell phone that's ringing. It's been in my hand, vibrating and tolling.

"Hello?"

"Ms. Kohan, it's Dr. Shaw's associate, Dr. Jeffries. He wanted me to call and give you an update."

My breath holds. The air stills. From somewhere in the distance, Aaron takes my hand.

"We're going to take a biopsy of her colon and abdominal tissue. But everything is going according to plan. We still have a few hours ahead of us, but he wanted you to know so far so good."

"Thank you," I manage. "Thank you."

"I'm going to get back now," he says, and hangs up.

I look to Aaron. I see it there, the love in his eyes. It mirrors mine.

"He said it's going according to plan."

He exhales, drops my hand. "We should get back," he says.

"Yeah."

We reverse the process. Elevator, door, street. When we get to the lobby of the hospital, someone calls my name: "Dannie!"

I turn to see David jogging toward us.

"Hey," he says. "I was just trying to check in. How's it going? Hey, man." He extends his hand to Aaron, who shakes it.

"I'm going to head back up," Aaron says. He touches my arm and leaves.

"You doing okay?" David folds me into a hug. I reach up and embrace him.

"They said it's going well," I said, although that's not entirely the truth. They said it's going. "I don't think they need to get into her stomach."

David's eyebrows knit. "Good," he says. "That's good, right? How are you?"

"Hanging in."

"Have you eaten?"

I shake my head.

David produces a paper bag with a Sarge's logo, my bagel with whitefish salad.

"This is my winner's breakfast," I say sadly.

"She's got this, Dannie."

"I should head back up," I say. "Shouldn't you be at the office?"

"I should be here," he says.

He puts a hand on my back and we go upstairs. When we get to the waiting room, Jill and Frederick are still on their cell phones. A pile of Scarpetta's takeout sits upright in a chair next to them. I don't even know how they got them to deliver this early—I'm not even sure they're open for lunch.

I brought my computer and I take it out now. The one good thing about the hospital: free and strong Wi-Fi.

Bella has told very few people. Morgan and Ariel, who I email now, and the gallery girls, for logistical reasons. I update them, too. I imagine these tiny, waiflike women contending with their beautiful boss having cancer. Does thirty-three seem ancient to them? They haven't even crossed twenty-five.

I work for two hours. Answer emails, punt calls, and research. My brain is a haze of focus and paranoia and fear and noise. At some point, David forces the sandwich on me. I'm surprised by my appetite. I finish it. David leaves, promising to come back later. I tell him I'll meet him at home. Jill steps out and comes back. Frederick goes in search of a charger. Aaron sits—sometimes reading, sometimes doing nothing but staring at the clock, at the big board where they list where patients are. Patient 487B, still in surgery.

It's creeping toward late afternoon when I see Dr. Shaw walking through the double doors. My heart leaps up into my ears. I hear the pounding, like gongs.

I stand up, but I do not run across the room to him. It's

strange the social normalcies we hold strong to, even in the midst of extraordinary circumstances. The rules we are unwilling to break.

Dr. Shaw looks tired, far older than his age, which I'd put at around forty.

"Everything went well," he says. I feel relief course through my body right along with my blood. "She's out and recovering. We were able to get all the tumor and any cancer cells to the best of our ability."

"Thank god," Jill says.

"She has a long road ahead of her, but today went well."

"Can we see her?" I ask.

"She's been through a lot. One visitor for now. Someone from my team will come over to take you back and answer any further questions."

"Thank you," I say. I shake his hand. So do Frederick and Jill. Aaron is still sitting. When I look back at him, I see that he is crying. He holds the back of his hand against his face, swallowing his sobs.

"Hey," I say. "You should go."

Jill looks at me but doesn't say anything. I know Bella's parents. I know being with her in the recovery room, unchaperoned, scares them. They don't want to make decisions about her care, not really. And so I will. I always have.

"No," he says. He shuffles his hands in front of his face, diverting attention. "You should go."

"She'll want to see you," I tell him.

I imagine Bella waking up in a bed. In pain, confused. Whose face does she want hovering above hers? Whose hand does she want to hold? Somehow, I know that it's his.

A nurse comes back. She wears bright pink scrubs and has a

stuffed koala clinging to the pocket of her shirt. "Are you the family of Bella Gold?"

I nod. "This is her husband," I lie. I'm not sure what the rule is for boyfriends. "He'd like to go back."

"I'll take you," she says.

I watch them disappear down the hallway. It's not until they're gone, and Jill and Frederick are cornering me, asking questions, demanding we get the nurse back, that I feel happy for Bella for the first time. This is the thing she's wanted forever. This, right here. This is love.

# Chapter Twenty-Four

Bella is supposed to spend seven days in the hospital, but because of her age and general health she's released after five, and on Saturday morning I meet her at her apartment. Jill has gone back to Philadelphia for the weekend to "take care of some business," but hired a private nurse who runs the place like military quarters. The apartment is spotless when I arrive, more orderly than I've ever seen it.

"She won't even let me stand up," Bella says.

Every day she has looked better. It's impossible to understand how she could still be sick, how there could still be cancer cells in her. Her cheeks are now rosy, her body has regained its color. She's sitting up in bed when I get there, enjoying scrambled eggs and avocado, a side of toast, and a cup of coffee on a tray.

"It's like room service," I say. "You always wanted to live at a hotel."

I set the sunflowers—her favorite—I brought on the nightstand.

"Where is Aaron?"

"I sent him home," she says. "The poor guy hasn't slept in a week. He looks way worse than I do."

Aaron has kept vigil at her bedside. I went to work, slogged through the days, and came in the morning and at night, but he refused to leave. Watching over the nurses, her monitors—making sure no misstep was made.

"Your dad?"

"He's back in Paris," she says. "Everyone needs to understand that I'm fine. Obviously. Look at me."

She holds her hands above her head in proof.

Chemo doesn't start for another three weeks. Long enough for her to recover, but not long enough for any cells to spread in a significant way—we hope. We don't know. We're all grasping. We're all pretending now. Pretending this was the hard part. Pretending it's over and behind us. Now, sitting in her sunny bedroom, the smell of coffee surrounding us, it's easy to forget it's a pretty, dressed-up lie.

"Did you bring it?" she asks.

"Of course."

From my bag, I produce the entire season of *Grosse Pointe*, a WB show from the early two thousands that performed so poorly it apparently doesn't warrant streaming on any service. But when we were kids, we loved it. It's a sitcom about the behind-the-scenes of a fictional WB show. We were so meta.

I ordered the DVDs and brought my old computer—the one with the DVD player from ten years ago—with me.

I take it out now and reveal it to her.

"You think of everything."

"Just about," I say.

I kick off my shoes and crawl into bed with her. My jeans feel too tight. I abhor people who walk around in workout clothes. It's the entirety of the reason I could never live in Los Angeles: too much Lycra. But even I have to admit, as I tuck my legs in underneath me, this would feel more comfortable with some stretch. Bella wears silk pajamas, embossed with her initials. She makes a move to get up.

"What are you doing?" I say, springing into action. I toss my body across hers like train tracks. I lunge.

"I need some water. I'm fine."

"I'll get it."

She rolls her eyes but tucks herself back into bed. I leave the bedroom and go into the kitchen where Svedka, the nurse, is furiously washing dishes. She looks up at me, her face practically murderous.

"What do you need?" she barks.

"Water."

She pulls a glass down from the cabinet—a green goblet from a set Bella bought in Venice. While the water is being poured, I look out over her living room, the cheerful color, the bright spots of blue and purple and deep forest green. Her window drapes hang in soft folds of violet silk, and her art, collected over the years from everywhere she's gone—high and low—lines the walls. Bella is always trying to get me to buy pieces. "They're investments in your future happiness," she tells me. "Only buy what you love." But I don't have the eye. Any art I own, Bella has picked out for me—usually gifted.

Svedka hands me the water glass. "Now move," she says, cocking her head in the direction of the bedroom.

I find myself bowing to her.

"She scares me," I say, handing Bella her water and getting back into bed.

"Leave it to Jill to find a way to imbue this situation with even more anxiety." She laughs—a tinkling sound, like twinkle lights.

"How did you even get these?" Bella asks me. She takes the

computer and opens it. The screen is dark, and she hits the power button.

"Amazon," I say. "I hope it works. This thing is centuries old."

It sputters to life, groaning at its own old age. The blue light flashes and then stills, then the screen appears in a flourish, as if presenting—*still got it.*

I tear the last of the plastic and pop in a DVD. The screen buzzes and we're met with old friends. The feeling of nostalgia—pleasant nostalgia—the kind imbued with warmth and not melancholy, fills the room. Bella settles herself down and nuzzles her neck into my shoulder.

"Remember Stone?" she says. "Oh my god, I loved this show."

I let the early two thousands wash over us for the next two and a half hours. At one point, Bella falls asleep. I pause the computer and slip out of bed. I check my emails in the living room. There's one from Aldridge: *Can we meet Monday morning? 9 a.m., my office.*

Aldridge never emails me, certainly not on a weekend. He's going to fire me. I've barely been in the office. I've been behind on due diligence and late to respond to emails. Fuck.

"Dannie?" I hear Bella call from the other room. I get up and run back to her. She stretches lazily, and then winces. "Forgot about the stitches."

"What do you need?"

"Nothing," she says. She sits up slowly, squinting her eyes to the pain. "It'll pass."

"I think you should eat something."

As if we're being bugged, Svedka appears at the door. "You want to eat?"

Bella nods. "Maybe a sandwich? Do we have cheese?"

Svedka nods and exits.

"Does she have you on a baby monitor?"

"Oh most likely," Bella says.

She sits up farther now, and I see that she's bleeding. There is a dark crimson stain on her gray pajamas. "Bella," I say. I point. "Stay still."

"It's fine," she says. "It's no big deal." But she looks woozy, a little bit nervous. She blinks a few times rapidly.

Ever alert, Svedka returns. She rushes to Bella, pushes up her pajamas, and, as if she were a clown, pulls gauze and ointment from her sleeve. She replaces Bella's bandages with fresh white wrappings. All new.

"Thank you," Bella says. "I'm fine. Really."

A moment later, the door opens. Aaron comes into the bedroom. His arms are laden with bags—errands, gifts, groceries. I see Bella's face light up.

"Sorry, I couldn't stay away. Should I make Thai or Italian or sushi?" He drops his bags and bends down and kisses her, his hand lingering on her face.

"Greg cooks," Bella says, her eyes still locked into his.

"I know," I say.

She smiles. "Do you want to stay for dinner?"

I think about the pile of paperwork I have, Aldridge's email. "I think I'm going to head out. You two enjoy. You might want to put on some armor before entering the kitchen," I say. I look toward the door at Svedka, who is scowling.

As I gather my things, Aaron climbs into bed with Bella. He gets on top of the covers, still in jeans, and he gently shifts her so she's in his arms. The last thing I see when I leave is his hand on her stomach—gently, tenderly, touching what lies beneath.

# Chapter Twenty-Five

It's Monday morning. 8:58 a.m. Aldridge's office.

I'm sitting in a chair, waiting for him to return from a partner meeting. I'm wearing a new Theory suit with a silk high-necked camisole underneath. Nothing frivolous. All severity. I'm tapping my pen to the corner of my folder. I've brought all our recent deals, the success I've helped and, in some cases, overseen.

"Ms. Kohan," Aldridge says. "Thank you for meeting me."

I stand and shake his hand. He has on a custom Armani three-piece suit with a pink-and-blue shirt and matching pink-trimmed detail. Aldridge loves fashion. I should have remembered that.

"How are you?" he asks me.

"Good," I say, measured. "Fine."

He nods. "Lately I've been noting your work. And I must say—"

I can't bear it. I leap in. "I'm sorry," I say. "I've been distracted. My best friend has been very sick. But I've brought all my case work to the hospital and we're still on schedule with the Karbinger merger. Nothing has changed. This job is my life, and I'll do whatever I can to prove that to you."

Aldridge looks puzzled. "Your friend is sick. What's wrong?"

"She has ovarian cancer," I say. No sooner are the words out than I see them, sitting on the table between us. They are bulking, unruly, bleeding. They ooze all over everything. The documents on Aldridge's desk. His gorgeous Armani suit.

"I'm very sorry to hear that," he says. "It sounds serious."

"Yes."

He shakes his head. "You've gotten her the best doctors?"

I nod.

"Good," he says. "That's good." His eyebrows scrunch, and then his face descends into surprise. "I didn't call you here to reprimand your work," he says. "I've been impressed with your initiative lately."

"I'm confused."

"I'll bet," Aldridge says. At this, he chuckles. "You know QuTe?"

"Of course." QuTe is one of our tech companies. They're primarily known as being a search function, like Google, but they're relatively new and building in interesting and creative ways.

"They are ready to go public."

My eyes go wide. "I thought that was never going to happen."

QuTe was created by two women, Jordi Hills and Anya Cho, from their college dorm room at Syracuse. The search function is outfitted with more youthful terminology and results. For instance, a search for "Audrey Hepburn" might lead you first to the Netflix documentary on her, second to *E! True Hollywood Story*, third to her presence in modern CW shows—and the ways to dress like her. Down the list: biographies, her actual movies. It's brilliant. A veritable pop-culture reservoir. And from what I understood, Jordi and Anya had no intention of ever selling.

"They changed their minds. And we need someone to oversee the deal."

At this, my heart starts racing. I can feel the pulse in my veins, the adrenaline kicking, revving, taking off—

"Okay."

"I'm offering you to be the key associate on this case."

"Yes!" I say. I practically scream. "Unequivocally, yes."

"Hang on," Aldridge says. "The job would be in California. Half in Silicon Valley, half in Los Angeles, where Jordi and Anya reside. They want to do as much work as they can out of their LA offices. And it would be quick; we'll probably begin next month."

"Who is the partner?" I ask.

"Me," he says. He smiles. His teeth are impossibly white. "You know, Dannie, I've always seen a lot of myself in you. You're hard on yourself. I was, too."

"I love this job," I say.

"I know you do," he tells me. "But it's important to make sure the job is not unkind to you."

"That's impossible. We're corporate lawyers. The job is inherently unkind."

Aldridge laughs. "Maybe," he says. "But I don't think I'd have lasted this long if I thought we hadn't struck some kind of deal."

"You and the job."

Aldridge takes off his glasses. He looks me square in the eye when he says: "Me and my ambition. Far be it from me to tell you what your own deal should be. I still work eighty-hour weeks. My husband, god bless him, wants to kill me. But—"

"You know the terms."

He smiles, puts his glasses back on. "I know the terms."

✦

The IPO evaluation begins in mid-November. We're already creeping further into October. I call Bella at lunch, while bent over a signature Sweetgreen salad, and she sounds rested and comfortable. The girls from the gallery are there, and she's going over a new show. She can't talk. Good.

I leave work early, intent on picking up one of David's favorite meals—the teriyaki at Haru—and surprising him at home. We've been strangers passing in the night. I think the last time I had a full conversation with him was at the hospital. And we've barely touched our wedding plans.

I turn onto Fifth Avenue and decide to walk. It's barely 6 p.m, David won't be home for another two hours, at least, and the weather is perfect. One of those first truly crisp fall days, where you could conceivably wear a sweater but because the sun is out, and still strong overhead, a T-shirt will do. The wind is low and languid, and the city is buzzy with the happy, contented quality of routine.

I'm feeling so festive, in fact, that when I pass Intimissimi, a popular lingerie company, I decide to stop inside.

I think about sex, about David. About how it's good, solid, satisfying, and how I've never been someone who wants her hair pulled or to be spanked. Who doesn't even really like to be on top. Is that a problem? Maybe I'm not in touch with my sexuality—which Bella, casually—too casually—has accused me of on more than one occasion.

The shop is filled with pretty, lacy things. Tiny bras with bows and matching underwear. Frilly negligees with rosettes on the hems. Silk robes.

I choose a black lace camisole and boy shorts, decidedly different from anything I own, but still me. I pay without trying them on, and then make my way over to Haru. I call in our order on the way. No sense in waiting.

✦

I can't believe I'm doing this. I hear David's key latch in the door and I'm tempted to run back into the bedroom and hide, but it's too late now. The apartment is littered with candles and the low stylings of Barry Manilow. It's like a cliché sex comedy from the nineties.

David walks in and drops his keys on the table, sets his bag down on the counter. It's not until he reaches to take off his shoes that he notices his surroundings. And then me.

"Woah."

"Welcome home," I say. I'm wearing the black lingerie with a black silk robe, something I got as a gift on a bachelorette weekend eons ago. I go to David. I hand him one end of the belt. "Pull," I say, like I'm someone else.

He does, and the thing comes apart, falling to the floor in a puddle.

"This is for me?" he asks, his index finger stretched out to touch the strap of my camisole top.

"It would be weird if it weren't," I say.

"Right," he says, low. "Yeah." He fingers the strap, edging it down over my shoulder. From an open window a breeze saunters in, dancing the candles. "I like this," he says.

"I'm glad," I say. I take his glasses off. I set them down on the couch. And then I start to unbutton his shirt. It's white. Hugo Boss. I bought it for him for Hanukkah two years ago along with a pink one and a blue-striped one. He never wears the blue one. It was my favorite.

"You look really sexy," he says. "You never dress like this."

"They don't allow this in the office, even on Friday," I tell him.

"You know what I mean."

I get the last button undone and I shake the shirt off him—one arm then the other. David is always warm. Always. And I feel the prickle of his chest hair against my skin, the soft folding my body does to his.

"Bedroom?" he asks me.

I nod.

He kisses me then, hard and fast, right by the couch. It catches me by surprise. I pull back.

"What?" he asks.

"Nothing," I say. "Do it again." And he does.

He kisses me into the bedroom. He kisses me out of the lingerie. He kisses me underneath the sheets. And when it's just us there, on the precipice, he lifts his face up from mine and asks it:

"When are we getting married?"

My brain is scrambled. Undone from the day, the month, the glass and a half of wine I had to prepare myself for this little stunt.

"David," I breathe out. "Can we talk about this later?"

He kisses my neck, my cheek, the bridge of my nose. "Yes."

And then he pushes into me. He moves slowly, deliberately, and I feel myself come apart before I even have a chance to begin. He keeps moving on top of me, long after I've returned to my body, to my brain. We are like constellations passing each other, seeing each other's light but in the distance. It feels impossible how much space there can be in this intimacy, how much privacy. And I think that maybe that is what love is. Not the absence of space but the acknowledgment of it, the thing that lives between the parts, the thing that makes it possible not to be one, but to be different, to be two.

But there is something I cannot shake. Some reckoning that has burrowed into my body, through my very cells. It rises now, flooding, probing, threatening to spill out of my lips. The thing I have kept buried and locked for almost five years, exposed to this fraction of light.

I close my eyes against it. I will them to stay shut. And when it's over, when I finally open them, David is staring at me with a look I've never seen before. He's looking at me as if he's already gone.

# Chapter Twenty-Six

I go down to Bella's and make her tens of peanut butter and jelly sandwiches—the only thing, really, I know how to "cook." The gallery girls come by. We order from Buvette, and Bella's favorite waiter brings it himself. And then the results of the surgery come back. The doctors were right: stage three.

It's in the lymph system, but not the surrounding organs. Good news, bad news. Bella starts chemo and impossibly, insanely, we continue wedding planning for two months from now: December in New York. I call the wedding planner, the same one a young woman at my firm used. He wrote a book on weddings: *How to Wed: Style, Food, and Tradition* by Nathaniel Trent. She buys me the book, and I flip through it at work, grateful for the environment, this animal firm where I work, that does not require or ask me to *ooh* and *aah* over peonies.

We choose a venue. A loft downtown that is, as Nathaniel tells me, the "best raw space in Manhattan." What he doesn't say: Every nice hotel is booked, this is the best we're going to get. Some couple called their wedding off and we got lucky.

The loft will mean more decisions—everything has to be brought in—but all of the available hotels are bland or too corporate, and we agree to follow Nathaniel's lead and end up with something that splits the difference.

At first, the chemo goes well. Bella is a champion. "I feel great," she tells me on her way home from the hospital after her second session. "No nausea, nothing."

I've read, of course, that the beginning is a lie. That there is an air of suspension. Before the chemicals reach your tissues, dig in, and start really doing their damage. But I am hopeful, of course I am. I'm breathing.

I'm reading over the IPO offering for QuTe. Aldridge has already been to California to meet with them. If I choose to, I'll leave in three weeks. It's the dream case. Young female entrepreneurs, a managing partner overseeing, complete access to the deal.

"Of course, you should do it," David tells me over a glass of wine and Greek salad takeout.

"I would be in LA for a month," I say. "What about the wedding? And what about Bella?" What about missing her doctors' appointments, not being here?

"Bella is doing well," David says, reaching over the question. "She'd want you to go."

"Doesn't mean I should."

David picks up his glass, drinks. The wine is a red we bought at a tasting on Long Island last fall. It was David's favorite. I remember liking it fine, which is the way I feel about it tonight. Wine is wine.

"You have to make choices sometimes for yourself. It doesn't make you a bad friend, it just means you put yourself first, which you should."

What I don't tell him—because I suspect, I know, that a lecture would follow—is that I don't put myself first. I never have. Not when it comes to Bella.

"Nate said that we should go with the tiger lilies and that no one does roses anymore," I say, skating to the next subject.

"That's insane," David says. "It's a wedding."

I shrug. "I don't care," I say. "Do you?"

David takes another sip. He appears to be really considering. "No," he says.

We sit in silence for a few moments.

"What do you want to do for your birthday?" he asks me.

My birthday. Next week. October 21. Thirty-three. "Your magic year," Bella told me. "Your year of miracles."

"Nothing," I say. "It's fine."

"I'll make a reservation," David says. He gets up with his plate and goes to the counter, refilling on tzatziki and roasted eggplant. It's a shame neither one of us cooks. We love to eat so very much.

"Who should we get to marry us?" David asks, and in the same breath: "I'll ask my parents for Rabbi Shultz's information."

"You don't have it?"

"I don't," he says, his back to me.

This is what marriage is, I know. Tiffs and comfortability, miscommunications and long stretches of silence. Years and years of support and care and imperfection. I thought we'd be long married by now. But I find, as I sit there, that a hitch of relief hits me when David still doesn't have the rabbi's information. Maybe he's still a step away, too.

✦

On Saturday, I go to Bella's chemo appointment with her. She chats amicably to a nurse named Janine, who wears white scrubs with a hand-painted rainbow emblazoned on the back, as she hooks her up to the IV. Chemo is in a center on East One Hundred Second Street, two blocks up from where her surgery was performed. The chairs are wide, and the blankets are soft on the third floor of the Ruttenberg Treatment Center. Bella has a cashmere throw with her. "Janine is letting me store a basket here," she tells me in a conspiratorial whisper.

Aaron shows up, and the three of us suck on Popsicles and pass the time. Two hours later, we're in an Uber going back downtown when Bella suddenly clutches my arm.

"Can we stop?" she asks. And then, more urgently, "Pull over."

We do, on the corner of Park Avenue and Thirty-Ninth Street, and she climbs over Aaron to retch in the street. She starts puking with ferocity; the remains of a technicolor Popsicle spew out with the bile.

"Hold her hair," I tell Aaron, who gently rubs her back in small circles.

She waves us off, breathing heavily over bent knees. "I'm fine," she says.

"Do you have any tissues?" I ask the Uber driver, who mercifully hasn't said anything.

"Here." He hands a box back. There are clouds on the cardboard.

I pluck out three tissues and hand them to Bella, who takes them and wipes her mouth. "Well, that was fun," she says.

She climbs back into the car, but there's a change in her. She knows now that what's to come is hers to face alone. I can't take this part from her, I can't even share it. I have the instinct to reach out, to try and keep the jaws open, but they have clamped shut too quickly. She leans on Aaron. I see the rise and fall of her body, matched in step to her breathing. The first evidence is in, and it isn't good.

Aaron helps her upstairs. Svedka is still there, washing dishes that have never been dirty. Bella hasn't fully recovered from surgery, and small things like a few stairs or bending down are still difficult. It will take her months to fully recover, and then there is the chemo.

"Let's get you into bed," I say.

Bella is wearing a blue lace Zimmermann dress with a butter-soft chocolate leather jacket, and I help her take them off. Aaron stays in the other room. When she's undressed, I can see her scars, some still bandaged, and how much thinner she has gotten in just a few short weeks. She must have lost fifteen pounds.

I smile, forcing the tide back down. "Here," I say. She holds her head out like a child, and I loop a long-sleeved cotton T-shirt over her head, then slide on some soft gray drawstring sweatpants. I pull down the freshly laundered duvet and tuck her inside, fluffing the pillows behind her.

"You're so good to me," she says. She reaches up for my hand, curls her tiny palm into mine. Bella has always had the smallest hands, too little for her body.

"You make it easy," I say. "You'll be better in no time."

We look at each other for a beat. Long enough for us to recognize the terrible fear we're both facing.

"I got you something!" Bella says. Her face breaks out into a smile. She tucks some hair behind her ears. Hair that will soon be gone.

"Bella, come on," I say. "That's not—"

She shakes her head. "No, for your birthday!"

"My birthday is next week."

"So it's early. I have an excuse to do things now, don't you think?"

I say nothing.

"Greg, can you come help me?"

Aaron comes into the room, wiping his hands on his jeans. "What's up?"

Bella sits up in bed, pointing excitedly to a gift-wrapped package that leans against her closet wall.

Aaron picks it up. I can tell it's not light. "On the bed?" he asks.

"Yeah, here." Bella removes a throw from her feet and moves her legs into a cross-legged position. She taps the space next to her, and I go to sit. "Open it."

The wrapping paper is gold, with a white-and-silver silk ribbon. Bella is a master gift wrapper, and it gives me some solace, some sign, that she did this herself. It feels like proof of stability, of order. I tear it away.

Inside is a large frame. A piece of art. "Turn it over," she says.

I do, with Aaron's help.

"I saw a print of this on Instagram and immediately knew you needed it. It took forever to find the Allen Grubesic one. I think he only made twelve. Everyone at the gallery has been trying to track it down for you, and we found it two months ago. A woman in Italy was selling it. We pounced. I'm obsessed. Please tell me you love it?"

I look at the print in my hands. It's an eye chart, and it reads: *I WAS YOUNG I NEEDED THE MONEY.* My hands feel numb.

"Do you like it?" she asks, her voice an octave lower.

"Yes," I say. I swallow. "I love it."

"I thought you would."

"Aaron," I say. I can feel him standing there. It seems crazy, impossible, that he doesn't know. "Whatever happened to that Dumbo apartment?"

Bella laughs. "Why do you call him Aaron?" she asks.

"It's fine," he says abruptly. "I don't mind."

"I know you don't *mind*," Bella says. "But why?"

"It's his first name," I say. "Isn't it?" I turn my attention to the gift. I run my hand over the glass.

"I bought it, the apartment," she tells me. The Aaron argument dissolves as quickly as it presented. "The rest is for me to know and you to find out."

I push the print to the side. I take her hands in mine. "Bella, listen to me. You cannot renovate that apartment. It will be a good investment as raw space. You bought it, fine, just sell it. Promise me you're not going to move in there. Promise."

Bella squeezes my hand. "You're crazy," she says. "But fine. I promise you. I'm not going to move in there."

# Chapter Twenty-Seven

The chemo goes from good to bad to gruesome quickly, too quickly. Next week she's sick, the following one she's weak, and after that she is sunken, her body practically concave. The one saving grace is that her hair doesn't fall out. Session after session, week after week, not even a strand.

"It happens sometimes," Dr. Shaw tells me. He comes to her chemo sessions to check up on her and run through any recent blood work. Today, Jill is there. Which might explain why Dr. Shaw and I are in the hallway, a whole room away from where Bella's mother pretends to be dutiful. "A patient who doesn't lose their hair. It's rare, though. She's one of the lucky ones."

"Lucky." I taste the word in my mouth. Rotted.

"Poor choice of words," he says. "We doctors aren't always the most sensitive. I apologize."

"No," I say. "She has great hair."

Dr. Shaw smiles at me. Colorful Nikes peek out from the bottom of his jeans. They point to some kind of life beyond these walls. Does he go home to children? How does he shake the everyday of these patients, shrinking inside?

"She's lucky that she has such a good support system," he tells me. It isn't the first time he's said it. "Some patients have to do this alone."

"She has two more weeks of this," I say. "And then she'll do another test?"

"Yes. We'll check to see if the cancer has been localized. But you know, Dannie, because it's in the lymph, it's really about containment. The likelihood of remission in ovarian cancers . . ."

"No," I say. "She's different. She has her hair! She's different."

Dr. Shaw puts a hand on my shoulder and squeezes gently. But he doesn't say anything.

I want to ask him more. Like whether he's ever seen a case like this. Like what we should prepare for. I want to ask him to tell me. Tell me what is going to happen. Give me the answers. But he can't. He doesn't know. And whatever he has to say, I'm not interested in hearing.

I go back in the room. Bella's leaning her head against the side of her armchair, her eyes closed. She opens them when I'm in front of her.

"Guess what?" she tells me, her voice sleepy. "Mom is going to take me to dinner and to see the Barbra Streisand musical. Do you want to come?"

Jill, dressed in black crepe slacks and a floral-print silk blouse with a pussy bow, leans over. "It'll be fun. We'll go to Sardi's before and have some martinis."

"Bella . . ." I can feel the anger start to simmer in me. She can barely sit up. She's going to go to dinner? To a theater?

Bella rolls her eyes. "Oh, come on. I can do it."

"You're not really supposed to be out right now. Dr. Shaw did say that, and he definitely mentioned that alcohol could interfere with your medi—"

"Stop! What are you, my parole officer?" Bella fires at me. It feels like a shot to the stomach.

"No," I say calmly. "I'm not trying to keep you from anything; I'm just trying to keep you well. I'm the one who has been here, and who has listened to the doctors."

Jill doesn't even bristle. She doesn't even seem to understand the slight.

"So have I," Bella says. She reaches down and tugs her blanket up. I see how thin her legs have become, like two arms. She notices me noticing.

"I'm going to get some iced tea," Jill says. "Bella, can I get you some iced tea?"

"Bella doesn't drink iced tea," I say. "She hates it. She always has."

"Well," Jill says. "Coffee, then!" She doesn't wait for a response, just saunters out of the room like she's in sweaters and headed now toward the shoe department.

"What is wrong with you?" Bella hisses when she's left.

"What is wrong with *me*? What is wrong with *you*? You can't do this tonight. You know that. Why are you acting this way?"

"Did it ever occur to you that maybe I don't need you to tell me how I feel? That maybe I know?"

"No," I say. "It didn't, because that's ridiculous. This isn't about how you feel, which, by the way, is like shit. You threw up three times in the car on the way here."

Bella looks away. I feel struck by sadness, but it does not push the anger out. Because that is what I feel: angry. And for the first time since her diagnosis, I let it take over. I let the righteous indignation burn a hole through me, through her, through this godforsaken chemical den.

"Shut up," Bella says. Something she hasn't said to me since we were twelve years old, in the back of my parents' station wagon, fighting over god knows what. Not her life. Not cancer. "I'm not your project. I'm not some little girl you have to save. You don't know what's better for me than I do." She struggles to sit up and winces, the needle in her arm shifting. I am overcome with a helplessness so deep it threatens to topple me into her chair.

"I'm sorry, Bella. I'm sorry," I say, gently now. For all the things she's going through, for everything. "It's okay. Let's just finish, and I'll take you home."

"No," Bella says. There is a ferocity in her tone that does not give. "I don't want you here anymore."

"Bells—"

"Don't 'Bells' me. You always do this. You've done this forever. You think you know everything. But it's my body, not yours, okay? You're not my mother."

"I never said I was."

"You didn't have to. You treat me like a child. You think I'm incapable. But I don't need you."

"Bella, this is insane. Come on."

"Please stop coming to these appointments."

"I'm not going to—"

"I'm not asking you!" she says. She's practically screaming now. "I'm telling you. You need to leave." She swallows. There are sores in her mouth. I can tell it takes effort. "Now."

I wander outside. Jill is there, juggling a coffee and a tea. "Oh, hello, darling," she says. "Cappuccino?"

I don't answer her. I keep walking. I keep walking until I start running.

I take out my phone. Before I am down the hall, before I have any clear grasp on what I'm doing, I'm scrolling to his name and hitting the green button. He answers after the third ring.

"Hey," he says. "What's wrong? Is she okay?"

I start to speak and then, instead of words, I'm met with big, hiccupping sobs. I crouch down in the corner of the hallway, let them rake over me. Nurses pass by, unmoved. This is the chemo floor, after all. Nothing new to see here. Just the end of the world over and over and over again.

"I'll be right there," he says, and hangs up.

# Chapter Twenty-Eight

"She doesn't mean it," Aaron says. We're sitting at a diner on Lexington, some late-night one named Big Daddy's or Daddy Dan's or something like that. The kind of place that can't afford to be downtown. I'm on my second cup of strong and bitter black coffee. I don't deserve cream.

"She does," I say. We've been going through this script for the last twenty minutes, since Aaron ran up to the hospital's double doors to find me crouching outside. "She always felt this way. She just never said it."

"She's scared."

"She was so angry with me. I've never even seen her like that before. Like she wanted to kill me."

"She's the one going through it," he says. "Right now, she has to think that she's capable of anything, even alcohol."

I ignore his attempt at levity.

"She is," I say. I bite my lip. I don't want to cry anymore. Not in front of him. It's too vulnerable, too close, too near. "I just can't believe her parents are behaving this way. You don't know what they're like—"

Aaron removes an invisible eyelash from his face.

"You don't know," I repeat.

"Maybe not," Aaron says. "They seem to care. That's good, right?"

"They'll leave," I say. "They always do. When she really needs them, they'll be gone."

"But, Dannie," Aaron says. He sits forward. I can feel the air molecules around us stiffen. "They're here now. And she really needs them. Isn't that what matters?"

I think about his promise on the street corner. I always believed it was just Bella and me. There was no one she could count on but me. There was no one who would really be there, forever, but me.

"Not if they'll eventually leave," I say.

Aaron keeps hovering closer. "I think you're wrong."

"I think you don't know," I say. I'm starting to believe it was a mistake calling him. What was I thinking?

He shakes his head. "You mistake love. You think it has to have a future in order to matter, but it doesn't. It's the only thing that does not need to become at all. It matters only insofar as it exists. Here. Now. Love doesn't require a future."

Our eyes lock, and I think that maybe he can read it there. Everything that happened. That maybe, somehow, he has reached back. That he knows. In that moment, I want to tell. I want to tell him, if only so he can carry this thing with me.

"Aaron," I start, and then his cell phone rings. He takes it out.

"It's work," he says. "Hang on."

He stands up and leaves the booth. I see him gesturing out by the glass doors emblazoned with the diner's name: Daddy's. The waitress comes over. Do we want any food? I shake my head. Just the check, please.

She hands me the bill. She hadn't expected us to stick around,

I guess. I leave cash on the table and get my bag. I join Aaron at the door, where he's hanging up.

"Sorry about that," he says.

"It's okay. I'm going to head out. I should go back to the office."

"It's Saturday," he says.

"Corporate law," I mutter. "And I've been gone a lot."

He gives me a small smile. He looks disappointed.

"Thank you for meeting me," I say. "Really, thanks for showing up. I appreciate it."

"Of course," he says. "Dannie—you can call me anytime. You know that, right?"

I smile. I nod.

The bells on the door jingle on my way out.

# Chapter Twenty-Nine

It's the first week of November, and Bella won't speak to me. I call her. I send David over with food. "Just give her a little time," he tells me. I don't express the absurdity of his statement to him. I can't even think it, much less say it out loud.

Dr. Christine is no more surprised to see me back in her office than I am to be there. She wants to know about my family, and so I tell her about Michael. I remember him less and less these days. What he was like. I try and focus on the details. His laugh, the strange way his forearms hung from his elbows, like there was just too much limb. His brown curly hair, like baby ringlets, and his wide brown eyes. How he used to call me "pal." How he'd always invite me to hang out in the tent in our backyard, even if his friends were over. He didn't seem to have any of the hang-ups older brothers usually have about their little sisters. We fought, sure, but I always knew he loved me, that he wanted me around.

Dr. Christine tells me I am learning to deal with a life I cannot control. What she doesn't say, what she doesn't have to, is that I'm failing at it.

I still go to the chemo appointments, I just don't go upstairs. I sit in the lobby and read through work emails until I know Bella's finished.

The following Wednesday, Dr. Shaw walks by. I'm sitting on a cement ledge, some fake foliage dangling below me, doing some paperwork.

"Humpty Dumpty," he says.

I look up, so startled I nearly fall.

"Hi," he says.

"Hi."

"What are you doing here?"

"Bella," I say. I gesture with my free arm, the one not holding my array of folders, upward, to the room where Bella lies, chemicals being pumped into her.

"I just came from there."

Dr. Shaw takes a step closer to me. He peers at my binder disapprovingly. "Do you need some coffee?" he asks.

I found some crappy vending machine stuff earlier, but it's wearing off quickly.

"It kind of sucks here," I say.

He holds a pointed finger out to me. "That's because you do not know the tricks. Follow me."

We wind through the ground floor of the treatment center to the back and down a hallway. At the end is a little atrium, with a Starbucks cart. I swear, it's like seeing a miracle. My eyes go wide. Dr. Shaw notices.

"I know, right?" he says. "It's the best-kept hospital secret. Come on."

He leads me to the cart where a woman in her mid-twenties with two French braids smiles wide at him. "The usual?" she asks.

He turns to me. "Don't tell anyone, but I'm a tea drinker. That's why Irina here has to know my order."

"The hospital is big on coffee?" I ask.

"More manly," he says, gesturing for me to step forward.

I order an Americano, and when our drinks are ready, Dr. Shaw takes a seat at a little metal table. I join him.

"I don't want to keep you," I say. "I appreciate the coffee referral."

"It's good for me," he says. He takes his lid off, letting the steam rise. "Do you know surgeons are notorious for having the worst bedside manner?"

"Really," I say. But I know.

"Yes. We're monstrous. So every Wednesday I try and have coffee with a commoner."

He smiles. I laugh because I know the moment requires it.

"So how is Bella?" he asks. His pager beeps and he looks at it, setting it on the table.

"I don't know," I say. "You've seen her more recently than I have."

He looks confused; I keep talking.

"We had a fight. I'm not allowed upstairs."

"Oh," he says. "I'm sorry to hear that. What happened?"

I'm cognizant of the time, of how little he has. "I'm controlling," I say, getting to the punch.

Dr. Shaw laughs. It's a nice laugh, odd in this hospital setting. "I'm familiar with this dynamic," he says. "But she'll come around."

"I don't know," I say.

"She will," he says. "You're here. One thing I've learned is that you can't try and make this experience above the simplicity of humanity, it won't work."

I stare at him. I'm not sure what he means, he can tell.

"You're still you, she's still her. You still have emotions. You'll still fight. You can try and be perfect, but it will backfire. Just keep being here, instead."

His pager goes off again. This time he snaps the lid back down on his cup. "Unfortunately, duty calls." He stands and extends his hand. "Hang in there," he says. "I know the road isn't easy, but stay the course. You're doing good."

I stay sitting near the Starbucks cart for another hour, until I know Bella has finished treatment and is safely out of the building. When I head home I call David, but there is no answer.

✦

The following week, I'm not at the hospital but instead on a plane with Aldridge to Los Angeles. Aldridge is seeing another client while we're out there, a pharmaceutical giant who sends their jet for our use. We board with Kelly James, a litigating partner I've never said more than twenty words to over the course of my nearly five years at Wachtell.

It's a ten-seater, and I take the one in the rear, by the window. I lean my head against the glass. I said yes to this trip without considering what it means. It is, of course, an answer to Aldridge's original question. Yes. Yes, I'll take on the case. Yes, I'll commit to this.

"You're doing the right thing," David told me last night. "This could be huge for your career. And you love this company."

"I do," I say. "I just can't help but feel like people here need me."

"We'll survive," he said. "I promise we'll all survive."

And now here I am, flying over an endless mountain range in pursuit of the ocean.

We're staying at Casa del Mar, in Santa Monica, right on the beach. My room is on the ground level, with a terrace that extends onto the boardwalk. The hotel is shabby-chic Hamptons meets European opulence. I like it.

We have a dinner meeting with Jordi and Anya tonight, but when I reach my room, it's only 11 a.m. We picked up half a day on our way across the country.

I change into shorts, a T-shirt, and a sun hat—my Russian Jew skin has never met a sun it particularly got on with—and decide to take a walk on the beach. The temperature is warm and getting hotter—in the mid-eighties by lunchtime—but there's a cool breeze off the ocean. For the first time in weeks, I feel as if I am not simply surviving.

We go to dinner at Ivy at the Shore, a restaurant down the street from Casa del Mar, but Aldridge still calls a car. Kelly is in town to see another client, so it's just Aldridge and me. I'm wearing a navy shift dress with lilac flowers and navy espadrilles, the most casual I've ever been in a work environment. But it's California, these women are young, and we're by the ocean. I want to wear flowers.

We get to the restaurant first. Rattan chairs with floral backs and pillows pepper the restaurant as diners in jeans and dinner jackets clink glasses, laughing.

We sit. "I'm going to insist on the calamari," Aldridge says. "It's delectable."

He's wearing a light gray suit with a purple paisley shirt. If you photographed us together, you might think it had been planned.

"Is there anything we should go over?" I ask him. "I have the company stats memorized, but—"

"This is just a get-to-know-you meeting, so they feel comfortable. You know the ropes."

"No meeting is 'just' anything," I say.

"That is true. But if you try for an agenda, you often get an undesired outcome."

Jordi and Anya arrive in tandem. Jordi is tall, in high-waisted pants and a cowl-neck sweater. Her hair is down and wet at the ends. She looks like a bohemian dream, and I am reminded, for not the first time, of Bella. Anya wears jeans, a T-shirt, and a blazer. Her hair is short and slicked back. She talks with her eyes.

"Are we late?" she says. She's skittish. I can tell. No matter. We'll win them over.

"Not at all," Aldridge says. "You know us New Yorkers. We don't know anything about your traffic patterns."

Jordi sits next to me. Her perfume is heady and dense.

"Ladies, I'd like you to meet Danielle Kohan. She's our best and brightest senior associate. And she's been a huge boon to your IPO evaluation already."

"You can call me Dannie," I say, shaking each of their hands.

"We love Aldridge," Jordi tells me. "But does he have a first name?"

"It's never to be used," I tell her, before mouthing: *Miles.*

Aldridge smiles. "What are we drinking tonight?" he asks the group.

A waiter materializes, and Aldridge orders a bottle of champagne and a bottle of red, for dinner. "Cocktails, anyone?" he inquires.

Anya gets an iced tea. "How long do you think this will take?" she asks.

"Dinner, or taking your company public?" Aldridge does not look up from his menu.

"I've been a big fan of yours for a while now," I say. "I think what you've done with the space is brilliant."

"Thank—" Jordi starts, but Anya cuts her off.

"We didn't do anything with the existing space. We created a new one," she says. She eyes Jordi as if to say, *Lock it up.*

"I'm curious, though," I say. I aim my question at both of them, equally. "Why now?"

At this, Aldridge looks up from his menu and grabs a passing waiter. "We'd like the calamari immediately, please." Aldridge winks at me.

Jordi looks to Anya, as if unsure how to answer, and I feel a question answered before it has been raised. I swallow it back down. Not now.

"We're at the point where we don't want to work as hard as we have been on the same thing," Jordi says. "We'd like the revenue to be able to turn our attentions to new ventures."

I feel the familiarity in her speech. The measured, calculated words. Maybe it's all true, but none of it feels authentic. So I push.

"Why give away control of something you own when you don't have to?"

At this, Jordi busies herself with her water glass. Anya's eyes narrow. I can feel Aldridge shift next to me. I have no idea why I'm doing this. I know exactly why I'm doing this.

"Are you trying to talk us out of this?" Anya asks. She directs her question to Aldridge. "Because I was under the impression this was a kickoff dinner."

I look at Aldridge, who stays silent. He is, I realize, not going to answer for me.

"No," I say. "I just like to understand motivation. It helps me do my job."

Anya likes this answer, I can tell. Her shoulders drop perceptively. "The truth is, I'm not sure. We've spoken a lot about this. Jordi knows I'm on the fence."

"We've been at QuTe for almost ten years," Jordi says, repeating what is no doubt a familiar line. "It's time for something else."

"I don't know why we have to give up control in order to have that," Anya says.

The champagne arrives in a flourish of glasses and bubbles. Aldridge pours.

"To QuTe," he says. "A smooth IPO process and a lot of money."

Jordi clinks his glass, but Anya and I keep our eyes on each other. I see her searching me, asking the question that will never be spoken at this table: *What would you do?*

# Chapter Thirty

Two hours later, I'm at the bar upstairs at the hotel. I should sleep, but I can't. Every time I try I think about Bella, about what a terrible friend I am to be this far away, and my eyes shoot back open. I'm leaning over my second dirty martini when Aldridge comes in. I squint. I'm too drunk for this.

"Dannie," he says. "May I?" He doesn't wait for my response but takes the seat next to me.

"Tonight was good," I say, trying for steady. I think I'm slurring my words.

"You were very engaged," he says. "Must have felt good."

"Sure," I deadpan. "Wonderful."

Aldridge's eyes flit down to my martini glass and back to me. "Danielle," he says. "Are you all right?"

I'm suddenly aware that if I speak I will cry, and I have never cried in front of a boss, not once, not even at the DA's office, where morale was so bad that we had a designated room for hysterical outbursts. I pick up my water glass. I sip. I set it back down.

"No," I say.

He gestures to the waiter. "I'll have a Ketel on the rocks, two lemons," he says. The waiter turns, but Aldridge calls him back. "No, actually, I'll have a scotch. Neat."

He takes off his suit jacket, drapes it over the empty stool next to him, and then goes about rolling back his sleeves. Neither of us speaks during this interval, and by the time the ritual is complete, his drink is in front of him and I no longer feel as if I'm going to cry.

"So," he says. "You can begin or I can do my ankle cuffs next."

I laugh. The alcohol has made everything loose. I feel the emotions there, right on the surface, not tucked and tidy where I normally keep them.

"I'm not sure I'm a good person," I say. I didn't know that's what was inside my head, but once I say it, I know it's true.

"Interesting," he says. "A good person."

"My best friend is very sick."

"Yes," Aldridge says. "I know that."

"And we're in a fight."

He takes a sip of scotch. "What happened?"

"She thinks I'm controlling," I say, repeating the truth.

At this, Aldridge laughs, just like Dr. Shaw. It's a hearty belly laugh.

"Why does everyone think that's so funny?" I ask.

"Because you are," he says. "You were quite controlling tonight, for example."

"Was that bad?"

Aldridge shrugs. "I guess we'll see. How did it feel?"

"That's the problem," I say. "It felt great. I loved it. My best friend is—she's sick, and tonight I'm in California, happy about some clients at dinner. What kind of a person does that make me?"

Aldridge nods, like he understands it now. Gets what this is about. "You are upset because you think you need to quit your life and be by her side."

"No, she won't let me. I just shouldn't be happy doing this."

"Ah. Right. Happiness. The enemy of all suffering."

He takes another sip. We drink in silence for a moment.

"Did I ever tell you what I originally wanted to be?"

I stare at him. We're not exactly braiding-each-other's-hair besties. How would I know?

"I'm assuming this is a trick question and that you're going to say lawyer."

Aldridge laughs. "No, no. I was going to be a shrink. My father was a psychiatrist, so is my brother. It's a strange career choice, for a teen, but it always seemed the right one."

I blink at him. "Shrink?"

"I would have been terrible at it. All that listening, I don't have it in me."

I can feel the alcohol weaving its way through my system. Making everything hazy and rosy and faded. "What happened?"

"I went to Yale, and my first day there I had a philosophy course. First-Order Logic. A discussion of metatheory. It was for my major, but the professor was a lawyer, and I just thought—why diagnose when you can determine?"

He stares at me for a long time. Finally, he puts a hand on my shoulder.

"You are not wrong for loving what you do," he says. "You are lucky. Life doesn't hand everyone a passion in their profession; you and I won that round."

"It doesn't feel like winning," I say.

"No," Aldridge says. "It often doesn't. That dinner, over

there?" He points outside, past the lobby and the palm tree prints. "We didn't cement that. You loved it because, for you, the win is the game. That's how you know you're meant for it."

He takes his hand off my shoulder. He downs the rest of his drink in a neat sip.

"You're a great lawyer, Dannie. You're also a good friend and a good person. Don't let your own bias throw the case."

✦

The next morning, I take a car up to Montana Avenue. It's overcast, the fog of the morning won't burn off until noon, but by then we'll already be up in the air. I stop at Peet's Coffee and take a stroll down the little shopping street—even though everything is still closed. A few Lycra-clad mothers wheel their distracted toddlers while they talk. The morning bike crew passes by on their way out to Malibu.

I used to think I could never live in Los Angeles. It was for people who couldn't make it in New York. The easy way out. Moving would mean admitting that you had been wrong. That everything you'd said about New York: that there was nowhere else in the world to live, that the winters didn't bother you, that carrying four grocery bags back home in the pouring rain or hailing snow wasn't an inconvenience. That having your own car was, in fact, your dream. That life wasn't, isn't, hard.

But there is so much space out here. It feels like there is room—to not have to store every single piece of off-season clothing under your bed. Maybe even to make a mistake.

I take my coffee back to the hotel. I walk across the concrete bike path, into the sand, and down to the ocean. Far to the left, I can see some surfers zigzagging through the waves, around one another, like their movements are choreographed. A big, oceanic ballet. Moving continuously toward the shore.

I snap a picture.

*I love you*, I write. What else is there to say?

# Chapter Thirty-One

"It's really a question of eggshell or white," the woman says.

I am standing in the middle of Mark Ingram, a bridal salon in Midtown, an untouched flute of champagne on a glass coffee table, alone.

My mother was supposed to come in, but the university called a last-minute staff meeting to discuss a confidential matter, re: donations for next year, and she's stuck in Philadelphia. I'm supposed to send her pictures.

It's now mid-November and Bella hasn't spoken to me in two weeks. She's finishing her second round of chemo on Saturday, and David tells me not to bother her until it's over. I've heeded his advice, impossibly. It's excruciating, not being there. Not knowing.

The wedding invitations have gone out, we're receiving RSVPs. The menu is set. The flowers are ordered. All that is left is getting a dress, so here I am, standing in it.

"Like I said, with this time frame it's really off-the-rack, so it's pretty much only the dresses hanging here." The saleslady gestures to the three dresses to our right—one eggshell, two white.

She crosses her arms, checks her watch. She seems to think I'm wasting her time. But doesn't she know? This is a sure sale. I have to leave with a dress today.

"This one seems fine," I say. It's the first one I've tried on.

I was never one of those girls who dreamed about her wedding. That was always Bella. I remember her standing in front of my mirror with a pillowcase over her head, reciting vows to the glass. She knew exactly what the dress would look like—silk organza with spools of unfolding tulle. A long lace veil. She dreamed of the decor: white calla lilies, puffy peonies, and tiny tea candles. There would be a harpist. Everyone would *ooh* and *aah* when she stepped out of the shadows and into the aisle. They'd stand. She'd float down to the faceless, nameless man. The one who made her feel like the entire universe was conspiring for her love, and hers alone.

I knew I'd get married in the way you know you'll get older, and that Saturday comes after Friday. I didn't think that much about it. And then I met David and everything fit and I knew it was what I had been looking for, that we were meant to unfold these chapters together, side by side. But I never thought about the wedding. I never thought about the dress. I never pictured myself in this moment, standing here now. And if I had, I never would have seen this.

The dress I wear is silk and lace. It has a string of buttons down the back. The bodice fits poorly. I don't fill it out properly. I shake my arms, and the saleswoman races into frame. She pinches the back of the dress with a giant clothespin.

"We can fix that," she says. She looks at me in the mirror. Her face betrays sympathy. Who comes here alone and buys the first dress they try on? "We'll have to rush it, but we can do that."

"Thank you," I say.

I feel like I might cry, and I do not want these tears being misinterpreted as nuptial joy. I do not want to hear her delighted squeals, or see her knowing glance: *so in love*. I turn swiftly to the side. "I'll take it."

Her face registers confusion, and then brightens. She's just made a sale. Three thousand dollars in thirteen minutes. Must be some kind of record. Maybe I'm pregnant. She probably thinks I'm pregnant.

"Wonderful," she says. "I love this neckline on you, it's so flattering. Let's just take some measurements."

She pins me. The curve of my waist and the length of the hem. The lay of the shoulders.

When she leaves, I look at myself in the mirror. The neckline is high. She is wrong, of course. It does not flatter me at all. It does nothing to show off my collarbones, the slope of my neck. For a brief, wondrous moment I think about calling David. Telling him we need to postpone the wedding. We'll get married next year, at The Plaza, or in Massachusetts at The Wheatleigh. I'll get a ridiculous dress you have to custom order, the Oscar de la Renta one with the brocade flowers. We'll have the top florist, the best band. We'll dance to "The Way You Look Tonight" under the most delicate strands of white-and-gold twinkle lights. The entire ceiling will be made of roses. We'll plan a honeymoon in Tahiti or Bora Bora. We'll leave our cell phones in the bungalow and swim out to the edge of the earth. We'll drink champagne under the stars, and I'll wear white, only white, for ten days straight.

We'll make all the right decisions.

But then I hear the clock on the wall. The *tick tick tick*ing of the second hand, bringing us closer and closer to December 15.

I take off the dress. I pay for it.

On my walk home, Aaron calls me. "We got the test results back from the last round," he says. "It's not good."

I should feel surprised, shouldn't I? I should feel like I'm stopped dead in my tracks. The world now, in light of this news, should slow down, stop spinning. The taxis should sputter still, the music on the street should stretch until silent.

But I'm not. I've been waiting.

"Ask her if she wants me there," I tell him.

He pauses. I hear a lapse in breathing, the white noise sounds of apartment motion, somewhere a few rooms over. I wait. After about two minutes—an eternity—he comes back to the phone.

"She says yes."

I run.

# Chapter Thirty-Two

To my relief, and also grief, she looks like she did three weeks ago. No worse, no better. She still has her hair, and her eyes still have that sunken, hollow quality.

She isn't crying. She isn't smiling. Her face looks blank, and it is this that terrifies me the most. Seeing her cry is not, out of context, a cause for alarm. She has always worn her emotions inside out, the soft, nubile vicissitudes subject to every change in wind. But her stoicism, her unreadability, I am not used to. I've always been able to look at Bella and read it all there, see exactly what she needed. Now, I cannot.

"Bella—" I start. "I heard—"

She shakes her head. "Let's deal with us first."

I nod. I come to stand next to the bed, but I do not sit on it.

"I'm scared," she says.

"I know," I say, gently.

"No," she says. Her voice gets stronger. "I'm scared of leaving you with this."

I don't say anything. Because all at once I'm twelve. I'm standing in the doorway of my room as my mother screams. I'm listening to my father—my strong, brave, good father—trying to make sense, asking the questions: "But who was driving?" "But was he going the speed limit?" As if it mattered, as if reason could bring him back.

I've always been waiting, haven't I? For tragedy to show up once again on my doorstep. Evil that blindsides. And what is cancer if not that? If not the manifestation of everything I've spent my life trying to ward off. But Bella. It should have been me. If this is my story, then it should have been mine.

"Don't talk like that," I say. But if I know Bella's tells, she, of course, knows mine. She is no less equipped than I am at reading the impressions of my moods and thoughts as they saunter and sprint across my face.

It works both ways.

"You're not going anywhere," I tell her. "We're going to fight this just as we always have."

And in that moment it's true. It's true because it has to be. It's true because there are no other options. Despite that chemo hasn't kept it at bay. Despite that it's spread to her abdomen. Despite. Despite. Despite.

"Look," she says. She holds up her hand. On it is an engagement ring, perched daintily on her finger.

"You're getting married?" I ask her.

"When I'm better," she says.

I get in bed next to her. "You got engaged and you didn't call me?"

"It happened at home last night," she tells me. "He was bringing me dinner."

"What?"

She looks at me, her eyebrows knit. "Pasta from Wild."

I make a face. "I still can't believe you like it there."

"It's gluten free," she says. "Not poison. They have good spaghetti."

"So anyway."

"So anyway," she says. "He brought me the pasta, and on top of the Parmesan was the ring."

"What did he say?"

She looks at me and she's right there—Bella, my Bella. Her face bright and her eyes lit. "You'll think it's corny."

"I won't," I whisper. "I promise."

"He told me that he's been looking for me forever and, even though the situation is less than ideal, he knows that I'm his soul mate, and that he was always fated to end up with me." She blushes pink.

Fated.

I swallow. "He's right," I say. "You always wanted someone who would just know it was you. You always wanted your soul mate. And you found him."

Bella turns to me. She takes her hand and places it on the duvet between us.

"I'm going to ask you something," she says. "And if I'm wrong, you don't have to answer."

I feel my heart rate accelerate. What if . . . ? She couldn't . . .

"I know you think we're really different, and we are, I get that. I'll never be someone who checks my weather app before I go outside or knows the number of days eggs can last in the fridge. I haven't strategically built my life the way you have. But you're wrong in thinking . . ." She wets her lips. "I think you're capable of this kind of love, too. And I don't think you have it."

I let that sit between us for a moment. "What's making you say that?" I ask her.

"Don't you think there's a reason you never got married? Don't you think there's a reason you've been engaged for almost five years? A five-year engagement was never in your plan."

"We're getting married now," I say.

"Because," Bella says. Her voice gets small. She seems to fold into herself next to me. "You think you're on a clock."

December 15.

"That's not true. I love David."

"I know you do," she says. "But you're not in love with him. You may have been at first, but if you were I never really saw it, and I don't have the luxury of pretending anymore. And what I realized is that you don't, either. If there's a clock ticking toward anything, it should be your happiness."

"Bella . . ." I feel something rise in my chest. And then it's tumbling out onto the duvet between us. "I'm not sure I'm capable of it," I tell her. "Not the kind you mean."

"But you are," she says. "I wish you knew that. I wish you understood that you could have love beyond your wildest dreams. Stuff movies are made of. You're meant for that, too."

"I don't think I am."

"You are. You know how I know?"

I shake my head.

"Because that's the way you love me."

"Bella," I say. "Listen to me. You're going to be fine. People do this all the time. They defy the odds. Every damn day."

She holds her arms out to me. I give her a careful hug.

"Who would have thought?" she says.

"I know."

I feel her shake her head against me. "No," she says. "That you'd end up being someone who believed."

And that's the thing I know more than anything, as I hold Bella's shrunken form in my arms. She is extraordinary. For once in my life, the numbers don't apply.

# Chapter Thirty-Three

Intraperitoneal chemotherapy and gardenias bring us into late November. The former is a more invasive form of chemo, where a port through which drugs are administered is essentially sewn into the abdominal cavity. It's more direct than previous rounds, and it requires Bella to lie flat on her back during the procedure. She's nauseous constantly, and throws up violently. The gardenias have somehow become our wedding flower—even though their life span is approximately five and a half minutes.

I'm dealing with the flowers on the phone at work when Aldridge stops by my office. I hang up on the florist with no explanation.

"I just got off an interesting phone call with Anya and Jordi," he tells me. He sits in one of my round gray chairs.

"Oh yeah?"

"I imagine you know what I'm going to say," he says.

"I don't."

"Think about it."

I rearrange a notepad and a paperweight on my desk. "They don't want to go public."

"Bingo. They've changed their minds." He clasps his hands and sets them on my desk. "I need to know if you've had any further contact with them."

"I haven't," I say. Just that one dinner, in which I could feel Anya's resistance. "But to tell you the truth, I'm not altogether convinced going public right now is the right move."

"For who?" Aldridge asks.

"All of us," I say. "I think the company, under their guidance, will grow increasingly profitable. I think they will employ us now, because they trust us, and I think when they eventually do go public, everyone will make a lot more money."

Aldridge takes his hands back. His face is unreadable. I keep mine steady.

"I'm surprised."

I feel my stomach tighten into familiar knots. I've spoken out of turn.

"And impressed," he says. "I didn't think you were a gut lawyer."

"What do you mean?" I ask.

Aldridge sits back. "I hired you because I could tell no one would ever get a mistake by you. Your work is meticulous. You read every single line of every single paragraph and you know the law backward and forward."

"Thank you."

"But even that, as we know, is not enough. All the preparedness in the world cannot stop the unexpected from happening. Truly great lawyers know every inch of their deal, but often they make decisions based on something else—the presence of an unknown force that, if listened to, will betray exactly the way the tide is turning. That's what you did with Jordi and Anya, and you were right."

"I was?"

Aldridge nods. "They're hiring us to replace in-house counsel, and they'd like you to head up the team."

My eyes widen. I know what this means. This is the case, the client. This is the thing I need before I make junior partner.

"One thing at a time," Aldridge says, reading me. "But congratulations."

He stands, so do I. He shakes my hand. "And yes," he says. "If this goes well, yes."

I check the clock: 2:35 p.m. I want to call Bella, but she had a session this morning and I know she'll be asleep.

I try David.

"Hey," he says. "What's wrong?"

I realize I've never called him during the day before. If I have something to tell him, I always email, or I just wait.

"Nothing's wrong."

"Oh—" he starts, but I cut him off.

"Aldridge just gave me my junior partner case."

"You're kidding!" David says. "That's great."

"It's the women who run QuTe. They don't want to sell right now, but they want me to head up legal."

"I'm so proud of you," David says. "Will it still involve being in California?"

"Probably a little bit, but we haven't gotten there yet. I'm just excited because it's the right thing, you know? Like, I felt it. I *knew* it was the right thing."

I hear background talking. David doesn't answer immediately. "Yeah," he says. "Good." Then: "Hang on."

"Me?"

"No," he says. "No. Listen, I have to go. Let's celebrate tonight. Whenever you want. Email Lydia, and she'll make a reservation." He hangs up.

I feel lonely then, the sensation of which spreads out like a fever, until the whole of my body is afflicted. I shouldn't. David is supportive. He's encouraging and understanding. He wants me to succeed. He cares about my career. He'll sacrifice for me to have what I want. I know this is the covenant we made: that we will not get in each other's way.

But, sitting here at my desk, I realize something else. We've been on these parallel tracks, David and I. Moving constantly forward in space but never actually touching, for fear of throwing each other off course. Like if we were aligned in the same direction, we'd never have to compromise. But the thing about parallel tracks is you can be inches apart, or miles. And lately it feels like the width between David and me is extraordinary. We just didn't notice because we were still looking at the same horizon. But it dawns on me that I want someone in my way. I want us to collide.

I call Lydia. I ask her to make a reservation at Dante, an Italian café in the West Village we both love. 7:30 p.m.

# Chapter Thirty-Four

I arrive at the restaurant—a corner one, tiny and candlelit, with old-fashioned red-checkered tablecloths—and David is already there, bent over his phone. He has on a blue sweater and jeans. The hedge fund is a less dressy environment than the bank he worked at before, and he can get away with jeans much of the time.

"Hi," I say.

He looks up and smiles. "Hey. Traffic was a nightmare, right? I'm trying to figure out why they closed down Seventh Avenue. We haven't been here in a long time. Since we first started dating," he says.

David and I were introduced through my old colleague Adam. We both worked as clerks at the same time in the DA's office. The hours were long and the pay was shitty and neither one of us was particularly suited for that kind of environment.

For about six months, I remember having a crush on Adam. He was from New Jersey, liked sitcoms from the seventies, and knew how to get the temperamental coffee maker to deliver a cappuccino. We spent a lot of time together at work, bent over our desks eating five-dollar ramen from the food truck downstairs. He threw a party for his birthday at this bar I'd never been to—Ten Bells on the Lower East Side. It was dark and candlelit. With wood tables and barstools. We ate cheese and drank wine and split bills we could not afford on credit cards we hoped we could one day pay off.

David was there—cute and a little bit quiet—and he asked to buy me a drink. He worked at a bank, and had gone to school with Adam. They had even been roommates their first year in New York.

We talked about the insane prices of rent, how it was impossible to find good Mexican food in New York, and our mutual love of *Die Hard*.

But I was still focused on Adam. I had hoped that his birthday might be the night. I had on tight jeans and a black top. I thought we'd flirt—scratch that, I thought we *had* been flirting—and that maybe we'd go home together.

Before closing, Adam sauntered over to us and slung an arm over David's shoulders. "You guys should get each other's numbers," he said. "Could be a match here."

I remember feeling devastated. That stabbing sensation you feel when the curtain is pulled back and what stands before you on the stage is the wide expanse of nothing. Adam was not into me. He had just made that very, very clear.

David laughed nervously. He stuck his hands in his pockets. Then he said: "How about it?"

I gave him my number. He called the next day, and we went out the following week. Our relationship built slowly, bit by bit. We went for a drink, then a dinner, then a lunch, then a Broadway show he had been gifted tickets to. We slept together on that date, the fourth. We dated for two years before we moved in together. When we did, we kept all of my bedroom furniture and half of his living room furniture and opened a joint bank account for household expenses. He went to Trader Joe's because I thought—and think—the lines are too long, and I bought the paper goods off Amazon. We RSVP'd to weddings, threw dinner parties with catered spreads, and climbed the ladders of our careers an arm's length away from each other. We were, weren't we? An arm's length away? If you can reach out and hold the other person's hand, does the distance matter? Is simply being able to see someone valuable?

"A pipe burst on the corner of Twelfth Street," I say. I take off my coat and sit down, letting the warmth of the restaurant begin to thaw out my bones. We're well into November now. And the weather has turned with us.

"I ordered a bottle of Brunello," he says. "We liked it the last time we were here."

David keeps a spreadsheet of really great meals we've had—what we drank and what we ate—for future reference. He keeps it accessible on his phone for such situations.

"David—" I start. I exhale. "The florist ordered us three thousand gardenias."

"What for?"

"The wedding," I say.

"I'm aware of that," he tells me. "But why?"

"I don't know. Some mix-up at the florist. They're all going to be brown by the time we take any photos. They last for like two hours."

"Well, if it's their mistake, they should cover the cost. Did you speak with them?"

I take my napkin and fold it over my pants. "I was on the phone with them but had to hang up to deal with work."

David takes a sip of water. "I'll handle it," he says.

"Thanks." I clear my throat. "David," I say. "Before I say this, you can't get mad at me."

"That's impossible to guarantee, but okay."

"I'm serious."

"Just say it," he says.

I exhale. "Maybe we should postpone the wedding."

He looks at me in confusion but something else, too. In the back of his eyes, behind the pupils and the firing optic nerve, is relief. Confirmation. Because he's known, hasn't he? He's suspected that I'd let him down.

"Why do you say that?" he asks, measured.

"Bella is sick," I say. "I don't think she'll be able to make it. I don't want to get married without her."

David nods. "So what are you saying? You want more time?" He shakes his head.

"That we postpone till the summer. Maybe even get the venue we want."

"We don't want this venue?" David sits back. He's irritated. It's not an emotion he wears often. "Dannie," he says. "I need to ask you something."

I stay perfectly still. I hear the wind outside howling. Ushering in the impending freeze.

"Do you really want to get married?"

Relief sputters and then floods my veins like a faucet after a water outage. "Yes," I say. "Yes, of course."

Our wine comes then. We busy ourselves with witnessing and then participating: the uncorking and tasting and pouring and toasting. David congratulates me on QuTe.

"Are you sure?" he says, picking the thread back up. "Because sometimes I don't . . ." He shakes his head. "Sometimes I'm not so sure."

"Forget about my suggestion," I say. "It was dumb. I shouldn't have brought it up. Everything is already set."

"Yeah?"

"Yes."

We order, but we barely touch our food. We both know the truth of what sits now between us. And I should be scared, I should be terrified, but the thing I keep thinking, the thing that makes me answer in the affirmative, is that he didn't ask the other question, the one I cannot conceive.

*What happens if she doesn't make it?*

# Chapter Thirty-Five

The chemo is brutal. Far, far worse than the last round. Standing up is hard for Bella now, and she doesn't leave the apartment except for treatment. She sits in bed, emailing with the gallery, looking over digital exhibits. I visit her in the mornings sometimes. Svedka lets me in, and I sit on the edge of the bed, even as she's sleeping.

She starts to lose her hair.

My wedding dress arrives. It fits. It even looks good. The saleslady was right, the neckline isn't as bad as I thought it was.

David does not mention the wedding to me for a week. For a week, I leave emails from the planner unanswered, dodge calls, hold off on writing checks. And then I come home from work to find him at the dining room table, a bowl of pasta and two salads set out in front of him.

"Hey," he says. "Come sit." *Hey. Come sit.*

Aldridge said I have a good gut, but I always thought the concept of intuition was bullshit. All you are feeling is an absorption of the facts. You are assessing all the information you have: words, body language, environment, the proximity of your human form to a moving vehicle, and deriving a conclusion. It is not my gut that leads me to sit down at that table knowing what is coming. It is the truth of what is.

I sit.

The pasta looks cold. It's been out a long time.

"I'm sorry I'm late."

"You're not late," he says. He's right. We didn't schedule anything tonight, and it's only eight-thirty. This is the time I'm usually home.

"This looks good," I say.

David exhales. At least he's not going to make me wait for it.

"Look," he says. "We need to talk."

I turn to face him. He looks tired, withdrawn, the same temperature as the food before us.

"Okay," I say.

"I—" He shakes his head. "I can't believe I'm the one who has to do this." His tone sounds just a little bit bitter.

"I'm sorry."

He ignores me. "Do you know what this feels like?"

"No," I admit. "I don't."

"I love you," he says.

"I love you, too."

He shakes his head. "I love you, but I'm sick of being the person who fits in your life but not your . . . fuck it, your heart."

I feel it in my body. It punches me right there, right on the tender underside.

"David," I say. My stomach clenches. "You do."

He shakes his head. "You may love me, but I think we both know you don't want to marry me."

I hear Bella's words echoed, here, with David. *You're not in love with him.*

"How can you say that? We're engaged, we're planning a wedding. We've been together for seven and a half years."

"And we've been engaged for five. If you wanted to marry me, you would have already."

"But Bella—"

"It's not about Bella!" he says. He raises his voice, another thing he never does. "It's not. If it were. God, Dannie, I feel horrible about all of this. I know what she means to you. I love her, too. But what I'm saying is . . . it's not the issue. This isn't happening because she got sick. You were dragging your heels way before that."

"We were busy," I say. "We were working. Life. That was *both* of us."

"I asked the question!" David says. "You knew where I stood. I was trying to be patient. How long am I supposed to wait?"

"Until the summer," I say. I smooth a napkin down on my lap. Focus on the plan. "What is the big deal with six months?"

"Because it's not just six months," he says. "In the summer, there will be something else, some other reason."

"There won't!" I say.

"There will! Because you don't really want to marry me."

My shoulders shake. I can feel myself crying. Tears run down my face in cool, icy tracks. "Yes I do."

"No," he says. "You don't." But he's looking at me, and I can tell he's not convinced of his own argument, not entirely.

He's asking me to prove him wrong. And I could. I can tell that if I wanted to, I could convince him. I could keep crying. I could reach for him. I could say all the things I know he needs to hear. I could lay out the evidence. That I dream about marrying him. That every time he walks into a room my stomach tightens. I could tell him the things I love about him: the curl of his hair and how warm his torso is, and how I feel at home in his heart.

But I can't. It would be a lie. And he deserves more than that—he deserves everything. This is the thing, the only thing, I have to offer him. The truth. Finally.

"David," I say. Start. "I don't know why. You're perfect for me. I love our life together. But—"

He sits back. He tosses his napkin onto the table. The proverbial towel.

We sit in silence for what feels like minutes. The clock on the wall ticks forward. I want to throw it out the window. Stop. Stop moving. Stop marching us forward. Everything terrible lies ahead.

The moment stretches so far it threatens to break. Finally, I speak. "What now?" I ask.

David pushes back his chair. "Now you leave," he says.

He goes into the bedroom and closes the door. I take the food and put it, mindlessly, into containers. I wash the dishes. I put them away.

Then I go to sit on the couch. I know I can't be here in the morning. I take out my phone.

"Dannie?" Her voice is sleepy but strong when she answers. "What's up?"

"Can I come over?" I ask her.

"Of course."

I travel the twenty blocks south. She's on the couch when I get there, not in bed. She has a colorful bandana on her head and the TV is on, an old rerun of *Seinfeld*. Comfort food.

I drop my bag down. I go to her. And then I'm crying. Big, hiccupping sobs.

"Shh," she says. "It's okay. Whatever it is, it's okay."

She's wrong, of course. Nothing is okay. But it feels so good to be comforted by her now. She runs her hands through my hair, rubs circles over my back. She hushes and soothes and consoles in the way only she can.

I have held her so many times. After so many breakups and parental disappointments, but here, now, I feel like I've had it backward. I thought I was her protector. That she was flighty and irresponsible and frivolous. That it was my job to protect her. That I was the strong one, counterbalancing her weakness, her whimsy. But I was wrong. I wasn't the strong one, she was. Because this is what it feels like—to take a risk, to step out of line, to make decisions not based on fact but on feeling. And it hurts. It feels like a tornado raging inside my soul. It feels like I may not survive it.

"You will," she tells me. "You already have."

And it's not until she says it that I realize I've spoken the words out loud. We stay like this, me in a ball in her lap, her curled over me, for what feels like hours. We stay long enough to try and capture it, bottle it, and tuck it away. Save enough of it to last, enough of it for a lifetime.

*Love doesn't require a future.*

For a moment in time, we release what is coming.

# Chapter Thirty-Six

I move into Bella's apartment the first week of December. To the guest room that still has clouds on the walls. Aaron helps me with the boxes. I do not see David. I leave a note on the table when my necessities are gone. He can buy me out or we can sell, whatever he wants.

*I'm so sorry,* I write.

I don't expect to hear from him, but he sends me an email three days later with some logistical things. He signs it: *Please keep me posted on Bella. David.*

All that time, all those years, all those plans, gone. We're strangers now. I cannot fathom it.

Hospital. Work. Home.

Bella and I are curled in her bed. We inhale early two thousands romantic comedies like popcorn kernels while she hurls, sometimes too weak to turn her head all the way to the side. She has no appetite. I fill up bowls and bowls of ice cream to the brim for her. They all melt. I throw their milky remains down the drain.

"Canker sores, open wounds, the taste of bile," she whispers to me, shivering under the blankets.

"No," I say.

"Chemicals being pumped through my veins, veins that feel like fire, fingers up my spine, grabbing at my bones, cracking them."

"Not yet," I say.

"The taste of vomit, the feeling of my skin crawling with fire. That it's getting harder to breathe."

"Stop," I tell her.

"I knew the breathing would get you," she says.

I bend down closer to her. "I'll be here for it all," I say.

She looks at me. Her hollow eyes are frightened. "I don't know how much longer I can do this," she says.

"You can." I say. "You have to."

"I'm wasting it," she says. "I'm wasting the time I have left."

I think about Bella. Her life. Dropping out of college. Flying to Europe on a whim. Falling in love, falling onward. Beginning projects and abandoning them.

Maybe she knew. Maybe she knew there wasn't time to waste, that she couldn't go through the motions, steps, build. That the linear trajectory would bring her only to the middle.

"You're not," I say. "You're here. You're right here."

Aaron sleeps next to her at night. Together with Svedka, we move around the apartment, choreographing our own silent dance of support.

✦

I come home from work the following week to find that the boxes in my room are gone. My clothes, my bathrobe, everything.

Bella is sleeping, as she has been for most of the day. Svedka comes in and out of her room, carrying nothing.

I call Aaron.

"Hey," he says. "Where are you?"

"Home. But my stuff isn't here. Did you move the boxes down to storage?"

Aaron pauses. I can hear his breath on the other end of the phone. "Can you meet me somewhere?" he asks me.

"Where?"

"Thirty-Seven Bridge Street."

"The apartment," I say. I feel a pull from deep down inside of me, far behind my sternum, the place where my gut might be, if I believed in its existence.

"Yeah."

"No," I say. "I can't. Something happened to my stuff and I have to—"

"Dannie, please," Aaron says. He sounds, all at once, a very long way away. A foreign country, the other side of a decade. "This is a directive from Bella."

How can I say no?

✦

Aaron is downstairs, outside the apartment when I get there, smoking a cigarette.

"I didn't know you smoked," I say.

He looks at the cigarette between his fingers as if considering it for the first time. "Me neither."

The last time we were here it was summer, everything was blooming. The river was wild in green and growth. Now—the metaphor is too much to bear.

"Thanks for coming," he says. He's wearing a jacket, open despite the cold. I can barely see out of my hood and scarf.

"What do you need?" I ask.

He tosses the end of the cigarette down, snuffs it out with his foot. "I'll show you."

I follow him back through the familiar door, into the building and up the rickety, wobbly elevator.

At the apartment door, he takes out the keys. I have the desire to put my hand over his, yank it away. Stop him from doing what he does next. But I'm frozen. I feel like I cannot move my arms. And when the door swings open I see it all, splayed out before me like the inside of my heart.

The renovation, exactly as it was. The kitchen. The stools. The bed over there, by the windows. The blue velvet chairs.

"Welcome home," he whispers.

I look up at him. He's smiling. It's the happiest I've seen anyone in months.

"What?" I ask him.

"It's your new home," he says. "Bella and I have been working on it for months. She wanted to renovate it for you."

"For me?"

"Bella saw this place ages ago when I was assigned the building renovation. Something about the layout and the light, the view and the bones of the old warehouse. She told me she knew you belonged here." He smiles. "And you know Bella, she wants what she wants. And I think this project has helped. It has given her something creative to focus on."

"She did all this?" I ask.

"She picked out everything," he says. "Down to the studs. Even when you guys were fighting."

I wander around the apartment, as if in a trance. It's all exactly the way I remember. It's all here. It has all happened.

I turn back to Aaron, standing with his arms crossed in the middle of the apartment. All at once it appears as if the world is rotating around us. Like we are the fulcrum and everything, everything is spinning outward from right here, taking its cues from us, and us alone.

I walk to him. I get close to him, too close. He does not move.

"Why?" I ask.

"She loves you," he says.

I shake my head. "No," I say. "Why you?"

I used to think that the present determined the future. That if I worked hard and long, I'd get the things I wanted. The job, the apartment, the life. That the future was simply a mound of clay waiting to be told by the present what form to take. But that isn't true. It can't be. Because I did everything right. I got engaged to David. I stayed away from Aaron. I got Bella to forget about that apartment. And yet my best friend is lying in bed on the other side of the river, barely eighty pounds, fighting for her life. And I'm standing here, the very place of my dreams.

He blinks at me, confused. And then he's not. And then it's like he reads the question there, and I see him uncurl, unfold himself to what I have really asked.

Slowly, gently, as if he's afraid he'll burn me, he puts his hands on my face in answer. They're cold. They smell like cigarette smoke. They are the deepest, truest form of relief. Water after seventy-three days in the desert.

"Dannie," he says. Just my name. Just the one word.

He touches his lips down to mine, and then we're kissing and

I forget it all, everything. I am ashamed to admit there is blankness there, in his kiss. Bella, the apartment, the last five and a half months, the ring that sits on her finger. None of it plays.

All I can think, feel, is this. This realization of everything that has, impossibly, turned out to be true.

# Chapter Thirty-Seven

He pulls back first. He drops his hand. We stare at each other, breathing hard. My coat is on the floor, crumpled like a body after a car crash. I turn my eyes from him and pick it up.

"I—" he starts. I close my eyes. I don't want him to say I'm sorry. He doesn't. He leaves it there.

I walk to the wall. I know what I'll find, but I want to see it. The final, culminating piece of evidence. There, hanging on the wall, is Bella's birthday gift: *I WAS YOUNG I NEEDED THE MONEY.*

"I don't know what to say," Aaron says from somewhere behind me.

I don't turn around. "It's okay," I say. "I don't, either."

"All of this—" he says. "It's all so wrong. None of this should be happening."

He's right, of course. It shouldn't. What could we have done differently? How could we have avoided this? This impossible, unthinkable end.

I turn around. I look at him. His golden, shining face. This thing that sits between us, now made manifest.

"You should go," I say. "Or I should."

"I should," he says.

"Okay."

"Your stuff is all unpacked. Bella hired someone to do the closet. Your things are all here."

"The closet."

His cell phone rings then, disrupting the air molecules, disentangling us from the moment. He answers.

"Hey," he says gently. Too gently. "Yes. Yes. We're here. Hang on."

He holds the phone out to me. I take it.

"Hi," I say.

Bella's voice is soft and bright. "Well," she says. "Do you like it?"

I want to tell her she's crazy, that I can't accept this, she cannot buy and gift me an apartment. But what would be the point? Of course she can. She has. "This is insane," I say. "I can't believe you did this."

"Do you like the chairs? How about the kitchen? Did Greg show you the green tile sink?!"

"It's all perfect," I say.

"I know the stools are a little edgy for you, but I think it's good. I think—"

"It's perfect."

"You always tell me I never finish anything," she says. "I wanted to finish this. For you."

Tears roll down my cheeks. I didn't even know I was crying. "Bells," I say. "It's incredible. It's beautiful. I could never. I would never— It's home."

"I know," she says.

I want her to be here. I want us to cook in this kitchen, making a mess of materials, running to the corner store because we don't have vanilla extract or cracked pepper. I want us to play in that closet, to have her make fun of everything I want to wear. I want her to sleep over, tucked in that bed, in safety, ensconced here. What could happen to her under my watch? What bad thing could touch her if I never, ever looked away?

But I understand she will not be. I understand, standing here now, in this manifestation of both dream and nightmare, that I will be here, in this home she built for me, alone. I am here because she will not be. Because she needed to give me something to hold on to, something to protect me. A literal roof over my head. Shelter from the storm.

"I love you," I tell her. Fiercely. "I love you so much."

"Dannie," she says. I hear her through the phone. Bella. My Bella. "Forever."

✦

Aaron leaves. I wander through the apartment, running my fingers over every surface. The green tile of the sink, the white porcelain of the tub. A claw-foot. I go through the kitchen—the cabinets stacked with pasta, wine, a bottle of Dom chilling, waiting, in the refrigerator. I go through the medicine cabinet with my products, the closet with my clothes. I run my hand over the dresses there. One is facing out. I already know which one it'll be. There's a note attached: *Wear this*, it says. *I always liked it on you.*

It's scrawled in her handwriting. Her loopy calligraphy.

I clutch it to my chest. I go to the window, right by the bed.

I look out on that view. The water, the bridge, the lights. Manhattan on the water, shimmering like a promise. I think about how much life the city holds, how much heartbreak, how much love. I think about everything I have lost there, this fading island before me.

# Chapter Thirty-Eight

It happens quickly and then slowly. We plummet fast, and then we exist at the bottom of the ocean for eight days, an impossible amount of time to breathe only water.

Bella stops treatment. Dr. Shaw speaks to us; he tells us what we already know, what we have seen up close with our own eyes—that there is no point anymore, that it is making her sicker, that she needs to be home. He is calm and collected, and I hate him, I want to ram him into the wall. I want to scream at him. I need someone to blame, someone to be responsible for all of this. Because who is? Fate? Is the hellscape we've found ourselves in the work of some form of divine intervention? What kind of monster has decided that this is the ending we deserve? That she does?

It moves upward, to her lungs. She ends up in the hospital. They remove the fluid. They send her home. She can barely breathe.

Jill isn't there. She's staying at a hotel in Times Square, and on Friday I find myself putting on my boots and coat and leaving Bella and Aaron alone in the apartment. I truck up to Midtown, through the lights of Broadway—all those people. They're about to go to the theater, see a show. Maybe this is a celebratory night. A promotion, a trip to the city. They're splurging on a feel-good musical or the latest celebrity play. They live in a different realm. We do not meet. We do not see one another anymore.

I find her at the W Hotel bar. I hadn't really known my plan, what I was going to do once I got there—call her cell? Demand her room number? But no further steps are necessary. She's sitting in the lobby, a vodka martini in front of her.

I know it's vodka because it's what Bella drinks. Jill used to let us have sips of hers when we were very young, and then make them for us later, when we were still not legal.

She has on an orange pantsuit, crepe silk, with a neck scarf, and I feel my stomach boil in anger that she had the energy to get dressed like this. That she has on accessories. That she still is able to believe it matters.

"Jill."

She startles when she sees me. The martini wobbles.

"How— Is everything all right?"

I think about the question. I want to laugh. What possible answer is there? Her daughter is dying.

"Why aren't you there?" I say.

She hasn't been downtown for forty-eight hours. She calls Aaron, but she hasn't actually made her physical presence known.

Jill opens her eyes wide. Her forehead doesn't move. An effect of injections, of the side of medicine she is fortunate enough to elect to use while her cells are not multiplying into monsters.

I sit down next to her. I'm wearing yoga pants and an old UPenn sweatshirt, something of David's I kept, despite.

"Do you want a drink?" she asks me. A bartender hovers at the ready.

"A gin martini," I find myself saying. I hadn't expected to stay. Just to say what I came to say and turn around.

My drink comes quickly. She looks at me. Does she expect me to toast her? I take a sip hastily and set it back down.

"Why are you here?" I ask her. The same question, a different angle. Why are you here, in this city? Why are you here, at this hotel where your daughter is not?

"I want to be close," she says. She states it matter-of-factly. No emotion.

"She's—" I start, but I can't. "She needs you there."

Jill shakes her head. "I'm just in the way," she says.

She's been ordering delivery to the apartment, sending in maid service. On Monday, she came with flowers and wanted to know where the cutting shears were.

"I don't understand," I say. "Frederick. Where is he?"

"France," she says simply.

I want to scream. I want to throttle her. I want to understand *how, how, how*. It's *Bella*.

I take another sip.

"I remember when you and Bella met," she says. "It was love at first sight."

"That park," I tell her.

Bella and I didn't meet at school, but instead at a park in Cherry Hill. We had gone for a Fourth of July picnic. My cousins lived out in New Jersey and they were hosting. We rarely visited them. They were conservative to our Reform and had a lot of opinions on the level of Jewish we were. But for some reason we weren't at the beach, so we went.

Separately, Bella and her family were at that same park, although they, like us, were setting up shop in a home twenty-five miles from there. They'd come for Frederick's work—some kind of company barbecue. We met by a tree. She was wearing a blue lace dress and white sneakers, and her hair was in a red headband. It was a lot for a little girl from France. I remember thinking she had an accent, but she didn't, not really. I had just never heard anyone speak who wasn't from Philadelphia before.

"She couldn't stop talking about you. I was afraid she'd never see you again, so we put her in Harriton."

I look up at her. "What do you mean, you put her in Harriton?"

"We weren't sure she'd make any friends. But as soon as she met you, we knew we couldn't separate you. Your mother said you were starting Harriton in the fall, and we enrolled her."

"Because of me?"

Jill sighs. She adjusts the scarf at her neck. "I've been less than a great mother, I know that. Less than good, even. Sometimes, I think the only thing I did right was give her you."

I feel the tears in my eyes spring up. They sting. Tiny bees in the lids. "She needs you," I say.

Jill shakes her head. "You know her so much better than I do. What could I possibly give her now?"

I lean forward. I put a hand on her hand. She's startled by the contact. I wonder when the last time anyone touched her was.

"You."

# Chapter Thirty-Nine

Jill comes home with me. She lingers at the door, and I hear Bella: "Dannie? Who is it?"

"It's Mom," Jill says.

I leave them be.

I go out. I walk. When my mom calls, I answer.

"Dannie," she says. "How is she?"

And then, as soon as I hear her voice, I start to cry. I cry for my best friend, who, in an apartment above, is fighting for the right to breathe. I cry for my mother, who knows this loss all too intimately. The wrong kind. The kind you should never have to bear. I cry for a relationship I've lost, a marriage, a future that will never be.

"Oh, darling," she says. "Oh, I know."

"David and I broke up," I tell her.

"You did," she says. She does not seem surprised. It is barely a question: "What happened?"

"We never got married," I tell her.

"No," she says. "I suppose you didn't."

There is silence for a moment.

"Are you okay?"

"I'm not sure."

"Well," she says. "That's better than some alternatives. Do you need help?"

It's just a simple question, one she has asked me over and over again throughout the course of my life. Do you need help with homework? Do you need help with that car payment? Do you need help carrying that laundry basket up the stairs?

I have been asked if I've needed help so many times that I have been allowed to forget the question, the significance of it. I see, now, the way the love in my life has woven into a tapestry that I've been blessed enough to get to ignore. But not now, not anymore.

"Yes," I tell her.

She says she will email David, she will make sure we get refunds where we can. She will handle the returns and the calls. She is my mother. She will help. That is what she does.

I go back upstairs. Jill is gone. Aaron is in the other room, maybe, working. I do not see him. At the door to the bedroom, I see that Bella is awake.

"Dannie," she whispers. Her voice is light.

"Yes?"

"Come up," she says.

I do. I come around to the other side of the bed, getting in next to her. It hurts for me to look at her. She's all bones. Gone are her curves, her flesh, the softness and mystery that has been her familiar body for so long.

"Your mom left?" I ask.

"Thank you," she says.

I don't answer. Just thread my fingers through hers.

"Do you remember," she says, "the stars?"

At first I think she means the beach at night, maybe. Or

that she doesn't mean anything. That she's seeing something I can't now.

"The stars?"

"Your room," she says.

"The stick-ons," I say. "My ceiling."

"Do you remember how we used to count them?"

"We never got there," I say. "We couldn't tell them apart."

"I miss that."

I take her whole hand in mine now. I want to take her whole body, too. To hold her. To press her close to me, where she can't go anywhere.

"Dannie," she says. "We need to talk about this."

I don't say anything. I can feel the tears running down my cheeks. Everything feels wet. Wet and cold—damp—we'll never get dry.

"What?" I say, stupidly. Desperately.

"That I'm dying."

I turn to her, because she can barely move anymore. Her eyes look into mine. Those same eyes. The eyes I have loved for so long. They are still there. She's still in there. It's impossible to think she won't be.

But she won't be. Soon, she won't be. She is dying. And I cannot deny her this, this honesty.

"I don't like it," I say. "It's bad policy."

She laughs, and then starts coughing. Her lungs are full.

"I'm sorry," I say. I check her pain pump. I give her a minute.

"I'm sorry," she says.

"No, Bella, please."

"No," she says. "I am. I wanted to be here for you for all of it."

"But you have," I say. "You've been here for everything."

"Not everything," she whispers. I feel her search for my hand under the sheets. I give it to her. "Love," she says.

I think about David, in our old shared apartment, and Bella's words: *Because that's the way you love me.*

"You've never had it," she says. "I want the real thing for you."

"You're wrong," I tell her.

"I'm not," she says. "You've never really been in love. You've never really had your heart broken."

I think about Bella at the park, Bella at school, Bella at the beach. Bella lying on the floor of my first New York City apartment. Bella with a bottle of wine in the rain. Bella on the fire escape at 3 a.m. Bella's voice on New Year's Eve, cracking through the Parisian phone. Bella. Always.

"Yes," I whisper. "I have."

Her breath catches, and she looks at me. I see it all. The cascade of our friendship. The decades of time. The decades to come—more, even, without her.

"It's not fair," she says.

"No," I say. "It's not."

I feel her exhaustion move over both of us like a wave. It drags us under. Her hand softens in mine.

# Chapter Forty

It happens on Thursday. I am asleep. Aaron is on the couch. Jill and the nurse are beside her. Those impossibly long, gruesome final moments—I miss them. I am in the apartment twenty feet away, not by her side. By the time I am awake, she is gone.

Jill plans the funeral. Frederick flies in. They obsess about the flowers. Frederick wants a cathedral. An eight-piece orchestra. Where do you find a full gospel choir in Manhattan?

"This isn't right," Aaron says. We are in her apartment, late at night, two days after she has left us. We are drinking wine. Too much wine. I haven't been sober in forty-eight hours. "This isn't what she would want." He means the funeral, I think, although maybe he doesn't. Maybe he means the whole thing. He would be right.

"So we should plan what she would," I say, deciding for him. "Let's throw our own."

"Celebration of life?"

I stick my tongue out at the word. I don't want to celebrate. This is all unfair. This is all not what should have been.

But Bella loved her life, every last moment of it. She loved the way she lived it. She loved her art and her travel and her croque monsieur. She loved Paris for the weekend and Morocco for the week and Long Island at sunset. She loved her friends; she loved them gathered; she loved running around the room, topping up glasses, and making everyone promise to stay long into the night. She would want this.

"Yes," I say. "Okay."

"Where?"

Somewhere high, somewhere above, somewhere with a terrace. Somewhere with a view of the city she loved.

"Do you still have those keys?" I ask Aaron.

✦

Two days later. December 15. We get through the funeral. Through the relatives and the speeches. We get through being relegated, if not to the back, then to the side. *Are you family?*

We get through the logistics. The stone, the fire, the documents. We get through the paperwork and the emails and the phone calls. *What?* people say. *No. How could it be? I didn't even know she was sick.*

Frederick will keep the gallery open. They'll find someone to run it. It will still bear her name. *The apartment isn't the only thing you finished*, I want to tell her. Why didn't I see it? The way she ran that place. Why didn't I tell her? I want to tell her now, taking inventory of her life, that I see all of it—all of her completion.

We gather at dusk. Berg and Carl, from our twenties in New York. Morgan and Ariel. The gallery girls. Two friends from Paris, and a few girlfriends from college. The guys from a reading series she used to participate in. These people who have all loved her, appreciated her, and saw different parts of her flourishing, pulsing soul.

We gather on that slice of terrace, shivering, coats bundled, but needing to be outside, to be in the air. Morgan refills my wineglass. Ariel clears her throat.

"I'd like to read something," she says.

"Of course," I tell her.

We gather in a little horseshoe. Spread out.

Of the two, Ariel is shier, a little more reserved than Morgan. She begins.

"Bella sent me this poem about a month ago. She asked me to read it. She was a great artist, but she was also a really great writer. Was—" She shakes her head. "Anyway, I wanted to share it tonight."

She clears her throat. She begins to read:

*There is a path of land that exists*
*Beyond the sea and the sky.*

*It is behind the mountains,*
*Past even the hills—*

*Those of luscious green that*
*Roll up into the heavens.*

*I have been there, with you.*

*It is not big, although not too small.*
*Perhaps you could perch a house on its width,*
*But we have never considered it.*

*What would be the use?*
*We already live there.*

*When the night closes*
*And the city stills,*

*I am there, with you.*

*Our mouths laughing, our heads vacant*
*Of all but what is.*

*And what is? I ask.*

*This, you say. You and I, here.*

We are all silent after she finishes. I know what place. It is a field, surrounded by mountains and fog, where a river runs through. It is quiet and peaceful and eternal. It is that apartment.

I pull my coat tighter around me. It's cold, but the cold feels good. It reminds me for the first time in a week that I am here, that I have flesh, that I am real. Berg steps forward next. He reads from Chaucer, a favorite stanza of hers from graduate school. He puts on a voice. Everyone laughs.

There is champagne and her favorite cookies from a bakery on Bleecker. There is also pizza from Rubirosa, but no one has touched it. We need her to return, smiling, full of life, gifting us back our appetites.

Finally, it is my turn.

"Thank you all for coming," I tell them. "Greg and I knew she'd want something with the people she loved that wasn't so formal."

"Although Bella loved black tie," Morgan chimes in.

We laugh. "That she did. She was a spinning, spiraling spirit that touched all of us. I miss her," I say. "I will forever."

The wind whistles over the city, and I think it's her, saying a final farewell.

✦

We stay until our fingers are frozen and our faces are chapped, and then it's time to go home. I hug Morgan and Ariel goodbye. They promise to come over next week and help us sort through Bella's stuff. Berg and Carl leave. The gallery girls tell me to come by—I say I will. They have a new exhibit going up. She was proud of it. I should see.

Then it's just the two of us. Aaron doesn't ask if he can come with me, but when the car arrives, he gets in. We travel downtown in silence. We speed across the Brooklyn Bridge, miraculously devoid of traffic. No roadblocks. Not anymore. We pull up to the building.

The keys, now in my possession.

Through the door, up the elevator, into the apartment. Everything I've fought against, now made manifest at my very own hands.

I take off my shoes. I go to the bed. I lie down. I know what is going to happen. I know exactly how we will live it.

# Chapter Forty-One

I must fall asleep because I wake up, and he's here, and the reality of it, of Bella's loss, of the last few months, swirls around us like the impending storm.

"Hey," Aaron says. "Are you okay?"

"No," I say. "I'm not."

He sighs. He walks over to me. "You fell asleep."

"What are you doing here?" I ask him, because I want to know. I want him to say it. I want to get it out, now, into the open.

"Come on," he says, refusing. Although if it's the refusal of the inevitable, or the unwillingness to answer the question, I do not know.

"Do you know me?"

I want to explain to him, although I suspect he understands, that I am not this person. That what has happened, what is happening, here, between us, is not me. That I would never betray her. But that she's gone. She's gone, and I do not know what to do with this—with everything she left in her wake.

He puts a knee on the bed. "Dannie," he says. "Are you really asking me that?"

"I don't know," I say. "I don't know where I am."

"It was a good night," he says, gently, reminding me. "Wasn't it?"

Of course it was. It was what she would have wanted. This gathering of what she stood for. Spontaneity, love. A good Manhattan view.

"Yeah," I say. It was.

I catch the TV. A storm is coming, circling its way closer to us. Seven inches of snow, they're predicting.

"Are you hungry?" he asks me. Neither of us ate tonight.

I wave him off. No. But he presses, and my stomach answers in return. Yes, actually. I'm starving.

I follow Aaron into the closet, itching to get out of this dress. He pulls his sweatpants, the ones he still has here from all the work he did on the apartment, out of the drawer along with a T-shirt he left behind. The only things here that aren't mine.

"I moved to Dumbo," I say, incredulous. Aaron laughs. It's all so ridiculous, neither one of us can help ourselves. Five years later, I have left Murray Hill and Gramercy and moved to Dumbo.

I change and wash my face. I put some cream on. I wander back into the living room. Aaron calls from the kitchen that he's making pasta.

I find Aaron's pants flung over the chair. I fold them and his wallet slides out. I open it. Inside is the Stumptown punch card. And then I see it—the photo of Bella. She's laughing, her hair tangled around her face like a maypole. It's from the beach. Amagansett this summer. I took it. It seems years ago, now.

We decide on pesto for the pasta. I go to sit at the counter.

"Am I still a lawyer?" I ask him, wearily. I haven't been to the office in nearly two weeks.

"Of course," he answers. He holds out an open bottle of red, and I nod. He fills my glass.

We eat. It feels good, necessary. It seems to ground me. When we're done, we take our wineglasses to the other side of the room. But I'm not ready, not yet. I sit down in a blue chair. I think about leaving, maybe. Not going through with what happens next.

I even make a move for the door.

"Hey, where are you going?" Aaron asks me.

"Just the deli."

"The deli?"

And then Aaron is upon me. His hands on my face, the way they were just weeks ago, on the other side of the world. "Stay," he says. "Please."

And I do. Of course I do. I was always going to. I fold to him in that apartment like water into a wave. It all feels so fluid, so necessary. Like it's already happened.

He holds me in his arms, and then he kisses me. Slowly and then faster, trying to communicate something, trying to break through.

We undress quickly.

His skin on mine feels hot and raw and urgent. His touch goes from languid to fire. I feel it around us, all around us. I want to scream. I want to tear us apart.

We make love in that bed. That bed that Bella bought. This union that Bella built. He traces his fingers over my shoulders and down my breasts. He kisses my neck, the hollow of my collarbone. His body on top of mine feels heavy and real. He exhales out sharply into my hair, says my name. We're going to break apart too quickly. I never want this to end.

And then it's over, and when it is, when he collapses on top of me—kissing, caressing, shuddering—I feel clarity, like it has clobbered me in the back of my head. I see it in the stars. Everywhere. All above us.

I knew it all five years ago; I saw everything. I even saw this moment. But staring at Aaron next to me, now, I realize something I did not know before, not until this very moment: 11:59 p.m.

I saw what was coming, but I did not see what it would mean.

I look down at the ring I am wearing. It is on my middle finger, where it has been since I put it on. It is hers, of course, not mine. It is the thing I wear to feel close to her.

The dress, a funeral shroud.

This feeling.

This full, endless, insurmountable feeling. It fills up the apartment. It threatens to break the windows. But it is not love, no. I mistook it. I mistook it because I did not know; I had not seen everything that would get us here. It is not love, this feeling.

It is grief.

✦

The clock turns.

# *After*

Aaron and I lie next to each other, perfectly still. It is not awkward, although we do not talk. I suspect we are, both of us, coming to terms with what we have just discovered: that there is nowhere to hide, not even in each other.

"She's laughing," he says, finally. "You know that, right?"

"If she doesn't kill me first."

Aaron lifts a hand to my stomach. He chooses, instead, to make contact with my arm. "She knows," he says.

"I'd imagine, yes." I roll to the side. We look at each other. Two people bound and tethered by our own grief. "Do you want to stay?" I ask him.

He smiles at me. He reaches over and tucks some hair behind my ear. "I can't," he says.

I nod. "I know."

I want to crawl to him. I want to make my bed in his arms. To stay there until the storm passes. But I can't, of course. He has his own to weather. We can help each other only in our history, not in our understanding. It is different. It has always been different.

I look around the apartment. This place she built for me. This haven.

"Where will you go?" I ask him.

He has his own place, of course. His own life. The one he was living this time last year. Before the tides of fate swept him up and deposited him here. December 16, 2025. *Where do you see yourself in five years?*

"You want to have lunch tomorrow?" he asks me. He sits up. Discreetly, under the covers, he pulls his pants back on.

"Yeah," I say. "That would be nice."

"Maybe we could make it a weekly thing," he says, establishing something. Boundaries, maybe friendship.

"I'd like that."

I look down at my hand. I don't want to. I want to hold it forever. This promise on my finger. But it is not my promise, of course. It is his.

I take it off.

"Here," I say. "You should have this."

He shakes his head. "She wanted you—"

"No," I say. "She didn't. This is yours."

He nods. He takes it back. "Thank you."

He stands up. He puts on his shirt. I use the time to get dressed as well.

Then he stops, realizing something. "We could drink some more wine," he says. "If you don't want to be alone?"

I think about that, about the promise of this space. This time. Tonight.

"I'm okay," I say. I have no idea if it's true.

We walk across the apartment silently, our feet light on the cool concrete.

He pulls me into a hug. His arms feel good, and strong. But gone is the charge, the kinetic energy pulling, asking, demanding to be combusted.

"Get home safe," I say. And then he is gone.

I stare at the door a long time. I wonder whether I will see him tomorrow, or whether I will get a text, an excuse. Whether this is the beginning of goodbye for us, too. I do not know. I have no idea what happens now.

I walk around the apartment for an hour, touching things. The marble countertops, the grainiest shade of green. The black wood cabinets. The cherrywood stools. Everything in my apartment has always been white, but Bella knew I belonged in color. I go to the orange dresser, and that's when I see a framed photo sitting on top of it. Two teenagers, arms wrapped around each other, standing in front of a little white house with a blue awning.

"You were right," I say. I start to laugh then. The hysterical sobs of someone caught between irony and grief. The woven tapestry of our friendship continuing to reveal itself even now, even in her absence.

Outside, across the street from the apartment, right by Galapagos, I can see it start to snow. The first fall of the year. I put down the picture. I wipe my eyes. And then I pull on my rubber boots. I grab my down jacket and scarf from the closet. Keys, door, elevator.

Outside, the streets are empty. It is late; it is Dumbo. It is snowing. But from a block over, I see a light. I turn the corner. The deli.

I wander in. There is a woman behind the counter, sweeping. But the place is warm and well-lit, and she doesn't tell me they're closed. They're not. I look up at the board. The array of sandwiches, none of which I've ever touched. I'm not hungry, not at all, but I think about tomorrow—about coming here and getting an egg salad on bagel, or a tuna on rye. A breakfast sandwich—eggs and tomatoes and cheddar and wilted arugula. Something different.

The door jangles behind me. A tinkling of holiday bells.

I turn around, and there he is.

"Dannie," Dr. Shaw says. "What are you doing here?"

His cheeks are red. His face open. He's no longer in scrubs, but in jeans and a jacket, open at the collar. He is handsome, of course, in the way familiarity is beautiful, if not a little worn, a little tattered.

"Dr. Shaw."

"Please," he says. "Call me Mark."

He extends his hand. I take it. We will stay in that deli until they close, sipping on coffee that turns cold, which is an hour from now. He will walk me home. He will say he is very sorry for my loss. That he never knew I lived in Dumbo. I will tell him I didn't. Not until now. He will ask if perhaps he can see me again, perhaps at that deli, when I am ready. I will tell him yes, perhaps. Perhaps.

But all of that is an hour from now. Now, on the other side of midnight, we do not yet know what is coming.

So be it. So let it be.

# *Acknowledgments*

A very special thanks . . .

To my editor, Lindsay Sagnette, who quite literally had me at hello. Thank you for sweeping me off my feet, and forcing me to use the phrase "the one." You are . . . and I am the lucky one.

To my agent, Erin Malone, who continues to support my career with sharp fangs, crazy good editorial skills, and real respect. Erin, thank you for believing in the things we can't yet see, and trusting me to be your true partner. I am lucky, and grateful. I'll say it here on them all: you are never getting rid of me.

To my manager, Dan Farah—thank you for your willingness to grow, your absolute commitment to my career and our relationship, and your unparalleled belief in my future. I'm proud of us.

To my agent, David Stone, for keeping everyone and everything in line. I need your wisdom, guidance, and support more than you know. Our grown-up forever.

To everyone at Atria, especially Libby McGuire, for welcoming me with such open arms.

To Laura Bonner, Caitlin Mahony, and Matilda Forbes Watson for carrying Dannie and Bella all over the world.

To Kaitlin Olson for your time and attention, and to Erica Nori for being the keyest (it's a word) member of this team.

To Raquel Johnson, because the truest love there is has always already belonged to us.

To Hannah Brown Gordon, first reader forever. Thank you for saying this was special, and different from any that came before. I needed it. I always need it.

To Lexa Hillyer for loving me with such compassion. My New York is our life together, and I'll treasure it always.

To Lauren Oliver for the revelation(s).

To Emily Heddleson for being the best research assistant (boss) in the biz.

To Morgan Matson, Jen Smith, and Julia Devillers for being such champions when the road got scary, and for telling me to leap.

To Anna Ravenelle for keeping me in line.

To Melissa Seligmann, who continues to inspire all my stories. You're it for me.

To Danielle Kasirer for your forgiveness. I'm so grateful for our story, every last chapter.

To Jenn Robinson for the warmest hugs and the sharpest bitch slaps. Thank you (f—you) for setting the bar so goddamn high.

To Seth Dudowsky, because I didn't know on that one, so I'm saying it here in this one. The longest phase.

To my parents, who show me over and over again what unconditional love looks like. Thank you for loving me, all of me, every single day. Blessed doesn't even begin to cover it. This is all because of you.

I ended the acknowledgments of my last book, *The Dinner List*, by saying "to any woman who has ever felt betrayed by fate or love. Hang in there. This isn't the end of your story." I now want to add: Even after midnight, especially after midnight. Continue moving toward that which is moving toward you.

# BONUS CONTENT

# Dannie's New York City Walking Tour

*Experience New York with* In Five Years*—follow Dannie's footsteps through the city. This walking tour is long, and though real New Yorkers do walk a lot (and fast!), feel free to substitute Ubers when preferred.*

Begin at the **Mark Ingram bridal salon in Midtown (515 Madison Avenue, second floor)** where Dannie bought her wedding dress. This exclusive bridal atelier serves customers by appointment only so plan ahead if you'd like to get inside. Otherwise, walk west and south to **51 West Fifty-Second Street**. This landmark skyscraper, designed by Eero Saarinen, has been home to Sony Music Entertainment, CBS, and **Wachtell, Lipton, Rosen & Katz**, the top law firm in the city and Dannie's dream job since she was ten years old. Continue south to where David proposed to Dannie at the **Rainbow Room (30 Rockefeller Plaza, sixty-fifth floor)**, now a private event space (and enjoy Rockefeller Center, with a McNally Jackson bookstore, while you're there). Continue south and west to the **W New York–Times Square (1567 Broadway)**, where Dannie met with Jill.

Stroll down Broadway to Forty-Second Street, then head east to the café tables at **Bryant Park**, Midtown Manhattan's iconic green space. Walk east through the park, exiting by the flagship branch of the New York Public Library, and continue east to Third Avenue. Walk south on Third; **Dannie and David's first apartment together** was on one of these Murray Hill blocks. Pause at **Sarge's Deli (548 Third Avenue)** to refuel with Dannie's favorite whitefish salad.

**Dannie and David's Gramercy apartment (2 Gramercy Park West)**, is your next stop: walk south on Third Avenue until you hit Twenty-First Street, and then head west to the elegant, exclusive park.

To get to **Bella's art gallery in Chelsea**, walk up to Twenty-Third Street and catch the M23 crosstown bus heading west. Get off at Tenth Avenue and walk just a little north and west to

**Oliander (530 West Twenty-Fifth Street).** Feel free to browse the nearby galleries along Twenty-Fifth and the neighboring streets, then to get to **Bella's brownstone** you've got two options: walk east and south to Eighth Avenue and Twenty-Third Street and ride the southbound C or E train two stops to West Fourth; or walk the High Line from Twenty-Third and Tenth down to Gansevoort and Washington. Either way you're ending up on **the corner of Bleeker and Charles (85 Charles Street).**

The West Village is known for a neighborhood feel and great restaurants; swing south to a tiny French café called **Buvette (42 Grove Street)** for a croque monsieur, then south again to **Snack Taverna (63 Bedford Street)** for Greek salad, souvlaki, lamb triangles, and stuffed eggplant. Or you can continue south and east into NoHo and find **Dante (79-81 MacDougal Street)**, the site of Dannie and David's dinner. Take MacDougal south to where it meets Prince Street, crossing Houston Street into SoHo. Then walk south and east to Dannie's favorite store, **Reformation (62 Greene Street)**, and continue east along Spring Street to Mulberry Street for arugula pizza at **Rubirosa (235 Mulberry Street).**

For your final stop in Manhattan, you'll see where Dannie and David first met: head back south on Mulberry to Broome Street, then follow Broome east to **Ten Bells on the Lower East Side (247 Broome Street).** Pause for oysters and wine, then catch the Brooklyn-bound F train at Delancey and Essex and ride two stops to York Street. **Bridge Coffee Shop in Dumbo (73 Bridge Street)** is just two blocks away from the subway station, and **the apartment in Dumbo**, our final location in more ways than one, is just two blocks north from there **(37 Bridge Street).**

BOOK CLUB FAVORITES

READER'S GUIDE

# In Five Years

## Rebecca Serle

*This reading group guide for* In Five Years *includes an introduction, discussion questions, ideas for enhancing your book club, and a Q&A with author Rebecca Serle. The suggested questions are intended to help your reading group find new and interesting angles and topics for your discussion. We hope that these ideas will enrich your conversation and increase your enjoyment of the book.*

# Introduction

*In Five Years* is a striking, moving love story about Dannie Kohan, a high-powered corporate lawyer who has everything planned out. The story opens on the day she interviews for her dream job, nails it, and gets engaged to her longtime boyfriend—all according to her five-year plan. That night, when she and her new fiancé get home, she falls asleep on the couch. But when she wakes up, she's suddenly in a different apartment, with a different ring on her finger, in bed beside a very different man. She looks over at the muted TV playing the news and sees the date: it's 2025, five years in the future.

After a very confusing hour, Dannie wakes up again back in her normal life. She tries to shake the dream—or was it a premonition?—by busying herself in work. She tells no one about it, not even her best friend, Bella. Then one day, four and a half years later, she comes face-to-face with the man from her dream. This stunning, heartbreaking story will leave you thinking about the unpredictable nature of destiny and make you want to call your best friend immediately.

# *Topics & Questions for Discussion*

1. From the very beginning of the book, we learn that Dannie has rules and plans laid out for everything in her life. Do you believe this helps or hinders her? How does her philosophy regarding keeping everything in its place change over the course of the novel?

2. To Dannie, the law is "like poetry, but poetry with outcome, poetry with concrete meaning—with actionable power" (page 10). Later she describes the law by saying that "everything is there in black and white" (page 142). How does the law empower Dannie? To what extent do you think the law shapes how rigidly she sees the world? As the book goes on, power is often taken out of Dannie's hands. Do you think her background makes this lack of control harder for her than it might be for others?

3. While Bella is a tragic character, she is not painted simply in an angelic light. Early on in the story, Dannie describes her as being "spoiled, mercurial, and more than a little bit magical" (page 6). Is Bella's portrayal as a complicated, sometimes flawed character unique given the ending of the book and the typical depiction of the tragic heroine?

4. The scene between Dannie and Aaron in Chapter 3 is mirrored by the same scene in Chapter 41. How did your impressions of the two characters change over the course of the book? Why do you think the author chose to frame the story with two identical scenes that will mean different things to the reader at different points in the story?

5. Bella gifts Dannie a print by the artist Allen Grubesic that reads: *I WAS YOUNG I NEEDED THE MONEY.* All the characters in the book are well-off financially by the time we meet them. What do you think the print's message means in the context of the story?

6. Dannie believes that "Bella lives in a world I do not understand, populated by phrases and philosophies that apply only to people like her. People, maybe, who do not yet know tragedy" (pages 44–45). How do you think the death of Dannie's brother at such a young age affects her outlook? Do you think she envies Bella for not carrying a similar burden, or does she look up to her for it? How do you think the fact that Dannie has already lost someone close to her affects her when Bella's diagnosis is revealed?

7. Bella introduces her new boyfriend as Greg, but, of course, Dannie already knows him as Aaron and has a hard time referring to him as anything other than Aaron. Why do you think he is introduced to the reader with two different names? Is Bella's version of him different from Dannie's version of him?

8. Dannie visits a therapist, Dr. Christine, once after her dream and once after she meets Aaron in real life. Why do you think she sees Dr. Christine only twice? What decisions does Dannie make after leaving these appointments?

9. How does Dannie and Bella's relationship change after Bella's diagnosis? How does it affect the other relationships in Dannie's and Bella's lives? Why do you think it's easier for Bella to be around Aaron than it is for her to be around Dannie?

10. Were you surprised that Dannie and Aaron kissed when he reveals that the apartment is a gift from Bella? Do you think it amounts to a betrayal of Bella's trust? How does Dannie and Aaron's connection to Bella intensify their own relationship?

11. Fate is a concept that is played with often throughout the novel. Dannie fights to change the fate she saw laid out in her vision. Aaron told Bella he was fated to end up with her. How do fate and free will interact in the novel? Do you think the book comes down on the side of one over the other?

12. Near the end of the book, Bella tells Dannie that she is meant to have love beyond her wildest dreams because "that's the way you love me" (page 205). How does the book portray the roles of romantic and platonic love? How did the book subvert the idea that the great love of Dannie's life would be one of the two men we were introduced to at the beginning of the novel?

13. Were you surprised that Dannie and Aaron did not end up together? What do you think this means for Dannie's journey and her future relationships?

14. Magical realism is an element of the story but only when it comes to Dannie's ability to see one evening five years in her future. Why do you think there's a magical component in this one instance but nowhere else? Did the book's hyperrealistic premise affect your expectations for how it would end?

# *Enhance Your Book Club*

1. Iconic New York City locations, restaurants, and shops are mentioned throughout the novel. Next time you visit New York City, take a walking tour to some of them, including the Rainbow Room, Buvette, Bryant Park, and Rubirosa. Find a full guide in the illustrated reading group guide on the author's website, rebeccaserle.com.

2. *In Five Years* often plays with preconceptions and blind spots when it comes to fate, love, and friendship. Consider your own opinions on the themes discussed in the book: Do you believe in fate over free will? Are any of the strongest relationships in your own life with someone other than a romantic partner? Where do you see yourself in five years, and how fixed is that vision of the future?

3. Read *The Dinner List* with your book club (if you haven't already!) and compare how the roles of love, friendship, and magical realism come into play in both of Rebecca Serle's recent novels.

# A Conversation with Rebecca Serle

**Q:** *In Five Years* and *The Dinner List* both take place in New York City, and the city is a central feature of both novels. How did you create such a sense of place for your books? Is the NYC of *The Dinner List* different from the one in *In Five Years*? Will you continue to write novels based in NYC, or will they be set elsewhere?

**A:** I have been in love with New York City since I was a little girl—Manhattan has always been almost a person to me. It's romantic, mercurial, and specific. The city is also the ideal place to set a book because it's so full of connection—street corners, cramped apartments, and subway cars. It's so easy to smack up against someone else's humanity there. Sabrina's New York in *The Dinner List* is less privileged than Dannie's and probably mirrors my early years in the city better. Both novels have lots of my old haunts, though! On every page you'll find my favorite restaurants, coffee shops, and bars where I, too, have experienced heartbreak. I lived it before I ever wrote about it, and I hope that comes through in my work.

I moved to Los Angeles this year, and my new novel takes place, in part, in California. I could see setting subsequent work in my new (very sunny) home.

**Q:** Dannie and Bella are such distinct characters. Why did you choose to portray them so differently? Do you think they help balance each other out? Who do you think you have more in common with: the pragmatic, by-the-numbers Dannie or the artistic, free-spirited Bella?

**A:** I knew that in order for the conceit to work, Dannie would have to be someone with an airtight life plan. She would have to know exactly what she wanted and was building toward. Dannie comes by her uptight nature honestly. She lost her brother when she was young and has had the need to control her life since, to make sure she is never struck down by tragedy again. I also knew I wanted to give her a counterpoint in Bella. Bella does not have any of Dannie's rules about life—she is open, creative, and impulsive. In many ways, Dannie's journey over the course of the novel is to embrace her own Bella-ness. I think I'm a pretty clear mix of the two, but, gun to my head, I'd say I'm more like Dannie.

**Q:** Is the relationship between Dannie and Bella reminiscent of any of the friendships in your own life?

**A:** The female friendships in my life are of paramount importance. They are my great loves. I think in some relationships I'm the Dannie and in some I'm the Bella. I turn to my friends for everything, like relationship advice and work input. I moved across the country this year and could never have done it without their support. I feel extraordinarily lucky to have them.

**Q:** The novel spans five years. How did you choose what to show us and what to summarize?

**A:** The plot doesn't really accelerate in a significant way until Dannie meets Aaron again. So I knew that what happened in the years between, while it was maybe interesting for Dannie's life, would not be particularly interesting for the purposes of our story. From there, I needed about six months to tell the story I wanted to tell, and to earn the emotional arc.

**Q:** Why did you decide to have Dannie be a lawyer? What research into law did you do in order to write about her career? Was it important to you to portray your two female lead characters as having high-powered, successful careers?

**A:** I am lucky enough to have a lot of super-successful women in my life, some of whom are corporate lawyers. I turned to them for advice and also did research into the firm where Dannie works. Before Dannie, I had never written a character who was so unapologetic about her desire for financial success. I found her voice very satisfying—and surprising!—to write. I love that about her, and a lot of her ambitions mirror my own.

**Q:** Neither Dannie nor Bella is particularly close with her parents, and there is an emphasis on chosen family—especially when it comes to their lifelong relationship with each other. Are these kinds of essential friendships something you've explored in your past novels? How is chosen family important in your own life?

**A:** I'm my parents' only child, and I think, as any only child knows, you need your friends to be like family. My girlfriends are my sisters, and they show up for me the way any blood relative would. I wanted to give Dannie and Bella that tie. Bella has been the great love of Dannie's life. I relate to that level of loyalty and heart connection. I believe very strongly in chosen family.

**Q:** Speak to your exploration of fate versus free will in your novel. Did you know from the beginning that Dannie's premonition would come to pass?

**A:** All of my novels since my very first book, *When You Were Mine*, are about the dialogue between choice and destiny. To me the most interesting question of our human existence is: "How much is in our control, and how much is going to happen regardless of what we do?" I knew that Dannie would live that hour and it would be exactly the same as the hour she lives at the beginning of the book, meaning all of the same things would happen. But I also knew it would mean something entirely different than what she'd been anticipating. That, to me, is really the thesis of the novel: we can think we know what is coming, but we can never know what it will mean.

**Q:** The book is framed as a love story, with two love interests Dannie must choose between. How did you want to subvert the traditional love story narrative? Do you think readers will expect the change that happens midway through the book?

**A:** I'm not sure! But I can say I'm far more interested in writing about the complicated dynamics between women than I am about traditional romantic notions of love between a man and a woman. I love a good love story, but my books tend to feature female friendships front and center. I still think the most important relationship in *The Dinner List* is the one Sabrina has with Jessica, even though her love story with Tobias takes up more page space. Bella is the most important relationship in Dannie's life, and I think that becomes clearer as the book goes on. That's not to say David and Aaron are unimportant—they are extremely important. They're just not as important as Bella.

**Q:** Was it challenging to write about Bella's diagnosis and subsequent struggle with cancer? What research into ovarian cancer did you do in order to portray it?

**A:** It was extremely challenging, and I almost didn't do it. For a while I tried to figure out a way for Bella not to have to get cancer, but I couldn't come up with anything that would be as powerful or turn Dannie's life upside down in the same way. Once I committed, I told my friend and fellow author Leila Sales how scared I was to write this. She told me to just stay close to Dannie, to write beside her, and to remind her that I was there. I still tear up thinking about that advice. It's a writing philosophy I'm bringing to all my subsequent work.

For research, I spoke to doctors, visited the hospital, and researched both Bella's diagnosis and treatment as best I could. I do not pretend to be a medical expert, and this book remains a work of fiction.

**Q:** Do you have any favorite books or movies that inspired you as you were writing *In Five Years*?

**A:** The novel opens with a quote from Nora Ephron. Her work in both film and books was hugely influential to me as a storyteller. In fact, she is one of the five people on *my* dinner list! I love any good New York love story. *Someone Great*, a film by Jennifer Kaytin Robinson, was a must-see of last year. The Modern Love column, as well. I've read it weekly for fifteen years.

**Q:** Why did you choose to use magical realism in the premises of both *In Five Years* and *The Dinner List*? What do these magical elements allow you to explore that you would not be able to otherwise?

**A:** The magical element allows for the conceit to be more magnified. The magic in my novels is never particularly overarching. It's really just the one thing that's injected into the narrative in a way that allows for expansion. For *The Dinner List*, it's the dinner table, obviously. But I think as time goes on we begin to forget the impossibility of this meal, and just start focusing on the relationships that are unfolding. Similarly in *In Five Years*, the magic is the flash forward. It's key to the plot, of course, but as Dannie integrates the experience into her life, so do we. It's simply a tool for us to get where we need to go.

**Q:** The premise of *The Dinner List* is based on the question "If you could have dinner with any five people, alive or dead, who would it be?" *In Five Years* is based on the question "Where do you see yourself in five years?" What attracted you to the idea of recasting these casual conversation starters as the jumping-off point for your recent novels?

**A:** *The Dinner List* took a long time to write, and in between when I began it and when I came back to finish it, my grandmother passed away. What was once a fun, zany conceit became very personal: What wouldn't we give to have one last dinner with a person we love whom we've lost? The book grew out of my desire to explore that idea. For *In Five Years*, the question came closely with the conceit. I knew I wanted to explore the idea of seeing a future that looks very different from the one we are planning. I am also fascinated by scientific data that is suggesting that the future in fact influences the present. Perhaps the choices we are making are not building a moldable future but are informed by one that has already solidified. It's intriguing stuff!